The Quince Seed Potion

The Quince
Seed Potion

A NOVEL

BRIDGE WORKS PUBLISHING COMPANY
Bridgehampton, New York

Published by Bridge Works Publishing Company,
Bridgehampton, New York,
an imprint of the Rowman & Littlefield Publishing Group, Inc.

Distributed in the United States by National Book Network, Lanham,
Maryland. For descriptions of this and other Bridge Works books, visit the
National Book Network website at www.nbnbooks.com.

FIRST EDITION

The characters and events in this book are fictitious. Any similarity to actual
persons, living or dead, is coincidental and not intended by the author.

Library of Congress Cataloging-in-Publication Data

Baharloo, Morteza, 1961–
    The quince seed potion : a novel / Morteza Baharloo—1st ed.
    p. cm.
    ISBN 1-882593-87-1 (hardcover : alk. paper)
    1. Iran—History—Pahlavi dynasty, 1925–1979—Fiction. 2. Iran—Hisotry—
Revolution, 1979—Fiction. 3. Indentured servants—Fiction. 4. Master and
servant—Fiction. 5. Rural conditions—Fiction. 6. Social classes—Fiction. 7.
Landowners—Fiction. I. Title

PS3602.A398Q56 2004
813'.6—dc22

                                                            2004009983

10 9 8 7 6 5 4 3 2 1

∞™ The paper used in this publication meets the minimum requirements of
American National Standard for Information Sciences–Permanence of Paper
for Printed Library Materials, ANSI/NISO Z39.48-1992.
Manufactured in the United States of America.

To my mother, Marzieh,

who taught me to combat the
perils of life with poetic satire,

and to my daughters,
Sahar and Yasmine,

whose conduct and thoughts are proof
that madness is hereditary.

The Quince
Seed Potion

Part I

Serving the Khans
Empire of Iran
1928–1951

Chapter 1

The household cock crowed, heralding the exact moment darkness surrendered to dawn, just as two tiny limbs emerged from the laboring woman's dark orifice. The half-somnolent state of Fatima, the Bald Doula, shattered. "I see them!" she yelled. "I see them! I see them!" she repeated, as if competing with the noisy cock.

The collective shouting of the female spectators blended with the painful cries of the woman now deep in labor and the clamor of the curious preadolescent girls observing their own procreative destinies.

As the neighboring cocks crowed in concert, the doula turned her attention from the spectators in the cramped room to the laboring woman. What she saw terrified her. Two miniature feet lurked at the edge of the orifice as if reluctantly contemplating exodus from the mother's womb. The doula cursed the infant for not following the normal instinctual birth, while gently manipulating its feet back into the womb and rotating the slippery creature. She raised her face toward the ceiling to plead for success.

"There is no God but Allah!" she shouted. Fatima's midwifery services would not be generously compensated if she delivered a dead child or if the mother died in labor. As a pious woman, she knew that the fate of both mother and fetus rested in God's hands, not her own. As such, she found the customary methods of payment unfair. Focusing on the financial incentives, she increased her vigor and administered her skills as best she could to save the infant and its mother, as well as her fee.

"Bring me the mortar and the pestle and an onion. Boil some water now, you lazy girls! Tell a Muslim *man* to grab a young hen and bring it to me. Now, I said! Now!"

The doula's efforts to rotate the infant proved effective, and he soon entered the world headfirst, his eyes open in an expression of shock, as if destiny were asking him enigmatic questions concerning the creator and the created. As Fatima held the infant aloft, she realized he was not breathing: there was no movement of his neonatal chest and certainly no sign of the universal complaint that most infants make upon entering the world.

The doula grabbed the onion from a pregnant woman who was watching the whole scene with fear and apprehension. In the pewter mortar, Fatima crushed the onion hurriedly with its matching pestle and then rubbed a generous dose of the crushed onions on the newborn's microscopic nostrils. Weakly, the infant began crying.

Next, the doula fetched a small opaque jar of lanolin from her satchel, turned the infant on his stomach, and lubricated his rectum. She then grabbed a struggling hen just delivered by a preadolescent boy. As the hen fluttered to escape her iron grip, Fatima dipped the bird's beak into the jar and rubbed the lanolin around the beak rapidly but thoroughly. Holding the hen's head in her strong clutches, she inserted the lubricated beak into the infant's rectum.

The doula's desire for monetary compensation was directly proportional to her vigor in pushing on the hen, whose beak was no longer visible. She willed the hen to arouse the desired response from the child by fighting futilely, ultimately forcing the exhalation of its air into the infant's lungs via his rectum. When the hen could no longer inhale air, it would reach the point of asphyxiation.

As the doula and the other women watched, the infant began to pant, a miraculous case of beak-to-rectum resuscitation, or perhaps a case of infantile perseverance, which resulted in the infant's survival and the hen's demise.

"It's a boy!" the women and the girls shouted as soon as the doula allowed them to observe the infant's genitals. The women's ecstatic screams masked the newborn's cries. Fatima immediately thought, *I can finally buy that head scarf, the gauzy one. I delivered a live boy!* The male infant would bring her a good bonus.

"Take him outside for some of God's air!" she commanded one of the preadolescent girls. The girl obediently took the slippery, onion-scented creature to the porch and laid him on a blanket.

The mother's sudden and intense hemorrhaging interrupted the doula's palpable relief. The pregnant woman who had brought the onion and three other women came to her rescue, but after an exhaustive effort, the doula announced, "She has entered the gate of heaven! May Allah's mercy and compassion be upon her! She has wasted away. She is gone, you miserable women! Cry, you mourners! Weep for the death of this woman!"

"I want to speak to her sister or mother," Fatima demanded authoritatively.

The pregnant woman replied, "Her mother is dead and her sister didn't show. I'm Kokab, her husband's brother's wife." Her own fear of coincidental death in labor became more noticeable, but the woman managed to conceal her jealousy at the birth of a male infant into her brother-in-law's family.

"Who's her husband?" the doula demanded.

"Zolfali!" another female voice shouted.

"Zolfali, the Bli—" Fatima did a lingual incision on the word "blind" and swallowed the latter half. She must not show disrespect to the person who would compensate her by calling him "Zolfali, the Blind Licker." After all, her name was likewise marred by anatomical problems. The locals called her "Fatima, the Bald Doula," a condition she suffered due to a dermatological disease. As she washed the infant in a pewter pan and poured water over him from a long-spouted ewer, she made a concentrated effort to weep. Fatima was uncertain of her fee now that one of her two patients had not survived.

The dead mother lay on the mattress covered in blood and other difficult-to-classify secretions. Her long black hair protruded from beneath her gauzy white head scarf. Tendrils of hair wreathed her head like deadly serpents.

"Send after the young dead bride's husband!" the doula commanded, trying to render the event more tragic by referring to the dead woman as a young bride. She had no cause to worry. Zolfali, the Blind Licker, ultimately paid the doula a fee equivalent to delivering a male infant, after discounting an arbitrary sum for the postpartum death of his wife. The doula, overjoyed at earning enough to purchase her gauzy head scarf, departed from the house of mourners in the village of Madavan outside the township of Kamab, Iran, three hundred kilometers from the

Fars provincial capital of Shiraz, on the tenth day of Teer, July 2, 1928.

DUE TO THE FATHER'S AMBIVALENCE in naming his son, Barat-Ali, Zolfali's brother, resorted to ridicule by naming the infant Sarv-e-ali, after the tall cypress tree of Ali, the first imam in Shiite Islam. Unfortunately Sarveali was an exceptionally small infant and became known instead as "Sarveali, the son of Zolfali, the Blind Licker." Zolfali, although unsighted, could lick his own forehead. His tongue could eject, as he put it, like a monkey's penis, pink and fleshy, and ascend to his forehead. Depending on an individual's anatomical, physiological, vocational, sexual, or criminal idiosyncrasies in rural areas during that era, one might easily be called "Ruhullah, the Bushy Eye-Browed Youth Killer," "Mustafa, the Epileptic," or even "Hassan, the Mare Mounter." Only in the mid-1930s did it become mandatory for citizens of Iran to choose a proper surname.

Alas, Zolfali died when the child was two years old. His maternal aunt and her husband, a shepherd, raised Sarveali as their own. One morning in the late spring of 1934, when Sarveali was about to turn six, his paternal uncle, Barat-Ali, the same relative who had named him, arrived at the shepherd's house. He said he had come to repossess Zolfali's herd of goats and sheep that Sarveali's aunt had claimed after her brother-in-law's death. Barat-Ali stated that he, a male blood relative, should become the boy's guardian.

Upon hearing this explanation, the maternal aunt shouted and pointed toward the open-air barn where the herd was kept: "So now that we've had the boy for five years, you've come to take him and his herd." Barat-Ali did not reply to the woman. Instead, he thought to himself, *Look at that herd! There must be a hundred in there!*

7

Barat-Ali's rogue nature and intractable greed were well-known. "Boy," he demanded to Sarveali, "go get your stuff ready and come with me . . . come with me and the herd. I'm your uncle, your father's brother, Mr. Barat-Ali." Sarveali began to cry, instinctively understanding the worst.

"Don't cry, dear nephew. I'll take care of you from now on. Go and pack up!" Barat-Ali said. He smiled as he stole another glimpse of his new herd.

As soon as he, the little boy, and the herd left the gate of Nasravan, Barat-Ali began to spout orders at Sarveali. Away they went to Madavan, the village where Sarveali had been born.

"What kind of a shepherd are you?" Barat-Ali ranted as the animals ran this way and that. "Can't you handle a few kids and lambs?"

Sarveali started crying again, but Barat-Ali had no intention of comforting the child. In the midst of his sadness, Sarveali was relieved that his miniherd had come with him. En route to Madavan, Sarveali focused his attention on a young, pearly white goat, his favorite since its birth. He watched the goat as it walked by a cluster of wild red anemones that had grown out of a mass of cow dung. As soon as Sarveali admired the flowers, his uncle, who was walking ahead of him, crushed them under his feet.

Barat-Ali's greed was defined by his name, which meant "promissory note bestowed by Imam Ali." His own father gave him his name at birth in an effort to encourage kismet to bequeath prosperity on the family. Barat-Ali had spent his entire life, according to his own proud confessions, attempting to gain prosperity by means of theft, deceit, extortion, and other charlatan acts. In this same rogue manner, Barat-Ali successfully gained guardianship of his nephew. Sarveali, in essence, was to become his uncle's "barat," a means of bringing him prosperity through the herd of sheep as well as any future wages the boy might earn.

As SOON AS THE JINGLING OF BELLS and the baaing and bleating of the herd sounded in Madavan, Barat-Ali's family appeared to welcome their leader, returning successfully.

"Get me some food, woman! I brought this whole herd all by myself." He managed to force the herd into an open-air pen at the back of his house, while his wife, the same pregnant Aunt Kokab who had witnessed Sarveali's birth, rushed to serve her husband. "Gholi, hey, Gholi, here's the boy, umm . . . I mean your cousin," Barat-Ali said.

Following behind his uncle, Sarveali saw the woman his uncle had addressed. Kokab returned Sarveali's gaze without a smile, not even a sham one. Sarveali then observed a fat boy close to his age, eating a flat loaf of bread rolled into a tubular shape. The first words the boy spoke to Sarveali were "I'm Gholi. Your baba is dead; mine is alive—hee hee." A hot tear ran down Sarveali's cheek, but before his sobs could develop into full-blown weeping, the entire family started at the screech of another child.

"Shut up, Yazgulu!" Kokab yelled as she turned toward a swinging hammock on the front porch. She walked toward the little girl and picked her up. The child's light henna hair and huge blue eyes terrified Sarveali. He had never seen a child with eye color that wasn't brown. He decided to minimize contact with this cousin, imagining she was a djinn.

The following morning, Sarveali started work. For three months, Sarveali's mornings, afternoons, and nights continued monotonously. Out with the goats and a shepherd in the morning, dried bread for lunch. Fat Gholi, who never accompanied Sarveali and the shepherd, made his cousin's life miserable every day before bedtime.

Close to autumn, Barat-Ali and Kokab heard a loud shattering noise on the front porch next to the swinging hammock. The noise was immediately followed by shouting and crying.

"He beat me, baba!" Gholi yelled.

"He called me 'fatherless'! And I did not beat him. He beat *me*," Sarveali replied defensively. As soon as he uttered the word "fatherless," his crying intensified.

Barat-Ali was not interested in mediating the squabble. He was merely interested in identifying the culprit who had broken his man-sized water vat.

"Who broke that vat?" Barat-Ali demanded.

"Sarveali! Sarveali did!" Gholi shouted.

In his mind, Barat-Ali instantly calculated the worth of the clay vat. His anger, directly proportional to the vat's value, caused him to strike Sarveali so hard on the chest that the child fell backward down three porch steps, landed on his buttocks, and skidded across the gravel. Defeat, pain, and humiliation coursed through Sarveali's veins. As if his tear ducts had been shattered, he began another long campaign of crying.

After the squabble, Barat-Ali and Kokab prepared for bed. Kokab could still hear Sarveali's sobbing. "Get rid of him," she said. "You should've let him stay with the other relatives! All you wanted was their herd!"

"Well, that fat boy *you* delivered can't do any shepherding!" Barat-Ali replied, as he fondled his wife's breasts. Feeling his penis stiffen, he said victoriously, "I know exactly where to take him, and I'll take him tomorrow!" Barat-Ali moved closer to his wife, but Yazgulu's violent screams from her hammock shattered the moment. Barat-Ali, frustrated by a seemingly intractable erect phallus, thought of an ersatz satisfaction. He surreptitiously fetched a jar of petroleum jelly, left the room, and entered Sarveali's chamber.

"Does your butt still hurt?" he asked solicitously.

Sarveali's response was incomprehensible.

"Turn around and take off your pajama bottoms. I'll put medicine on it."

Sarveali felt something greasy on his behind, then a queer pain between his buttocks; it was a pain much worse than the blow he had received earlier.

Chapter 2

The following day, Barat-Ali delivered six-year-old Sarveali into indentured servitude. Sarveali always remembered that painful day—emotionally painful because he was told to offer his pet white goat as a gift to the Great Khan, the ruling landowner on whose estate he would be employed, and physically painful because he still felt a strange ache inside his anus, which was exacerbated by frequent waves of nausea.

After two hours of walking with the snowcapped Zagros Mountains in the distance, they reached the Great Khan's estate. Barat-Ali grabbed the door knocker and beat its triangular-pointed tip solidly against the steel circle mounted on the wooden door. Sarveali observed the knocker's semicircular movement, followed by a succession of loud metallic sounds that vibrated against his eardrums. A guard opened the door and allowed them to enter the vestibule of the guardhouse. Once inside, Barat-Ali asked for permission to speak to the head factotum of the estate. As they waited, Sarveali noticed a juniper-lined road that led from the guardhouse and disappeared around a curve. On both sides of the road, hundreds of young green fruits hung from citrus trees in the estate's orchard. From around the curve of the orchard, a dark-skinned, narrow-mustachioed gentleman approached. When he arrived, he raised his visored hat for a moment, scratched his head, and replaced his hat. A khaki shirt, trousers, and knee-high brown leather boots completed the factotum's attire.

"Mirza Sheikhak, salam!" Barat-Ali exclaimed. He grabbed Sheikhak's right hand and kissed it. Sheikhak grimaced and said nothing.

"Mirza Sheikhak, please protect this orphan, the son of my dead brother, Zolfali; he has no one and nothing in the world, except for the Great Khan's generosity," Barat-Ali wheedled, determined to simultaneously rid himself of Sarveali and secure financial gain. So it was that holding the neck of his pearly white goat, Sarveali was first exposed to the word "orphan" while being introduced to Mirza Sheikhak Yazdani, the head factotum of the estate.

Sheikhak's grimace intensified. Barat-Ali decided to increase his efforts and heighten Sarveali's status as an object of misery. He yelled, "Kiss Mirza Sheikhak's hand, you insolent idiot of a child!" At that moment Sarveali finally released the pearly white goat and proceeded toward Sheikhak to kiss his hand, which was extended at Sarveali's eye level.

Sheikhak nodded in a wry gesture that indicated he wished for Barat-Ali's disappearance. He was wary of Barat-Ali's peculiar looks, particularly his deep-set small eyes, features he had commonly seen among pederasts. He seemed to remember Barat-Ali had a reputation as such. *I could use this boy as Teimour Khan's personal servant; he must be about the same age,* he thought. *At least I can free the orphan from this boy fucker!*

Barat-Ali continued, "His kismet is firstly in Allah's hand and secondly in yours, Mirza Sheikhak. Make him the servant of the Great Khan's household. Let him grow up, become a man, marry, and die here. All the boy wants is to serve you and your masters." He thought of Sarveali's future compensation and added, "Whatever Allah, the khans, and *you* think is right for his salary, you can forward to me for safekeeping . . ."

"What did you say, child seller?" Sheikhak harshly interrupted. Although he had no inclination to hire Sarveali initially, he realized the boy would become prey to his uncle's pederasty if, of course, he had not already. Reluctantly, he surmised that Sarveali would be better off employed by the estate.

"Well, Mirza Sheikhak, I beg your forgiveness. I know a midget orphan brings nothing to the grand estate. Please forget his salary, if you don't wish to pay. It's better for him to be under the shadow of your kindness than wandering about in the wilderness."

"Bite your tongue, you blasphemous one! Do you think that the Great Khan and his dynasty are in need of gratis servitude from the likes of you?" the factotum cried. "Don't worry, we'll send you his salary." He was appalled at the greedy relative who would receive Sarveali's full salary, but knew he could do little to reverse this onerous practice.

"What's your name, boy?" Sheikhak asked Sarveali in a theatrical manner. His intention was not only to cheer the orphan but also to demonstrate his hierarchical superiority.

"Sarveali," the six-year-old replied in a barely audible tone. Sheikhak laughed thunderously.

"Was there a drought of names when Zolfali, the Blind Licker, named you?" "Sarv-e-Ali," he enunciated and continued. "God, give mercy to the garden, whose *'sarv'* is this pale, midget soul . . . What a name!"

The child's threshold of humiliation collapsed and he burst into radical weeping. His tears, combined with a greenish nasal discharge, created a salty amalgamate that Sarveali tasted as it ran into his mouth.

"Don't cry, my boy, I was teasing!" Sheikhak changed his cadence into a poetic tone. Fear of Sheikhak's loud chants compounded Sarveali's sadness. He started to hiccup.

"Dear boy, our business will not be consummated if you're going to be such a fragile sissy." Sheikhak patted Sarveali on the head and, as his preceptor, ordered the new apprentice to follow him to the servant quarters. Sarveali followed Sheikhak into the kitchen, where they found Barat-Ali squatting in front of a tray full of food on a short-footed stool.

"Are you still here? Get lost, you greedy child seller!" Sheikhak growled at Barat-Ali.

Sheikhak ordered the cook to prepare some food for Sarveali. The plate contained steamed, saffron-infused basmati rice: some grains were dyed light yellow, some amber, and some orange from saffron. Pistachios, walnuts, and raisins, exuding an exotic aroma and taste, mingled with the rice. This dish so impressed Sarveali's virgin palate that the mere mention of its name, *keshmesh polo,* caused his mouth to water. Later in life, it would become his culinary specialty.

Sarveali ate furiously, as if he feared that the joy of feasting might halt without warning. His gastronomic pleasure was so great that he almost forgot the persistent pain between his buttocks.

After the rice, Sheikhak handed Sarveali something that looked identical to chicken feces. But Sarveali trusted the factotum, and his taste buds were immersed in yet another delicacy: baklava from the central city of Yazd. The sweetness carpeted his tongue and throat while cardamom, jasmine, and clove lifted his soul.

The factotum's directive quickly brought Sarveali back to reality: "You are to be in the service of Teimour Khan, the young prince. You understand? If he tells you to eat shit, you do it! If he tells you to go get water from Daghestan, you do it! If the *khanzadeh* desires butterfly kisses from Kandahar, you get them! If he orders you to walk on fire, you do it! If . . ." Sheikhak interrupted himself and asked Sarveali, "Do you understand?"

Although Sarveali did not know where Daghestan or Kandahar was, swallowing the very last bit of the baklava, he replied, "Yes, Mirza Sheikhak."

"Now follow me, and you'll learn your first assignment." Sheikhak, carrying a plate of baklava, walked away from the kitchen and toward a grand two-story edifice on the same juniper tree–bordered path surrounded by citrus trees. They removed their shoes, placed them on the kilim doormat, and entered. The marbled foyer felt cool on Sarveali's bare feet.

Inside, multicolored rugs imprinted with images of goats, chickens, flowers, faces of lovers, strange beasts, and lions stared up at him. Half-naked women winked at him from the wallpaper. They walked toward the rug-covered stairs and up to the second floor. As Sarveali surveyed the foyer from his aerial view, he realized that he had never been so high in his life.

Sheikhak opened a gigantic double door, and heaven exhaled its perfumed essence on the face of the novice servant. In a moment of astonishment, Sarveali saw thousands of stars glittering and glowing at him. He later realized that what he had interpreted as a grand cosmos were merely hundreds of crystal clusters hanging from an Austrian chandelier.

Further into the room, soft velvet armchairs shaped like obese women offered a welcoming embrace. The Great Khan, lord of the estate, lay on a sofa, reading from a stack of oversize papers as tall as Sarveali himself. Later Sarveali learned that they were newspapers, written in Persian, from Shiraz, Tehran, Baku, and Bombay. Sarveali surreptitiously touched the corner of a sofa; the softness galvanized his small body.

Sheikhak placed the baklava dish on a round table in front of the sofa and introduced the boy to the Great Khan as "the son of Zolfali, the Blind Licker," without mentioning Sarveali's actual name. He told the Great Khan that Sarveali would be Teimour Khan's new "small servant." The Great Khan did not cease his reading, but that did not keep his nose from registering the boy's body odor.

"Tell the boy to bathe and give him one of these baklavas."

Sheikhak chuckled and led Sarveali from the room as he whispered, "God's grace is with you today, boy!"

The Great Khan had suffered from extreme melancholy since the postpartum death of his wife. Their marriage had been the only one in the family to experience a genuine foundation of conjugal love, as most of the Great Khan's cousins and relatives had entered into loveless, contractual, and clan-based marriages.

Sheikhak told Sarveali that the Great Khan's marriage had produced only two offspring. The birth of the first son, Changiz Khan, had planted the seed of paternal resentment and competition. It became apparent that the

Great Khan and his elder son experienced only one mutual feeling in their father–son relationship—resentment of the second son's birth. That tragic labor caused the loss of a lover and goddesslike mother. As a result, Teimour Khan, the younger son, was born hated and despised by his father and only brother.

Outside the Great Khan's chamber, Sheikhak ordered an attendant to take Sarveali to the bathhouse. The attendant barely spoke to Sarveali en route to the *hammam*. As soon as they arrived, the attendant ordered Sarveali, "Take off your clothes and put this around 'that place,'" handing Sarveali a red loincloth. Sarveali did so, but with a queer anticipation of pain. The attendant lifted him into the warm-water reservoir; the soapy solution irritated and intensified the pain in Sarveali's anus. The attendant had already noticed Sarveali's rectal bleeding, so he applied a soothing, cooling salve before taking Sarveali back to the manor house. Immediately Sheikhak led Sarveali to another room, where he met Teimour Khan, a handsome, light-skinned boy his own age. The young khan's combed-back, light brown hair crowned his face, which was adorned with two rosy cheeks. When Sheikhak greeted the young Teimour Khan, the boy merely looked at the factotum blankly and then returned to gazing out his bedroom window at his father's 1932 Packard as the uniformed chauffeur washed it. Sarveali was almost paralyzed with excitement and could not say a word beyond his initial "hello." He noticed that although master and servant were of the same age, wealth had made one beautiful, fair, soft, and alert, while poverty had left the other ugly, dark-skinned, and confused.

As for Sheikhak, he knew that the young Khan felt peevish but was not certain about the cause. He theorized that his young master dreaded starting school that year. All he desired, lately, was to cruise the boulevards of Shiraz in the Packard. Also, Teimour Khan envied Changiz Khan, his brother, eight years his senior, who was now attending Zagros School, a preparatory school in Tehran. Changiz Khan preferred to stay in Tehran and showed little interest in visiting his brother.

In the midst of Sheikhak's ruminations regarding his masters' fraternal conflict, Teimour Khan spoke. "Tell my father I want to be driven to Shiraz now! Why is it that I can't be taken in the Packard to Shiraz right now?!" The six-year-old stamped his foot and crossed his eyes at the factotum. He ignored Sarveali completely.

"I will tell your father, my master," Sheikhak assured him. "Does the young master have any orders for his new servant?"

For the first time, Teimour Khan noticed the other little boy, and the first stage of a boyhood bond began with Teimour Khan granting Sarveali the privilege of fetching him a glass of water. Sarveali, in ecstasy at his first task, proudly accompanied Sheikhak to the kitchen, where he poured water into a tall glass and placed it on a silver tray.

Upon serving the water, the first gulp of which caused an ephemeral smile to appear on Teimour Khan's face, Sarveali received a reward so potent that it eradicated his pain. His bruised soul was soothed, at least temporarily, by the approving smile of his master.

A week later, school started on September 23, 1934, the first day of *Mehr*. Sarveali's duty was to awaken the young master at 7:00 A.M. and make certain that Teimour Khan was prepared for his breakfast, which he would serve to his master by 7:30. Sarveali's own breakfast, which he devoured while the young master dressed, consisted of whatever

19

Teimour Khan could not eat. Auspiciously, their tastes were symbiotic: the master enjoyed the yolk and the servant, the whites.

On that first day, Sheikhak was prepared by 8:00 A.M. to train the master/servant duo for their task of getting to school. He had begun to develop a fatherly feeling toward Sarveali, the fatherless boy paired with himself, a sonless man. Sheikhak was quite pleased with Sarveali's progress and the little master's satisfaction with his abilities. Holding Teimour Khan's left hand with his right and ordering Sarveali to carry Teimour Khan's parchment-colored briefcase, Sheikhak led the two boys toward the gate of the estate to show them the route. Sarveali held the briefcase, stuffed with new books, blank notebooks, pencils, and other supplies, and felt proud that he resembled a student. He remembered how humiliated he had felt, starving, when he was beaten by Barat-Ali; he concluded that pride did not mix well with hunger.

They left the bliss of the estate to enter the 1930s township of Kamab and its quintessential dirt-covered streets and labyrinthine alleys that easily turned alluvial with rain. The name Kamab, which means "water deficient," was at odds with the condition of its namesake. Sporadic epidemics of trachoma, diphtheria, and syphilis, as well as natural disasters, further plagued the municipality.

Sheikhak took a right turn and charged toward the main square behind which stood the Shahr-Azad School. The school had inherited its name from a pre–Greek invasion Persian prince. The ancient town's ruins demonstrated a civilization that most likely had been more advanced 2,500 years earlier. The main square now resembled a deformed octopus with eight disproportionately sized legs. One main street, four curvaceous wide alleys, and three ultra-convoluted narrow ones—all tortuous—formed the eight legs that culminated in the nucleus of the town. The end of one wide alley formed a minibazaar, covered by domed ceilings with breastlike peaks on the roof. This constituted the commercial center of Kamab. The citizens perceived the *bazaarcheh* as a center for commercial deception. Since Iranian towns like Kamab had been historically invaded and conquered and their citizens repeatedly raped and brutalized by domestic warlords and foreigners, the merchants had developed the philosophy that raping the township's citizens and bumpkins of the surrounding villages, through trade, was merely an act of tradition. When the trio reached the opening of the *bazaarcheh*, they were fallen upon by merchants, who considered Sheikhak an indispensable customer, although he was implacable in his purchasing demands. They wheedled him constantly to win his business.

"*Ass-salam-ul-alaik*, Mirza Sheikhak, the grand emissary of the Shirlu dynasty!" the grocer said.

But Sheikhak was too hurried to exchange pleasantries. The school was located on the other side of the bazaar, so the three continued on their journey down the graveled main street. Black-chadored, crowlike women, who had already started their morning confabulation rituals, carried freshly baked hot bread to their homes. Sheikhak eyed the huge jugs of rose water; jute sacks full of sun-dried grapes, dried figs, and apricots; and other covert items hidden in the kilim-style woven satchels that held the villagers' cargo.

When they passed the board of education office, the trio came upon Hedermaneh, the female lunatic, who suddenly appeared from a side alley. She prepared to lift her oversize, multilayered skirt to expose her genitals, which she referred to as her "elephant eye."

"Get lost, you filthy Arab woman!" Sheikhak said as he moved forward to shield the boys. "You are scaring the prince of the Shirlus." He threw a coin at the woman, who then disappeared down a side alley. Neither Sarveali nor Teimour Khan understood the little scene, but both understood that money had won the day.

"They're all harmless . . . no need for fear," Sheikhak consoled the two frightened boys. "If I notice that anyone in the school or on the streets harms the little Khan, I'll personally behead them. If one strand of hair is missing from your princely head, I'll kill them all. You just tell me if someone is bold enough to harass you." He knelt down and faced the little Teimour Khan, holding his shoulders with both hands. Teimour Khan, slightly embarrassed by his fear, tried to emanate an expression of childish confidence. A *khanzadeh* of the Shirlu dynasty should never be terrified. But Sarveali, deprived of any such self-esteem, felt more apprehensive than before.

Sheikhak gave his last instructions to Teimour Khan. "Do not drink the water at school. Only drink out of the canteen in your bag. Do not touch anyone, especially those with trachoma. Sit only by your cousins. When you get hungry, there are some walnut-stuffed, sugar-coated dates in your bag."

On orders from Sheikhak, Sarveali waited outside the school by the oversize wooden door, whose steel knocker was as big as his head. He was even more terrified now that Sheikhak and his master had disappeared. Remembering that Sheikhak's protectionist lecture about beheading hurtful beasts only pertained to the defense of his master and not to him, he shuddered at the semispherical heads of the nails mounted on the thick sycamore door. All at once the nail heads became the eyes of a giant ghoulish face staring at him. He pressed his small, dark body against the ghoul-face door; on his back, he felt the metallic cold of the semispherical nail heads. He prayed for Sheikhak's return.

After leaving the *khanzadeh* with the principal, Sheikhak walked toward the front gate where Sarveali had been ordered to wait. As soon as Sheikhak opened the gate's door, Sarveali lost his balance and fell onto his buttocks in the gravel. The familiar pain in his anus started him crying again.

"Now what, you son of Zolfali, the Blind Licker?" Sheikhak queried. Immediately regretting his words, he fetched a walnut-stuffed, sugar-coated date from his pocket, gave it to the little boy, and emphasized that as a servant of the powerful Great Khan, he was not to be alarmed by anyone or anything, that the whole town respected and feared the Great Khan. "You be a good servant," he said, "and in return, you'll receive money and protection." This was Sarveali's first exposure to the primary principle of feudalism.

Chapter 3

For the next six years, at the feet of Sheikhak, Sarveali learned the intricacies of indentured servitude and its heroic features. It was difficult for the factotum not to take advantage of Sarveali's boyhood innocence by concocting farragoes of truth and fiction about his duties. He would occasionally remind Sarveali of the boy's elevated hierarchical status as the personal servant of the Great Khan's son and forbid the boy to interact with the other children on the estate. "Your master is Teimour Khan, and you do nothing other than serve him. There'll be no playing around with those other servant children! What if your master needs you to tie his shoes or sharpen his pencils when you're enjoying yourself?"

Once, during the summer of Teimour Khan's third grade when Sarveali was nearly eight, Sheikhak concocted a particularly memorable fabrication for his innocent servant-in-training. He spun a long tale about a servant of a Shirlu khan who died while rescuing his master in a great flood. Pausing to inhale a minute dose of air, Sheikhak said, "This is what you should do for your master; be willing to kill yourself so he may live, Tall Cypress!"

Sarveali was entranced by the story and lost himself in a dream: *I am waiting in the rain outside the classroom door at my master's school with a pitcher of rose water. The rain is pouring down hard, as Mirza Sheikhak said . . . maybe even harder. I look up, and I see the roof of the classroom crumbling. I run and pull my master out. When I die trapped in the rubble, then people will say nice things about me.*

DREAMS LIKE THIS ONE HELPED SARVEALI EXCEL in his servile duties. By the time he was twelve he had memorized every corner of the route that Teimour Khan and he had taken religiously every school day for the past six years. He was no longer afraid of the lepers and ruffians and he only laughed when the lunatic Hedermaneh accosted them. He knew the exact spot where he once saw a snake devour a rat. He also remembered seeing the wife of a distant relative of his master's walking with her maid, the spike of one of her high-heeled shoes lanced through a lizard's abdomen.

Chagrined, he remembered that, when he was almost nine years old, a perfectly shaped chunk of chicken feces had deceived him into thinking it was one of those baklavas he had received from Sheikhak on his first day of employment. He had genuflected to grab the treat from the ground, but upon attempting to put it in his mouth, received a hard slap on the face from Teimour Khan. The blow swiveled his head forty-five degrees on his neck, and the chicken shit went flying through the air.

Teimour Khan's sixth grade year was now nearing its end, signaling the end of his primary schooling. Sarveali, who had grown very little and seemed stunted, remained illiterate, while his master, now a tall, handsome preadolescent, was about to take his final examination for upper school. One evening prior to the exam, Sheikhak played a trick on Teimour Khan and Sarveali. Emboldened by wine, he told them about the magic of Saint Elias: "If you wash and sweep the alleyway in front of the estate every day before dawn for sixty days, Saint Elias will make any of your wishes come true."

"Any wish?" Teimour Khan asked.

"Yes, my master, any wish! The saint himself has told me so. We are close friends, you see," Sheikhak added.

"How could the saint be your friend? You are a mere servant! Besides, I don't believe in such rubbish," Teimour Khan replied; nevertheless, he did not wish to completely discount the saint's influence. Teimour Khan yearned to score highest on the final examination to win the status of valedictorian for the district.

"My master, you are correct that I'm a mere servant," Sheikhak demurred, bowing slightly from his squatting position on the rug. "But I have major connections within the circle of saints. Indeed, if my memory serves me right, knowing that I am a servant of this august household, the saint mentioned that, for my masters, he might make some concessions. You can, for instance, give the early morning washing and sweeping privilege to someone else." He paused and then ordered Sarveali, "Tall Cypress of Shiraz, run outside and see if there is a full moon tonight!" Sheikhak winked at Teimour Khan while pointing his head in Sarveali's direction. Sarveali yelled in response, "Yes, it's full!"

"You'll then be the privileged one attending to the saint's needs," Sheikhak announced.

Sarveali nodded.

Close to bedtime, Sarveali brought Teimour Khan his water pitcher and glass, and his master reinforced his desire for Sarveali to carry out the predawn task.

"It's important that you do this every day before the cock's crow," Teimour Khan said. "I *must* become the valedictorian, and that's what the saint will give me after seeing the washed and swept alleyway in front of our house. You best do a perfect job! No laziness!"

Overjoyed with excitement at such an opportunity, Sarveali did not sleep that night lest he violate the saint's time threshold.

On that first day, Sarveali had barely finished the post-irrigation sweeping of the alleyway as the first rays of the sun hit the shiny stones. At that moment, tens of neighborhood cocks crowed as if, in their ensemble, they were congratulating Sarveali for completing his task. His soul felt galvanized as his first mission was accomplished. He impatiently waited for Teimour Khan to witness his success.

Teimour Khan, observing the flawlessly clean space in front of the door, tried to conceal his satisfaction. But instead of praising his servant's efforts, he said, "Do the same but better, cleaner, shinier! And do it for fifty-nine more days. If you have to, lick the stones and then shine them with oil—after you've rid them of rough edges with emery paper. Make the stones of the alleyway stand out for the saint!"

For the next fifty-nine days, Sarveali developed a relationship with every single stone. Some stones had eyes that gazed at him and others, smiling lips. A few stones had coarse edges that no sandpaper could soften. When he awoke the last day of work, he felt faint from a fear of tardiness. He noticed that the world's luminosity was a shade or two closer to dawn. A sense of guilt, mixed with fear of punishment, made him sweep with even greater vigor, raising massive clouds of dust into the air. The lighter particles of dust danced upward, while the heavier ones started their downward descent, resulting in a phantasmagoric dance. From the dust haze, Saint Elias emerged, paralyzing Sarveali so that he fell to his knees. The broom dropped from his hands as the ghostlike saint walked toward him. His bushy white eyebrows, white beard, green turban, huge paunch, black cloak, and yellow slippers were barely visible behind the dust cloud. Sarveali fought for air. He closed his eyes, for he knew Saint Elias had come to express his outrage at Sarveali's tardiness.

"You son-of-a-whore!" Sarveali heard, and felt a hard slap on his cheek. He was still not courageous enough to open his eyes. He gathered all of his courage to say, "Saint Elias, please forgive me! I overslept!"

"Saint Elias?! You are calling *me* Saint Elias? You insolent, blasphemous bastard!" the voice said as Sarveali was slapped on the other cheek.

"I'll tell Mirza Sheikhak to beat the shit out of you if you dust the alley one more morning!" the voice continued. Sarveali remained kneeling with his eyes closed until he could no longer hear the saint's footsteps. When Teimour Khan appeared, ready to take his final examinations, he did not seem to notice Sarveali's agitation.

The results of the examination were issued three weeks later, and Teimour Khan was indeed the valedictorian of the district. Upon learning of his status, Teimour Khan promptly contested Sheikhak's theory of sainthood and its ability to create miracles. "My intelligence and genius won me the valedictorianship, not your stupid saint!" he said to Sheikhak.

And when Sarveali complained to Sheikhak, "Your saint friend slapped me twice and hard," Sheikhak smiled and said, "I will tell my friend to be gentler to the Tall Cypress of Shiraz from now on! Also, my dear, when a saint slaps you on one cheek, you need to immediately turn the other."

TEIMOUR KHAN WAS TO ATTEND Avicenna Preparatory School in Shiraz the following autumn. Sarveali and Teimour Khan continued their servant–master relationship, but by now Sarveali had cultivated an unrequited fascination for Teimour that verged on religious worship. He thought his master the most handsome, intelligent person on earth. His face, body, attire, aroma, agility, diction, and mannerisms stimulated a potent enthrallment in Sarveali. He determined that his entire purpose in life was to please his master, which the little Khan stonily accepted as his due.

One early afternoon, Sarveali heard Sheikhak calling to him: "Tall Cypress of Shiraz! Come here!" When Sarveali entered the room, he was surprised to find the chief factotum and the local prostitute in bed together.

"Hey, you nice little boy, come here!" the woman, known as Madame Illuminator, whispered. As if a huge ewer full of poison had poured onto his flesh, Sarveali recoiled.

"Go to the angel, tall graceful one!" Sheikhak reinforced with a chuckle. Although his feet seemed stuck in a viscous ground of fear and reluctance, Sarveali moved toward the couple. Madame Illuminator immediately grabbed his penis and held it between her index finger and thumb, pressing it gently through the cotton fabric of his pants.

"What a little chickpea you have there!" she said laughing, wafting toward him her alcoholic breath.

"Perhaps it's a lentil? Or a vetch pea?" Sheikhak laughed and, in reaction, Sarveali jerked himself away from the woman's fingers and ran toward the door.

"Come back! I was teasing you," Madame Illuminator called after him.

Sarveali darted from the room, ran toward the back of the orchard, found the tallest date palm tree, and sat on the ground next to its trunk, his face between his knees. He felt massive shame and humiliation. Until the light grew dim, he watched a family of nightingales perched within the cleft leaves indulge themselves on remnants of dates. Finally walking back toward his quarters, he met up with Sheikhak.

"Where were you? You're lucky that Teimour Khan was away. What if he needed you?" Then patiently and kindly, the factotum said, "And don't worry about your chickpea; someday it will grow into a cobra."

THE ESTATE WAS IN HIGH EXCITEMENT, for soon Changiz Khan, the Great Khan's older son, would arrive home. He had earned his preparatory school diploma a few days after Teimour Khan finished his primary school examinations. The Great Khan received a telegraph, which Sheikhak read loudly: "Arriving on the 13th of *Teer* to Kamab 1200 hours via Khashayar Khan's auto. Sincerely, Changiz Shirlu."

Teimour Khan's vexation escalated when he heard this news, as he had never stopped being jealous of his older brother. He was thinking about his position with his father being downgraded as Sarveali was tying his left shoe into a perfect butterfly-shaped knot. Sarveali looked up and asked, "Teimour Khan, do you think they're coming in Khashayar Khan's Mercurochrome?"

Teimour Khan urgently needed to relieve his aggravation. He looked down at Sarveali, now tying his right shoe, and slapped the other boy's left cheek as hard as he could.

"You retarded midget! The car is a Mercury, not a Mercurochrome. Now get out!" Sarveali rushed out of the room, confused about any difference in mispronunciation.

Sheikhak, arriving late to the servants' chamber that night, was unaware of Sarveali's earlier punishment. As Sarveali sleepily rubbed his left cheek, Sheikhak told the boy, "One day, you will prepare for Teimour Khan's return from preparatory school."

On the day of Changiz Khan's arrival, the Great Khan, Teimour Khan, and some of the servants, Sheikhak and Sarveali included, along with several other relatives in a cavalcade of four automobiles and several carriages, left the township for the Kamab Gorge. Sarveali was proud that the leading automobile was the Great Khan's Packard. Khashayar Khan's Mercury, carrying its owner, the chauffeur, and Changiz Khan, finally arrived around four in the afternoon. The crowd cheered and sacrificed a calf in front of the automobile's bumper. Sarveali, from the vantage point of the roadside, watched his master. Teimour Khan remained silent, neither smiling nor grimacing at the arrival of his brother.

The Great Khan and his relatives greeted Changiz Khan by kissing him on both cheeks and bestowing occasional hugs. When Changiz Khan reached Teimour Khan, the two greeted each other warily. It was Teimour Khan, however, who did not return his older brother's kisses.

As Changiz Khan prepared to drive the family Packard home, Sarveali knew in one glance that Teimour Khan was enraged. In spite of Changiz Khan's invitation, Teimour Khan refused to ride back with his brother in the Packard; instead, he chose to ride in the Mercury. As the procession reversed its direction and the Packard passed, Sarveali issued a covert, boyish malediction on Changiz Khan: "I hope he becomes bald . . . oh no! What blasphemy! God of Shirlus, please forgive me!" he immediately pleaded. His allegiance, no matter how trod upon it was, would always be to Teimour Khan.

As soon as the caravan reached the estate, Teimour Khan rushed to his room, Sarveali following him.

"You stupid midget, bring me some mint potion. My stomach is growling!" Sarveali had never concocted mint aqua vitae, so he raced to find Sheikhak, who was working in the cellar of an outbuilding.

"How do I make this mint-water thing? Teimour Khan wants it *now!*" Sarveali pleaded.

Sheikhak downed several gulps of the red wine he was preparing for the Great Khan and his guests and then slowly, as if his command of motor skills had diminished, told Sarveali the precise proportions of the water versus mint distillate.

"What's a dis—till—ate? And where is it?" Sarveali wailed.

Sheikhak walked to the back of the cellar, grabbed a small bottle, and handed it to Sarveali. He then hesitated and said, "You know what, Great Cypress? I'll make the potion for the prince."

Sheikhak mixed the aqua vitae in a tall crystal glass, poured crushed ice from the icehouse into it, and, in slow motion, handed it to Sarveali. Sarveali put the glass on a tray and held it with one hand as he ran across the courtyard to the main building, entered the front door, and ran upstairs to present the concoction to Teimour Khan.

The aroma of mint rising from the glass caressed Sarveali's nostrils. When he arrived with the tray, Teimour Khan was simultaneously enraged and pleased by Sarveali's fifteen-minute delay: enraged because his spasmodic guts were still bothering him but pleased because he had an excuse to give Sarveali a whipping. Converting all his fraternal rage into a potent muscular power in his right leg, Teimour Khan kicked Sarveali in his buttocks as hard as if he were shooting a soccer ball into a penalty goal.

Sarveali glanced at the white plaster near his face as he fell, and it oddly reminded him of the pearly white goat of his childhood. His face struck against the wall with full force and ricocheted onto the carpeted floor.

From some hidden depths of his being, the twelve-year-old remembered the queer pain he had experienced so long ago in the epicenter of his rectal region, the exact spot where the pointed tip and welt of Teimour Khan's boot had just landed. The pain of the insult was so great that he burst into tears. Without looking at Teimour Khan, Sarveali ran from the room.

In the hallway, Sarveali heard Changiz Khan's voice.

"Who is that child, and why is he crying?"

"He's the son of Zolfali, the Blind Licker," Sheikhak mumbled. "I don't know why he's crying." So it was that Changiz Khan saw Sarveali for the first time. Through his tear-infused vision, Sarveali gave Changiz Khan a brief glance. "He's not bald yet!" he thought, as he ran toward his chamber.

That night, Sheikhak advised Sarveali that as a good servant, he must be a receptacle for his master's rages when needed. "You know, he's become a young man, and young men at times get upset about a few things. And when a *khanzadeh* sees his arms grow with muscles, the first thing he needs to do is severely beat his personal servant. So remember, Tall Cypress, whenever he's angry, you should make yourself available so he can unload his aggression on you."

"Aggression?"

"Yes, so he might give you a few whippings, but you should be *man* enough to take it. It won't kill you; it will make your skin thicker, it'll make you more muscular, and it'll make your bones stronger," Sheikhak continued. "When his Eminence's royal hand lands on your cheek, it's like a divine gift from a saint, especially now that he's seen and felt his large and hard muscles," Sheikhak clarified.

So it was that Sheikhak and Sarveali discussed the centuries-old class structure between peasant masses and their tribal elites in rural Iranian society. Both were oblivious to the modern age that was sweeping their country in the midst of World War II. If either had been told that radical change would ultimately force an end to their centuries-old traditions, one would have denied it and the other—naive and unlettered—would not have comprehended it.

Chapter 4

Four months after his return, twenty-year-old Changiz Khan was betrothed to fifteen-year-old Bibi Golnar Khanom Shirlu, his paternal *and* maternal cousin. Their impending nuptials caused Sarveali to develop a strange feeling of envy on behalf of his master. He wished for Teimour Khan to marry also. When Teimour Khan announced he would not attend the wedding, Sarveali waited eagerly to learn of Teimour Khan's grand plan to free himself from the obligation. His master's solution was to fabricate symptoms of *sarsam*, an illness diagnosed by delirium and frenetic behavior. Sheikhak immediately sent for Dr. Pezeshkian, the new physician who made house calls. The clinician could not substantiate Teimour Khan's self-diagnosis, although he did find before him a precocious young man who could memorize the symptoms of encephalitis.

Anticipating orders from the young master or the physician, Sheikhak ordered Sarveali to remain in Teimour Khan's room during the examination. "I don't wish to go where the commoners go. I wish to rest from my *sarsam*," Teimour Kahn announced to the physician, who smiled gently and took a red bottle from his briefcase. He administered a tablespoon of the bottle's contents to Teimour Khan.

"Here's some chloral hydrate syrup, a sedative and hypnotic that should give you ample rest." When Sarveali saw the syrup, its color like red wine, flow from the translucent bottle, he wished he were ill so that he could taste it. Teimour Khan did not go to the wedding. The drug-induced sedation lasted an entire week, until the newlyweds returned home.

Bibi Golnar Khanom arrived at the estate as the first female-in-residence since the death of the Great Khan's wife. Sheikhak, although obedient and respectful, was secretly agitated that he could no longer entertain Madame Illuminator or continue his usual inebriated episodes. Still, he prepared to feign any amount of virtuousness, if necessary.

Changiz Khan's bride became known as *the* Bibi, or "lady of the house." She was tiny with large honey-colored eyes, and she reminded Changiz Khan of his late mother. He hoped this commonality would fill the void he had felt since her death and that by extension Golnar Khanom would become a suitable companion. Sarveali, however, had lived many years solely in the world of men and was initially terrified of the Bibi. But slowly his fear turned into ambivalence and compliant servitude.

Filling the role of matriarch for the estate, the Bibi initially received a modicum of respect from her new brother-in-law. She was only three years older than Teimour Khan and was the daughter of his late uncle. He dined with the couple and on occasion played backgammon and read with the Bibi the poems of the tenth-century poet Hafez. Within a month, the backgammon and poetry sessions ended; Teimour Khan's resentment of his brother had seemingly transferred to his young bride. The young prince began to receive his meals in his room alone. Soon he began to address the Bibi with only the impersonal "cousin."

Chapter 5

In 1925, almost fifteen years before Changiz Khan's marriage, Reza Shah toppled the last shah of the Qajar dynasty, ending its two-hundred-year reign, and founded the Pahlavi dynasty. Declaring himself a nonrevolutionary reformer, Reza Shah began to introduce reforms that he hoped would elevate Iran, formerly known as Persia, to a level of modernity comparable to the Western world's. In his path of reform, the Shah attacked the corrupt traditional bureaucracy, the usurious bazaar merchants, and the fundamentalist fanaticism of the clergy.

As Changiz Khan and his father became closer, they often discussed politics. "In Iran, progressive Westernization, like kicking these backward mullahs' asses, requires a strong king like Reza Shah!" Sarveali did not understand the discussion or his master's false optimism, but he enjoyed listening. What Changiz Khan and his father did not anticipate, however, was that the Shah, an autocratic nationalist who developed a strong local police force and an army, as well as his own secret police, wished to disarm and weaken the tribal khans, of whom the Shirlus were paramount leaders.

Soon after Changiz Khan's wedding, Reza Shah directed a military attack against most of the tribal khans. The Shirlus were completely unprepared for the end of a four-dynasty era that had cemented the intimate relationship of the tribal upper class with the royal courts. Sarveali became an unwitting observer to the change.

One day, in the late summer of 1940, Sarveali and Teimour Khan returned home from visiting Khashayar Khan's walnut groves. They were met by Changiz Khan, who was pale and agitated, and the Bibi, weeping.

"They have arrested my great-uncle!" the Bibi cried. Changiz Khan said nothing. The Great Khan had been taken away and the estate ransacked. Troops had broken down the front door of the manor house. The chandelier was shattered into thousands of shards and the furniture tossed into a pile. Only Sheikhak had been heroic during the Great Khan's arrest: he punched a uniformed military officer for showing disrespect to his master. Sheikhak too was immediately arrested. Sarveali was only partially relieved to hear that Sheikhak had declared his intention to mirror the destiny of his master. If the Great Khan was to be arrested and imprisoned, then so should he. This loyalty inspired young Sarveali. He told himself that when the time came, he too would fight and die for his master.

Teimour Khan, however, showed no reaction to his father's fate. He was more upset to discover that the soldiers had broken the windshield and headlights of the Packard and ripped the leather seats.

"They even broke the taillights!" Sarveali cried.

Teimour Khan slapped Sarveali in the face.

"Shut up! I can see that! Do you think we're blind *and* deaf?"

Sarveali concluded that Teimour Khan would beat him whenever his amorous feelings for the Packard were adversely affected. When his master's attention returned to the disfigured car, Sarveali quietly slipped away to the orchard. He wept alone against a palm tree trunk. *I deserved it! Why should I shout in front of my master?*

Someday in life, he thought, *I too will slap a uniformed officer to show the master my loyalty.* He continued to paint in his mind a parallel picture of himself and the missing Sheikhak.

Within months, the Shirlu families were told they had the option of being exiled from their land to Tehran or to a neighboring city. Exile became a symbol of hope for them. Even though they bemoaned their fate, they accepted the alternative to imprisonment and prepared to uproot themselves and their possessions.

Will I be exiled too? Sarveali wondered. Unfortunately for his adventurous spirit, Changiz Khan and his family were exiled not to Tehran but Shiraz, which was closer to Kamab. Teimour Khan had been planning to attend secondary school there in any event.

After a few days, the family was informed that the Great Khan had been imprisoned in Tehran, nearly eight hundred kilometers from Shiraz. "Informing you. Bahador Shirlu under arrest at Qasr Prison. Servant Yazdani exiled to the Neishapour outskirts," reported the telegraph from the Ministry of Defense. Sheikhak's heroic defense of his master had won him an exile's sentence to a remote village far away from Tehran. But according to letters Sheikhak wrote to Changiz Khan, he did not complain, but merely stated that he had been provided a home in the village along with an adequate stipend from the government. He also wrote about meeting an elderly man who played a three-string *seh-tar* and claimed to be the descendant of Omar Khayyam. *I wish my father was Omar Khayyam and not stupid Zolfali, the Blind Licker,* Sarveali thought in response to the implausible story. He wished that Sheikhak was with him. Now he had no one to whom he could turn.

Sarveali still longed to accomplish an act of heroism like Sheikhak's, even if it meant imprisonment. Then khans and servants would say, "Oh, yes, it was Sarveali who courageously beat the gendarme to protect the Khan and was sent away to a strange village for years." Although that opportunity never seemed to appear, Sarveali remained hopeful.

As the time came for the family to vacate the Kamab estate, Changiz Khan ordered that all furniture and valuables be stored or crated for transportation to Shiraz. He ordered all the buildings boarded up. Uniformed personnel were assigned to guard the estate because the Shirlus lands had been sequestered, not seized, by the state. But the family could not continue to cultivate the land, and no one knew how long the imprisonment of the Great Khan or the deposed family's exile would last. It was not clear to anyone when or if they would ever return to the estate.

Changiz Khan ordered the chauffeur to immediately transport the Bibi, Teimour Khan, Sarveali, and the Bibi's maid to Shiraz with the Dodge truck. During the ride, Teimour Khan was silent. He hated the lowly vehicle, but the Packard was too damaged to make the trip.

As they drove the streets of Shiraz, they first coursed Karim Khan Zand Boulevard. Sarveali said the name over and over to himself, relishing the words on his tongue. He was awed by the neon signs, colors, shapes, and exotic people. When he saw a cluster of red and blue lights flashing, he said to himself, *God must have landed here, shit these shiny, sparkling turds, and flown away.*

Changiz Khan joined the family two weeks later, just before the government deadline to leave Kamab. He left with a sizable sum of cash from the Great Khan's safe and a crock of gold and silver coins he had hidden under a weeping willow outside the cemetery where their ancestors were buried. Changiz Khan was determined not to lower the family's aristocratic standards; according to his calculations, the family could survive for a decade by selling the retrieved coins to Jewish merchants in Shiraz or Isfahan. After a week in Shiraz, he purchased a furnished house on Karim Khan Zand Boulevard across from Avicenna Preparatory School, where Teimour Khan was enrolled.

Sarveali's excitement at living on the very boulevard whose name fascinated him showered him with happiness. When they arrived at the residence, he noticed that the vestibule where the guards' chambers were located was a miniature version of the guardhouse at the Kamab estate. A familiar cool late summer breeze drifted over his face as the family toured the quarters, the garage, and the servant chambers until they reached the kitchen. Past three outdoor stoves and a cement-floored modern kitchen with indoor stoves, a tall fat object stared at them. When the Bibi opened the kerosene-fueled Kelvinator refrigerator, revealing wire shelves, Sarveali thought it looked like a giant ghoul exposing its rib cage.

This new urban establishment seemed glorious to everyone. Outside the kitchen, a large circular, shallow pool, four meters in diameter with a water-ejecting fountain in the center, stood in the middle of the yard. Past the pool was a rectangular rose garden. In the very middle of the garden, a dying jasmine tree straggled.

"We have only twelve rooms in the house and two *panj-dari* (a room with five doors); the one downstairs has an indoor basin." Changiz Khan showed them the basin with a fountain ejecting and splashing water. "And here is Karim Khan Zand," Changiz Khan said, pointing at a mural of a bearded man smoking a *nargillah*.

This Karim Khan is part of our house as well as outside, Sarveali thought. It seemed that Karim Khan winked at him.

The excitement of the new home made Sarveali forget his anguish at losing Sheikhak because it imparted a fresh feeling, a new beginning. He took a special interest in the jasmine tree, which seemed dead. The tree's only living branch protruded from the base of its trunk; the rest of the branches were dead. But the tree continued to stand, like a man-size skeleton. When Sarveali bent down to examine the branch, he noticed it spanned the length of his arm. He decided he would make it his personal project to revitalize the imprisoned tree in honor of Sheikhak.

FOUR DAYS AFTER MOVING into the house at Shiraz, Teimour Khan started school. Sarveali was uncertain how to move forward now that his old preceptor was no longer there to advise him. How would he help his master in a metropolitan area like Shiraz? For the first three days, Sarveali carried Teimour Khan's briefcase as he had before, even though the school was just across the boulevard from the new house.

"Walk behind me!" Teimour Khan cautioned. "I don't want people to see me with you!" Sarveali did as he was commanded without question.

One afternoon, when Sarveali waited to greet Teimour Khan after school, he noticed that his master had made new friends. Two classmates, one dark-skinned and the other lighter in complexion, were laughing with his master. Teimour Khan gave his briefcase to Sarveali and pointed for him to walk behind. Sarveali followed them to Café Reza, where they took a table by the window. "Stand at attention next to me," Teimour Khan ordered.

When the waiter brought the three boys their delights, Sarveali's mouth watered as though his heart had melted into his salivary glands. The young men were devouring the famous Shirazi *paloodeh,* an iced noodle dessert. *Snow-white doves flying into a warm nest,* Sarveali imagined hungrily. Teimour Khan poured sour cherry syrup on top from a small bottle that looked to Sarveali like a baby Arab in a *kaffiyeh.*

It's a little baby Arab full of blood, Sarveali thought, as the other two boys poured lemon juice from a bigger bottle on their *paloodeh.*

Teimour Khan could feel that Sarveali was going mad at being tempted by the gustatory delight, so he dipped his spoon into his dessert and scooped a large portion of the sour cherry–*paloodeh* until drops of the red fluid diluted by melted ice danced from the angel-haired starch. He lifted the spoon in front of Sarveali's mouth and held it for several seconds as if his actions were frozen. Sarveali opened his mouth instinctually, anticipating the *snow dove* would fly into the *nest* of his mouth. Teimour Khan tilted the spoon slowly so that its content would fall to the floor. But Sarveali leaped forward and, just as the bite of *paloodeh* was in midair, gobbled the delicacy like a frog catching a fly. The other boys laughed thunderously, and Sarveali realized they thought he was a dolt. As he blushed in embarassment, Teimour Khan came to a conclusion. There was no need to beat his servant. He had discovered the joy of inflicting psychological misery and humiliation.

NINE MONTHS LATER, at the end of Teimour Khan's first school year, the Great Khan died in prison of a pulmonary embolism caused when the prison executioner injected air into his veins. The young Changiz Khan and Teimour Khan did not pose a threat to the Shah, so they stayed free. Only the Great Khan had remained imprisoned with the other tribal leaders to prevent the possibility of uprisings.

Sheikhak died six months after his master and was buried in his village of exile. Mourning his late preceptor, the only father he had ever known, Sarveali suspected that Sheikhak's grief over the Great Khan's murder caused his death, and more than ever hoped he could die for his own master. When he thought of the Khan's family members branding Sheikhak's death as the ultimate servile martyrdom, Sarveali cried into his pallet many nights. But the young khans showed little emotion for their dead father, as Changiz Khan formally succeeded his father as head of the clan.

Chapter 6

In 1942, when Teimour Khan and Sarveali were fourteen years old, the British forced Reza Shah into exile in South Africa. The Shah, a known German sympathizer, had announced Iran's neutrality in World War II, incurring English wrath. The crown prince, Mohammad Reza Shah, became monarch at age twenty-two, about the same age as Changiz Khan. The young Shah gave amnesty to all tribal leaders, and the Shirlus decided to repatriate to their estates and lands.

Changiz Khan planned to spend his time revitalizing the neglected property in Kamab. The citrus trees and date palms had withered and died. After Changiz Khan returned from his first trip to the estate, while he and the Bibi were drinking tea, Sarveali heard, "The whole place needs to be redone. The building is fine, but the orchard is completely gone."

Changiz Khan continued, "The rooms next to the guardhouse became the fucking soldiers' latrine. Shit smell wafted over me when I entered the estate. And, yes, there was not a single juniper left. These exiles accomplish nothing for the state, except the death of people like my poor old father, destruction of our lands, and starvation of the peasants . . ."

He spent the next year repairing the country estate, planting new orchards, and redeveloping their old land, while the family continued living in Shiraz. Everyone, Sarveali most of all, looked forward to going home. But when Sarveali witnessed Changiz Khan in his new role as master of the estate, he bemoaned Teimour Khan's subservience. He dreamed of Teimour Khan driving his new Jeep through his own vast fields of cotton and wheat or grand citrus orchards. Once he even sinfully envisioned himself sitting next to Teimour Khan as he drove.

IN 1944, AS TEIMOUR KHAN WAS about to graduate from preparatory school, he and his friends decided to play a trick on Sarveali. They would force the servant to accompany them to a brothel in Shiraz, which they had been patronizing for three months. Since the incident when Madame Illuminator, the prostitute in Kamab, had held Sarveali's "chickpea" penis, he had avoided women and felt ashamed to be near them. A peculiar revulsion toward any and all of the female staff seemed as insoluble as oil and water. When a group of *khanzadehs*, including his master, proposed the following: "Sarveali, we are taking you to heaven," Sarveali swallowed mightily. "I have a backache, dear Khan. I can't go with you!"

"You have a backache because you jack off too much!" the boys shouted in hideous glee. Instantly Sarveali felt his feet fail him and his hands become too powerless to resist. When they reached the brothel, the chauffeur purchased prostitutes from the head madam, and Sarveali was assigned the cheapest. Without indulging in any female companionship himself, the chauffeur walked back to the car to wait.

The head madam directed her high-paying customers to the Kings Quarters, a venue for the younger, more desirable prostitutes. Sarveali was pointed toward a corridor where the low-cost prostitutes waited for their customers in roofless cubicles with walls barely tall enough to cover the bed and its occupants. A short while later, from Sarveali's cubicle, Teimour Khan and his cousins heard a hullabaloo.

"Get this midget and his date-seed dick out of my room!" the prostitute shouted. Her voice echoed through the corridors of the brothel. "He couldn't even get it up!" she yelled.

The *khanzadehs* had a good laugh at Sarveali's sexual humiliation. Sarveali, however, felt a pseudo-victory. *At least it's not a "chickpea" anymore,* he thought. *It's grown into a "date seed."*

Teimour Khan bade Sarveali hold his clothes outside his prostitute's chamber in the first-class quarters. Sarveali dutifully sat outside the door and listened to the grunts and groans produced by his master's fierce copulation.

With a peculiar mixed feeling of pride and sadness, he thought, *Oh, if I could just have what my master has, just for a couple of hours,* placing his master's shirt, scented with cologne, to his face. Immediately he felt a stiffness in his phallus. Alas, on that day it was too late to do him any good.

But Sarveali was proud of his master for more than his sexual prowess. Teimour Khan had matured into a handsome sixteen-year-old with slicked-back hair and a Douglas

Fairbanks mustache. What Sarveali found even more amazing was that his young master had developed literary, artistic, and intellectual aspirations as well. Although Sarveali understood nothing, Teimour Khan was forever lecturing him about the surrealists and dadaists. He read books and periodicals and was fascinated by the avant-garde movement in Europe.

Once during a hunting trip, Teimour Khan captured a baby boar, brought it to the Shiraz mansion, and named it Donghozi. He put Sarveali in charge of attending to the baby.

When Sarveali was bathing Donghozi, he observed the animal staring into his eyes. That night, Sarveali experienced a nocturnal emission while dreaming that Donghozi had sodomized him ferociously. He interpreted this dream to mean that his master's animal served as an extension of Teimour Khan. Sarveali felt a familiar pain followed by a familiar joy. He continued to admire Teimour Khan and thought of nothing but serving him. He hardly noticed that Teimour Khan returned his unconditional loyalty and servitude with a mixture of ambivalence and abhorrence.

One afternoon in December 1944, when Sarveali brought Teimour Khan's polished boots to his room, he heard his master shouting, "Switzerland, take me away!" Sarveali was shaken by his master's news. Determined to leave what he called "philistine" Iran, Teimour Khan had answered an advertisement in the local newspaper placed by a Swiss school announcing its new faculty of pharmacology. The school was accepting new students, and Teimour Khan initiated correspondence with it immediately. Although World War II was continuing in Europe, he made plans to emigrate to Switzerland, a neutral country, ostensibly to pursue a course of study in pharmacology. His true intent, however, was to pursue literature, sculpture, painting, and other pleasures of intellectual life. Changiz Khan not only forbade studying useless subjects such as the arts but also considered Teimour Khan an idiot to set out for a continent ravaged by war. Sarveali was crushed by the news and prayed that he could accompany his master on his journey.

Chapter 7

In the summer of 1945, shortly before the end of World War II, Teimour Khan finished preparatory school at age seventeen, one year earlier than most of his classmates. On the day he was to leave for Switzerland, the pregnant Bibi ordered Sarveali to prepare the ritual farewell tray. Her pregnancy surprised Sarveali; he had always seen her relationship with her husband as one with no love or affection. Sarveali's hopes to accompany his master vanished like a straw in a storm. He began to assemble the contents of the silver tray—a miniature Koran, a bowl of water with rose petals, a small brazier with four ovoid-shaped molten red charcoals with burning wild rue, and a small vase of jasmine flowers. The Koran was used to bless the traveler, and the rue to dispel bad omens. Teimour Khan whispered a poem to himself:

Sometimes you're the fire that burns,
Sometimes the wild rue that fumigates.

Sarveali could not comprehend Teimour Khan's metaphor; he simply offered the tray to his master in humility. The poem had pierced his heart and burned his bowels. Teimour Khan ceremoniously climbed into his brother's new Studebaker without a backward look as Sarveali sobbed copiously. The chauffeur drove through the gate of the estate, leaving Sarveali to follow the car through the gate and onto the street, until his master disappeared into the haze.

Teardrops plopped into the water bowl Sarveali still held. He poured the bowl of water on the ground, completing the superstitious ritual that protects the traveler from harm. But the ritual did not protect him against his unprecedented sadness. Once again, he felt like an orphan. He attempted to fill his servile vacuum by taking on new duties—now for Changiz Khan—but his new master seemed oblivious. Sarveali performed his duties unenthusiastically since the magnetic connection he had felt for Teimour Khan had been broken. His body remained in Kamab, but his heart never stopped yearning for his old master.

MEANWHILE, CHANGIZ KHAN'S MARRIAGE never warmed up; it was as loveless as the hundreds of other arranged marriages in that circle of Turko-Persian life. For Sarveali, this relationship justified his lack of interest in women, as a cold-blooded wife and a disinterested husband typified marriage. But when a beautiful girl with tulip-red cheeks, little Bibi Naz Khanom, was born in late winter, Sarveali saw that some good could come from the most loveless of marriages.

During this time, the family continued to live in the Shiraz mansion, while Changiz Khan spent a great deal of his time at the Kamab estate, overseeing the restoration.

Sometimes Sarveali accompanied his master; more often he stayed in Shiraz with the Bibi and her infant daughter. He could not help but notice the increased level of activity in Changiz Khan's life as he started a personal campaign to re-create the glory of the Shirlus. He approached the American troops currently deployed in Iran and proposed that he supply their needs for wheat and barley. Changiz Khan also experimented with developing a citrus business and cotton farms and utilizing modern agricultural machinery. Free of his father's restrictions and his brother's condescension, Changiz Khan excelled in these ventures. He also formed ties with local politicians, as well as those in Tehran, some of whom had been his classmates at Zagros School.

In October 1946, although the relationship between the Bibi and Changiz Khan remained cold, the Bibi delivered a set of twin boys, Virasb and Lohrasb. It was as if the couple felt they must prove the legitimacy of their union by procreation. The Bibi's life continued in caring obsessively for the newborns and her daughter and in an exaggerated altruism toward the sick and poor peasants of the area.

Longing every day for news about Teimour Khan, Sarveali listened carefully as Changiz Khan read aloud the letters he received from his brother, which reported that he was actively pursuing his education in pharmacology. Sarveali hoped his old master would ask about him, but Teimour Khan's correspondence included no mention of his former servant. If his master had gotten involved with the intelligentsia and the avant-garde of Europe, Teimour Khan never mentioned them, either.

FOR TWELVE YEARS, SARVEALI HAD HEARD LITTLE from his uncle. Barat-Ali had attempted two or three visits before the

Great Khan's imprisonment but Sheikhak had not granted him entrance. However, Barat-Ali had been receiving Sarveali's salary every month, but as Sarveali approached the age of eighteen, that financial arrangement would come to an end. Sarveali hoped that with his imminent financial security the coming year would be a pleasant one.

Twelve days after the Iranian New Year in the spring of 1946, on the sidewalk of the Karim Khan Zand Boulevard, Sarveali came upon a group of gypsy women selling metal handicrafts. They lined up pewter mortars and pestles, *kabab* skewers, and braziers on the sidewalk.

"Hey, mister!" one of the gypsies shouted at Sarveali. "Come and buy skewers so you can grill some *kababs* for your woman! This one is a liver *kabab*, and this thick one is for gizzards."

"I don't have a woman!" Sarveali said, annoyed. He was reminded of a project that the dead Sheikhak had given him—to search for a blue stone in cock gizzards, considered an aphrodisiac.

As he reached to examine some offal, the gypsy grabbed his hand. "Let me see your palm. I can tell your future for two *qerans*." Before Sarveali could say no, the gypsy had coerced him into a soothsaying session.

"You don't have a knotted hand; you have a pointed one," she said. "Your palm is square. Look at your knobby knuckles. Your Jupiter finger says it all . . . the square nails . . ."

"Jupi—what?"

"Someone close to you will marry you to a girl whose beauty will make you suffer for the remainder of your life. It's in your stars." She rubbed Sarveali's palm with her hennaed fingers. Sarveali shuddered as much from the flirtation of her touch as her fearful augury.

That evening, on the rooftop where he often slept, he watched the full circle of the moon worshiped by millions of stars. *Are these my stars? The ones the gypsy was talking about?*

Under those stars, the indigo sky, and the full moon, dialogue wafted over him from a nearby outdoor cinema. He thought of the gypsy. Her words echoed in his head. *Am I really destined to marry?* He feared and abhorred women. *How could I marry someone I didn't like?* His favorite people were men—Teimour Khan, his mentor, Sheikhak. As he cried, the moon metamorphosed into a blurry shape and disappeared.

"Someone is coming tomorrow to ruin my life!" Sarveali groaned. "And this coming year will not be nice after all. My master is gone. Like the gypsy whore said, it'll be the *worst* year of my life!"

Chapter 8

The next day, who should appear at the Shiraz mansion but Barat-Ali, Sarveali's shameless uncle. Sarveali listened to Barat-Ali, who still looked very much as he had twelve years earlier except for his graying sideburns, as he entreated Changiz Khan.

"Great Khan of the Shirlus, I have come to obtain your royal permission for a holy cause," Barat-Ali said breathlessly. "Although it might be a petty one for Your Khanate, it's an important one for your petty servant, Sarveali, who's the dust on the bottom of your shoes!" Sarveali felt doom down to his toes.

"Sarveali?" Changiz Khan asked.

"Yes, my master. Sarveali. You don't want to have a bachelor servant at his age, do you, my master? What would people say about someone who's not married, yet works for a great khan like your majesty? I wish to give my daughter's hand to Sarveali, my nephew. I beg for your royal permission."

Changiz Khan wanted to depart immediately. Barat-Ali's aggressive stench, a combination of sheep dung and body sweat, was becoming more intolerable by the moment. The Khan imagined his forthcoming poker game—a full house, straight flush, and a pile of varicolored chips in front of him. Impatient, he did not stop to analyze the man's proposition. He simply consented to it.

"Well, many happy returns!" he said to Sarveali. And to his uncle, "We will handle the expense of the wedding." Immediately he got into his Studebaker and rode away to his poker party.

Sarveali rushed to the kitchen to await his uncle. He was filled with dread. Marriage? To some woman his uncle knew?

Barat-Ali saw in his nephew the same small dark eyes he remembered from his dead brother, short stature, large nose, thin, cracked lips and skin a shade too dark. "How ugly he's become; but my light-skinned daughter must marry this midget."

As for Sarveali, he could only remember the night when he was six years old and his uncle had visited him with the petroleum jelly. He knew now what the visit had been about, and he suddenly hated his uncle. As Barat-Ali kissed him on the mouth, Sarveali felt a vomitus liquid rise to his lips.

An aroma from the kitchen interrupted the false affection. "Umm . . . What's that heavenly smell?" queried Barat-Ali. "Treat your uncle to some of it. I just brought a big fat lamb all the way from Madavan. The fucker shit all over me and the entire ride tried to eat the trucker's cottonseeds."

After Barat-Ali had eaten and drunk an entire pitcher of *doogh*, a yogurt soda, in one gulp, he opened his mouth to start his lecture but emitted a thunderous belch instead. The noise traveled across the yard, hit the walls of the guardhouse, and ricocheted back, enabling Sarveali to hear it twice. Barat-Ali started again, pleased with his gaseous relief. "You are my nephew, my late brother's son. I love you like my own as I've proven to you over the years. I freed you from your mother's sister and her bastard husband . . ."

Sarveali was sucked back into the memory of his childhood. He remembered his little herd of goats and his favorite white kid. He remembered his fat cousin Gholi who had abused him, the little "reddish-yellow" girl, Yazgulu, with the henna-colored hair and startling blue eyes, whose appearance had always scared him.

"Now, I worry about you. You're a bachelor at the age of twenty . . ."

"I'm only eighteen!"

"Even better! What will people say about a young man of eighteen who's not yet married? You just tell me, my nephew, what will people say?"

"I don't know."

"They'll say that the bachelor is 'unnatural,' that the person is afraid of women. They'll say . . ."

Sarveali could not listen to the rest of his uncle's rant. "I'm not 'unnatural,' and I'll marry whenever my master tells me to do so!" Poor Sarveali had fallen easily into Barat-Ali's trap.

"Well, the great Changiz Khan gave the 'royal demand.' He will pay for the wedding, and he demanded that his servant marry immediately! Can you imagine Changiz Khan having to struggle with the reputation that he has a faggot for a servant?"

"The Khan said that?" Sarveali asked. He thought again of the gypsy woman and her prediction.

"Yes, Changiz Khan ordered you to marry my daughter, Yazgulu. I swear on the grave of my late brother, your father, Zolfali, that the Khan said so."

"Who? Yazgulu? The little loud baby?" Sarveali asked. She had the ability to terrify him to no limits, and now he was being "ordered" to marry her.

"Yes, Yazgulu, my daughter! Your cousin! She's fourteen now. Babies grow. Even you've grown, but not by much, I can see," Barat-Ali said, smirking at the nephew who was still a head shorter than he.

THAT NIGHT, SARVEALI AND BARAT-ALI SLEPT together in Sarveali's room in the servants' chambers. In the middle of the night, Barat-Ali's hand clutched Sarveali's buttocks. Sarveali moved away. Minutes later, his uncle reached toward his penis and testicles. Again Sarveali remembered his last night in Madavan so many years earlier. He pushed his uncle away, rose immediately, and lay down under the once-dying jasmine tree in the courtyard. The branch, once the length of his arm, had grown twice as tall as he. The tree branches, leaves, and blossoms muffled the sound of Sarveali's vomiting from the family.

Chapter 9

The next day, Barat-Ali, accompanied by Sarveali and carrying Changiz Khan's gift of five hundred toumans in cash and checks, traveled back to Madavan by truck and donkey cart. Along the way, Sarveali vomited up his breakfast, Changiz Khan's leftovers. Sarveali vomited again when they reached Barat-Ali's door.

"Stop throwing up, boy; it's a bad omen," Barat-Ali said. Gholi heard his father's voice and opened the door.

"Welcome, cousin Sarveali." Sarveali saw a fat man, taller than he, his eyes buried in his fat cheeks. This was what his cousin Gholi, the boy who had treated him so badly when they were children, had turned into . . . a pillar of lard.

And while, to Sarveali's relief, he saw neither Yazgulu, his intended, nor her mother Kokab, that night, he could not purge his anxiety. He felt as pale as the hay he slept on. His only mild consolation was that for the first time in his life, he would be the cynosure of a major event, his own wedding, and that his masters and their relatives would attend. And since it was his unquestioned duty to serve the Shirlus and promote their reputation as the most prosperous and powerful family in Kamab, to a degree that thought soothed his pain.

"My master doesn't want to have single servants. I must marry soon, so I won't embarrass him," he said to himself, but his self-deception was only mildly successful.

Wedding preparations started immediately. The following morning, Barat-Ali, Gholi, and Sarveali went to Kamab via donkey cart to buy provisions. Cone-shaped sugar loaves from the bazaar were the first purchase Barat-Ali made for the wedding; the cones served as invitations to the wedding and as a metaphoric gesture of the "sweet life" that was about to begin.

Early in the morning, on the first day of the wedding festivities, Barat-Ali, Sarveali, and Gholi, fatigued by the previous day's activities, went to the rooftop to observe and evaluate the first wave of attendees. Sarveali watched the surrounding villagers straggle in on foot, horse, and donkey to congregate in Madavan's main square. The villagers' interest in attending a wedding such as this was not only that they might pay their respects to Sarveali and his bride, but also to indulge and satisfy their own hunger. The meals they devoured at such grandiose feasts were often their only substantial ones in an entire year.

The first grand feast was served at lunch. The guests attacked the food like carnivores on helpless prey, their appetite enhanced by aromatic spices and herbs. Sarveali did not recognize many of the guests, but he watched as some of the gluttonous participants became immobile. Finally, many unbuttoned their trousers to release their bellies and, unable to contain the high tide rising in their mouths, vomited into a makeshift vomitorium established near the latrine.

Barat-Ali, who had returned from his first course to stand by Sarveali's side, claimed, "Look at how they are eating! It's only because it's free. These people would hang themselves if they were given a free piece of rope."

Sarveali almost laughed in his uncle's face. *He likes free things more than any of them, such as the twelve years of my salary and sweat money,* he thought. *And he is the biggest stomach worshiper I've ever seen, probably number one among all of them.*

Gholi arrived at that moment, eating a chicken leg. He tied a green handkerchief around Sarveali's left arm. "This is an expensive *silk* armband for the groom! Now everyone knows who you are!" Barat-Ali laughed at Sarveali, who did not know that the armband was not silk but a shiny faux muslin.

As Sarveali, ornamented with his new armband, walked through the crowd, he concluded that the wedding was indeed a reward bestowed on him by Changiz Khan. This thought pained him all the more as he realized that his fear of impotence, disinterest in cohabitation, and abhorrence of his uncle and his family, not to mention his childhood fear of Yazgulu, had transformed the celebration into a period of personal mourning. Perhaps it would be less onerous if he could see and talk to Yazgulu in advance of the ceremony, so they could come to an understanding. But he was still afraid of her, and her mother had given her instructions. "Don't show your face. It's a bad omen. Especially don't show your face to that man before he becomes your husband!" Indeed, since Sarveali had arrived at the Madavan village, he had been forbidden to look upon his bride.

Barat-Ali and Gholi greeted a group of people carrying musical instruments and directed them to their designated position. The loudest noise came from the *serna* player who blew mightily into the mouth of the oboelike instrument. Two *serna* players complemented the *tymbal* players. The *sernas,* which the players blew into fiercely, were almost a meter long. Sarveali was fascinated with their length and thickness; their phallic shapes amused him. "What kind of filthy man am I, having these thoughts at my own wedding?" he murmured to himself.

ON THE SECOND MORNING, Barat-Ali and Sarveali arose early and went to the rooftop to see if the dignitaries had arrived. About 9:00 A.M., Sarveali observed a caravan of Jeeps carrying mostly the Shirlu Khans, their families, and guests. "What are you doing, Mr. Pygmy Groom? Your master is coming. Run with me, now!" Barat-Ali sped down the stairs.

Since they rarely saw cars in the rural villages of Iran in 1946, children ran after the caravan for kilometers, inhaling dust and gasoline or diesel exhaust. Their goal was to catch up to a car and thump it on the side or on the fenders, as if touching the vehicles made them their own.

Barat-Ali and Sarveali observed the automobiles from afar. "The green Jeep is Changiz Khan's, of course. The red one is Tahmour Khan's. That long one is Sahtiar Khan's . . . that one way in the back belongs to Fereidoon Khan . . . and more are coming!" Barat-Ali said, doing a gleeful dance. "But where in the fuckhole is Gholi?"

"I'm coming. I'm coming!" Gholi yelled, lumbering after them.

Barat-Ali genuflected before Changiz Khan and kissed the top of the khan's boots. He shouted at Sarveali and

Gholi. "You insolent idiots! Bend down and kiss your grand master's feet! You are nothing but the dust he sets his footsteps on!"

Sarveali remembered the first day at the Shirlu estate and how his uncle had insisted that he kiss Sheikhak's hand. Thoughts of Sheikhak made Sarveali long for him still. His protector had taught him some useful lessons. He could not overlook the way that Barat-Ali's embellished adulations always netted him some gain. He was sure his uncle expected more than fees for the wedding; surely he hoped for land or a sum of cash.

THE ARISTOCRATS WERE DIRECTED TO THEIR CHAMBER, a makeshift salon in Barat-Ali's house. In the evening, the venue for the khans changed to the rooftop of the house, where they had an aerial view of the celebration. The bibis stayed mostly within the salon where their maids fanned them with woven straw fans.

Yazgulu remained in the second room of the house. She was visited by adolescent boys who delighted in her beauty, and by some of the ladies, including the Bibi, who would become her employer after the marriage. The Bibi and her two babies, the twins Virasb and Lohrasb, were accompanied by the Bibi's daughter, who sat next to her mother and observed every inch of Yazgulu's multicolored bridal costume. Yazgulu's hair stuck out through her gauzy head scarf; her red cheeks, which matched her red silk overall, shone. Underneath the overall, she was wearing six layers of skirts, so thick that her upper body sat elegantly on a cone of fabric. Instantly Yazgulu and the Bibi felt a mutual affection.

Leaving the rooftop on an errand, from his bride-to-be's room Sarveali heard a delicate, female voice speak in

64

a Madavani accent. Through the chamber window, he saw a graceful young woman in multicolored apparel over layered skirts. Her henna hair was visible through the transparent gauze of her head scarf. "She must be Yazgulu," Sarveali guessed. Shockingly, he felt a strange wave of sensuality. *Could Yazgulu's beauty convert me into a proper husband?* he wondered.

He returned thoughtfully to the rooftop where the guests, drinking cognac, single-malt scotch, and Shiraz red wine, were discussing the imminent departure of the Iranian Jewish population to the new state of Israel. Changiz Khan asked Sarveali if he would like to apprentice to Ishaq Shamoun, the Jewish community leader known to be an expert oenologist, before the community's departure. Sarveali decided that winemaking would be a step up in his duties, and was pleased and proud his master thought that well of him. Shyly, with downcast eyes, he said, "Yes, my master." Perhaps this wedding would not be such a terrible ordeal after all.

Chapter 10

With the application of cosmetics, Yazgulu, as a living representation of the Persian goddess Anahita, became a bride of captivating beauty. Her eyes, the envy of gazelles and blue as the Caspian, were said by the townspeople to melt the snow on top of the Zagros. The crimson tulips in her cheeks now blazed blood red with ocher and rouge. Her rosy lips, open to protest the manipulations performed on her by an inquisitive spinster and subordinate beauticians, revealed pearly, straight teeth. She did not speak. Instead, she closed her kohl-streaked eyelids while tears flowed down her cheeks in coal-tar rivulets.

From a makeshift bath chamber outside, Sarveali watched as Yazgulu's female relatives escorted her through the village on a white mare. The mare walked with grace as if she knew that the nymphet enthroned upon her was as well endowed as she was. Adolescent boys and older men watched Yazgulu with carnal desire, and unwed girls and their mothers looked at her with envy.

Sarveali awakened that morning fatigued from a strange nightmare. He dreamed that Barat-Ali and Gholi had savagely beaten him. They undressed him and robbed him of his belongings, and raped him with the handle of a shovel to excavate eighteen golden pomegranates from his anus. The pomegranates ruptured, and thousands of pearls poured from the fruits. When the pearls became frozen teardrops that thawed and disappeared, the excitement of his dream ended.

The second nightmare was set at the local saint's tomb, an *imamzadeh,* where the mullah, an Islamic cleric, stole a stack of bills from Sarveali while chanting Koranic verses. He awoke feeling as if a leopard had attacked him.

After having the surreptitious view of his future bride, Sarveali took a bath in a man-sized pot in the bath chamber, a tent. Logs burned beneath the belly of the pot. Shampoo made from cedar leaves, a bar of soap as big as a brick, a coarse loofah, and a pewter bowl were arranged for his use.

Once undressed, Sarveali regarded his penis. "Do not fail me tonight," he pleaded. As though comprehending his plea, Sarveali's member shrank immediately. Sarveali sighed heavily as he climbed into the bath pot. An adolescent boy arrived at the tent carrying the groom's folded clothes. Sarveali suddenly produced the necessary erection, stimulated by the youth, the emollient feeling of the soap, and the thermal energy of the warm water. After about fifteen minutes, Sarveali heard Gholi asking his father, "All that's left are the 'henna slapping' and the 'mullah's thing,' right?" A henna application ceremony and the legalization of the marriage contract were the only formalities yet to be done.

"Yes, and then we'll all be relieved. We had disaster coming our way, but we got rid of it," Barat-Ali said. "The poison arrow of an already deflowered, spoiled sister-bride almost did us in. Thank God and the imams we were saved by my brilliant plan of having this idiot marry *your* sister. Now shut your fat mouth!" Sarveali could not quite decipher "poison arrow" and "spoiled," and before he could gather his thoughts, his uncle and cousin were upon him.

Sarveali's ceremonial henna coloring, symbolically intended to mask biliousness and melancholy with the "henna red" of excitement, was applied that night. The topical application of the dye was performed in public for the groom and in private for the bride. Sarveali's pale skin, representing potential humiliation at wedding-night impotence, was so stubborn that it repelled the pigments. "It's like pouring water over skin greased with wool fat," Gholi derided him. It took several applications of henna to paint Sarveali's hands and forehead.

Meanwhile, in Yazgulu's room, ladies-in-waiting performed her henna art ceremony. Like Sarveali, Yazgulu was pale with anxiety, which the ladies attempted to mask in the same way—by repetitive applications of ocher, rouge, henna, and gentle slaps on her cheeks.

While Yazgulu received the henna application in her room, the other women prepared the main salon for the wedding ceremony. They spread the green velvet nuptial tablecloth in the middle of the room. On the tablecloth, they placed items pertinent to the customs: a silver candleholder with three tapered candles; a silver-framed mirror, placed in front of the candleholder directly facing the bride; and a huge Koran.

Now the wedding room became available for the bride, the groom, the mullah, and the rest of the nuptial party— all female—who were present to witness the ceremony. At most weddings, the mullah and the groom comprised the entire male population among a colony of females. But as if social status had defeated sexual segregation, for Sarveali's ceremony, near-adolescent and semipubescent males of aristocratic ancestry were also allowed in the chamber.

Sarveali was directed to the wedding chamber after his henna application and found himself in a roomful of cheering males and females. Yazgulu sat on a short-footed stool facing the silver-framed mirror. Sarveali had not seen her, other than the glimpse through the window, in twelve years. He remembered her as a loud two-year-old creature screaming from her infamous hammock. When he looked at her closely now, sitting on a stool with her face cast down, he saw a beauty so intense that his childhood fear of her strange reddish-yellow hair and big blue eyes transformed into a peculiar new fear. *She's so beautiful, so what did Uncle and Gholi mean when they called her spoiled? I might become her lawful husband, but can I ever be her legitimate husband? She still scares me.*

Sarveali was directed to a stool next to his bride. The mullah walked into the room slowly and theatrically. He straightened the cloak over his shoulder in a pseudo-elegant manner. Everyone looked at the cleric; for the moment, he had become the cynosure of the ceremony. Sarveali wondered when, as the groom, *he* would garner that attention. To him, the only positive thing about his marriage ceremony was that the khans and the bibis would pay him some attention for a small while.

Sarveali wondered what the mullah was thinking. He noticed the cleric manipulating his crotch under his cloak, and wondered, *Is this man of God having sinful and devilish thoughts about my bride?* A wave of fear mixed with jealousy overtook him. But before he could contemplate his first episode of frightful suspicion, the mullah began his sermon.

Chanting verbose Arabic verses that nobody, perhaps not even he himself, understood (the audience spoke Persian or Turkish), the man of God soon had the wedding guests emitting loud and repetitive yawns.

One old bibi dozed off and started snoring. After a minute, as if her sleep apnea woke her, she cried out in Turkish, "When is he going to shut up?" Even Sarveali, who was trapped in a sea of anxiety, laughed. Then he heard the old bibi continue, "This is a wedding, not some Friday prayer at the mosque! God forbid the day these turban-headed fools take over our lives." The room exploded in laughter. Sarveali knew the mullah did not understand Turkish, but he suspected that the woman's meaning dawned on the cleric as he discontinued the Koranic part of the ceremony. He hurriedly switched to reading the contract in classical Persian, in a peculiar, pontifical Arabic accent:

Will the wise, virtuous, virgin Miss Yazgulu Jokar, daughter of Mr. Barat-Ali Jokar, allow me to be her power-of-attorney in administering this holy matrimony on this propitious, auspicious, prosperous, felicitous, hallowed, glorified, consecrated, and praised moment? Are you prepared, you, the wise, virtuous, virgin Miss Yazgulu Jokar, the daughter of Mr. Barat-Ali Jokar, of Madavan to wed Mr. Sarveali Jokar, the son of Zolfali Jokar, the head factotum of his eminence, Changiz Khan Shirlu? Will the wise, virtuous, virgin Miss Yazgulu Jokar accept one mesghal (5 grams) of gold, one volume of the Holy Koran as collateral for Mr. Jokar's marriage proposal? Am I now your attorney-in-fact?

The mullah read the contract three times before Yazgulu whispered yes and began to cry. She bent her head down toward her lap, then raised it and glanced sideways at Sarveali. He observed the look on his bride's face and gave her a sympathetic smile.

But how can I comfort her? I've never talked with or dealt with any woman since I left my aunt's! he thought. The ephemeral sensuality he had experienced seeing Yazgulu for the first time disappeared like steam rising from a hot teacup, overtaken by his familiar apprehension.

Meanwhile, after Yazgulu's barely audible "yes," the mullah went to work, dipping his pen into the inkwell to write the contract. He registered various names, dates, and facts in an oversize logbook. After a few signatures and fingerprints, the marriage was formally legal. The cleric called out enthusiastically. "Felicitation and blessedness to all!"

At that moment, a group of preadolescent and semipubescent *khanzadehs,* involved in a game of hide-and-seek, ran near the matrimonial tablecloth, accidentally hitting the inkwell. It flew into midair, landing on the mullah's open logbook and splashing its contents on the page where the wedding had just been registered. Only seconds after Sarveali's marriage became official, its documentation was blackened out entirely. Like a believer desperately wishing for a miracle, Sarveali hoped that the accident would be seen as an omen bad enough to annul the marriage. If the annulment did occur, he was sure that Yazgulu, still sobbing, would not complain.

However, the mullah simply rewrote the document and Sarveali Jokar's marriage to Yazgulu Jokar was official once more. The crowd cheered loudly. *Tymbal* and *serna* music escalated. Sarveali was taken to the rooftop with Changiz Khan and his cousins so he could pay them respect and gratitude. Yazgulu, her mother, and the ladies-in-waiting went to Yazgulu's room to transform it into the nuptial chamber. Many offerings, including a postnuptial financial foundation, ten hectares of nearby land, fifty sheep, and 150 toumans, were given to the couple by the invitee khans. All of the offerings were intercepted by Barat-Ali, to the dismay of the bridegroom.

The moment neared for the ritual copulation within the nuptial chamber. *I hate myself,* Sarveali thought. *Any natural man waits his whole youth for a moment like this. Look at me, scared to death! It's because I'm not a real man, I'm sure!*

He reluctantly dragged his feet to the chamber, noticing two male attendants outside the entrance staring at him with peculiar glee. Inside, Yazgulu, fully clothed but with only one layer of skirt under her original overall, lay on the bed. Her chamber had been decorated as a bower walled with shiny silk fabric and illuminated with two miniature lanterns. A tribal rug with a colossal male lion in its center hung over the window. Two mattresses lay side by side, stuffed with feathers from poultry sacrificed for the wedding feasts. Underneath the mattresses, layers of myrtle leaves and rose blossoms waited for their scent to be inhaled by the couple.

Unknown to Sarveali, Yazgulu held hidden in one hand a calico cloth blotted with dove blood. Tradition demanded that a bride demonstrate a bloodstained cloth the morning after the nuptial night as evidence of her loss of virginity.

Yazgulu's sad face assumed an ambivalent mask, and she turned her back on her husband. Sarveali, pleased that his bride was not scrutinizing his many physical deficiencies, thought of his dilemma. How could he change himself from an impotent man into a copulative one? He prayed that the aphrodisiacs he had consumed for the previous three days would infuse him with an ad hoc virility. A glimmer of hope empowered him to remove his trousers, cough quietly, and get into bed beside his wife.

The velvet bedcover and aroma of myrtle and roses lifted Sarveali's spirits, returning him to the Shiraz brothel where, as an adolescent, he had waited patiently for Teimour Khan, holding the khan's cologne-scented clothes. He immediately developed an erection. Emboldened, he reached across to the adjacent mattress and tapped his wife on the shoulder. Yazgulu moved as far away from him as she could, but Sarveali felt he had worked too hard for his erection not to be fulfilled. He moved toward his wife again. Once more, the scent of attar of rose and myrtle intensified and his penis became steel hard. He touched his wife's shoulder, moving down to her left hand, which was holding a piece of cloth. Yazgulu pulled her hand away as if terrified of her new husband and placed it under the mattress.

Sarveali grabbed his bride's other hand and placed it on his penis. Yazgulu held the erect penis for a few seconds as if she were choosing a twig for kindling. Sarveali then lifted the skirt beneath Yazgulu's overall and tried to find a way into her vagina. Fumbling, ignorant of how to proceed, he could not locate her orifice. Yazgulu shouted in pain as his penis plunged at her, causing an involuntary spasm of the muscles surrounding her vagina.

Only too aware of his failures, Sarveali moved back to his side of the mattress, humbled by his awkwardness. *This woman is more than scary. She doesn't even have one—a vagina!* But as his penis reverted to flaccidity and the light of reason seemingly flashed on him for the first time, he shouted at his new wife in outrage. "So that's what your father and brother meant when they said you were

73

'spoiled.'" Instead of responding, Yazgulu showed her blood-clotted piece of calico to Sarveali and cried out, "Be quiet! See what you've done! Now give this to the attendants outside!" Terrified at the sight of what he imagined was his wife's blood, Sarveali thought he must have been mistaken about his penetration of Yazgulu and ran out the door where the two men yanked the calico from his trembling fingers. With glee, the men shouted in unison. "Sarveali has become the groom of the virgin!" The crowd cheered. The ceremonial announcement of the "virginity monitors" and the cheers of the crowd relieved Sarveali. He *must* be a legitimate groom who had deflowered his bride. He retreated to the kilim beside the bed. Yazgulu was already asleep. Overcome by fatigue and sudden doubts about his "virgin" bride, Sarveali lapsed into a fitful slumber.

Chapter 11

On a predawn Sunday two weeks later, Ishaq Shamoun awaited the new bridegroom at the guardhouse of the Kamab estate as Changiz Khan ordered. Shamoun had been assigned to give Sarveali a tour of a local vineyard, in his capacity of winemaker to the khans. It was a trip the Jew treasured, as it could very well be his last before he emigrated to Israel. Sarveali welcomed the reprieve from his matrimonial chaos.

"Good morning to you, young, fresh-looking groom!"

"Hello, Mr. Shamoun," Sarveali replied weakly. He felt dishonest being addressed as a groom, since his recent marriage had still produced no copulation.

"Go fetch your donkey, young man." Shamoun gathered all his effort to lift his heavy body onto his red-tailed donkey. After much struggle, the oenologist managed to defeat gravity and overcome the animal's rebellion. Sarveali joined him, and they trotted toward the north gate of Kamab.

Shamoun rode in front of Sarveali and immediately began to address the servant. Shamoun's henna-dyed hair and beard matched his donkey's natural red tail, and both man and mount swayed and trembled as he spoke.

"I am losing my patience with all the paperwork from the Promised Land," Shamoun complained over his shoulder.

"Who promised you land?" Sarveali asked in a confused state, thinking of the ten hectares given to him as a wedding present, the land his uncle had possessed as his own.

"The state of Israel," Shamoun whispered, as if to avoid detection by eavesdropping bigots. Sarveali, whose knowledge of post–World War II geopolitics was not highly defined, comprehended little of Mr. Shamoun's comments. He remained quiet. Shamoun interpreted Sarveali's silence as resentment toward him, an Iranian citizen, who dared to abandon his own country.

"You know, my dear young groom, the Muslims still consider us Jews *najes*. Dirty, unclean, and untouchable. In the old days before His Majesty's father became the Shah, Jews couldn't go out on rainy or hot days lest the germs of their *najes* bodies touch a Muslim's. Even in this rural area, the only ones who'd do business with us were the khans and the bibis; the merchants of the bazaar would *sell* to the Jews but never buy anything. Thank God we could send our nephew to a school in Isfahan built by a Jewish convert. It's this nephew of mine who's arranged for us to emigrate."

Shamoun paused tactfully and switched to oenology. "King Jamshid, the founder of viniculture, was the inventor of wine. Ancient Persia was under Jamshid's reign for seven hundred years, according to legend," Shamoun declaimed pedantically. Behind him, Sarveali tried his best to hold these facts in his brain.

"Wine became an important piece of the fabric of Persian life, but it was ripped to shreds with the introduction of Islam. Persian rituals, which required wine, were altered by substituting vinegar."

Sarveali's confusion intensified as a brisk breeze took the fragments of Shamoun's speech and blew them in the opposite direction, exacerbating the lecture's lack of clarity. Sarveali allowed himself to daydream, as Shamoun, oblivious, continued with his talk.

"Nearly twenty-five centuries ago, Cyrus the Great issued Persian citizenship to the Jews of Babylon—my ancestors. We had fled from the Holy Land in the Great Diaspora only to become slaves in Babylon. And when the Arabs invaded Persia, hell began for us again. And now that we have our Promised Land back, we are repatriating to Israel." Shamoun slowed so Sarveali could catch up with him and returned to the subject of grapes.

"The most important aspect of winemaking is the quality of the grapes. There is only one legitimate type of wine, the ruby red made from the *yaghut* grape," Shamoun said, salivating at the very mention of the magnificent liquid. "These grapes are inedible due to their sour and vitriolic taste." Once again, Sarveali looked dazed and confused.

"I mean you can't eat these grapes like you eat the sweet *askari* grapes. You need to boil some grape leaves, pour the broth over the grapes, and hang them or store them in a jug where wine was stored before . . ." Shamoun paused and said, "I hope I'm not talking too much." Sarveali lifted his head and cried, "No!" even though the oenologist's ramblings were beyond his depth.

"Now, if your master ever wants to grow the grapes, you'll need to know the following: if you dig the base of the vine and put approximately one *mesghal* or five grams of opium therein, its fruit will yield an antidote against snakebites, scorpions, and other creatures; if you plant lily flowers in the middle of the vineyard, the grapes will be sweet; if you plant a pomegranate tree next to a grapevine, the grapes will have a musky aroma; if you plant the grapevine in a barley farm, it'll survive for decades . . ." Sarveali tried to stay awake.

Finally, they arrived at the vineyard of Haji (he had made a pilgrimage to Mecca) Matroorabi where, in the shade of a pergola where the grapevines twined around the beams and columns, Shamoun placed two clay cups on the floor and held a jug in his arms as if it were a beloved child. He even kissed it on the neck.

"This is a vintage from five years ago," he said with misty eyes.

"But what is it?" Sarveali asked.

"Shamoun's 'Khan Grade' wine!" the man said. "Drink to the health and prosperity of Changiz Khan, the success of your marriage, and luck for me in the Promised Land." Shamoun lifted his filled cup to the sky and cried, "Long live the Shirlus! Long and happy life for Sarveali and his bride, with many healthy children!"

Sarveali lifted his cup but no words came to his tongue, so he downed the first gulp. His virgin salivary glands found the taste of fermented grapes very much to his liking.

"Don't drink this lovers' potion too fast, and don't get too attached to its taste either. It should be drunk drop by drop. And when this jug is finished, there will never be another. Shamoun will not be here to make the wine of the khans. Unless! Unless, young man, you listen to my instructions carefully. If you don't do what I tell you, after I'm gone, the centuries-long institution of winemaking in Iran will disappear for good."

Sarveali downed several more gulps despite Shamoun's advice. The anxiety Sarveali felt about learning something as complicated as winemaking made him forget even Shamoun's last sentence. If Changiz Khan expected him to learn the art, he would try his best, but so far he felt he had not learned much.

"This potion will make you become a good lover—not that you need it. I'm sure you're a virile young groom. It also makes you so courageous that you could kill your enemy without any reservation."

This old Jew's teaching me so many good things, Sarveali thought, remembering a dollop of information at last. *I'll be brave enough to kill someone once I drink some of this potion.*

The two men enjoyed the rest of the wine, their repose under the shade of the grape arbor quite delicious. The wine placed Sarveali on a mass of clouds and reminded him that he *had* managed a few erectile episodes since his wife's rejection the first night. He had even made Yazgulu feel the stiffness of his member to prove his capability. By demonstrating his erections and making Yazgulu feel them, Sarveali felt he was taking the first steps toward a successful conjugal relationship. Alas, the episodes always failed to attract the already disinterested Yazgulu. Copulation never followed the foreplay.

Sarveali was startled back to the present by the loud snoring of his oenology instructor, accompanied by yells of outrage nearby. Running to its source, Sarveali discovered Shamoun's donkey ferociously copulating with a female donkey. The owner of the female donkey, incensed by the violation, grew even angrier when he recognized its owner. In the midst of Sarveali's instant thought, *Even the Jew's donkey does it and I cannot,* the duo heard, "You Jewish son-of-a-whore! Can't your *najes,* untouchable, Jew donkey refrain from fucking my innocent Muslim one?" The man rushed toward Shamoun. But somehow reassured by the collateral of his new Israeli citizenship, Shamoun lifted his pomegranate stick in the air and landed several strokes on the head of the female donkey's proprietor.

"Be quiet, you son-of-a-whore! Don't you know this gentleman is the factotum of Changiz Khan Shirlu?" Shamoun exclaimed.

Taking advantage of Shamoun's pause in blows, the Muslim and his freshly bred donkey fled; when they had put sufficient distance between themselves and Shamoun and Sarveali, the rider threw a stone back in their direction.

"Fuck all Jews!" he yelled and trotted off.

Shamoun looked sadly at Sarveali. "For the first time, maybe in the twenty-five centuries since Jews have been in this country, I fought back. Maybe it was because of the dream I had under the arbor. I dreamed I beat up some Arab youths in the Jerusalem bazaar." Sarveali did not know where Jerusalem was, but his own life had been so servile that he had never imagined that his betters might suffer too. He nodded mutely.

"I apologize, Sarveali. You shouldn't have to hear such profanity." They made their way back to the estate in silence, each wrapped in his own fantasy.

SARVEALI'S SHORT APPRENTICESHIP PROVED less than successful. He liked Shamoun's wine very much, but one day was not enough to learn the profession competently. When it came time to taste the wine of his own making, Sarveali nervously served Changiz Khan. His hand shook as he poured the first bottle from the vat. The brown, murky color and acidic aroma were nothing like the ruby, aromatic love potion he had tasted with Shamoun.

His master took one gulp of the wine and spat it all over the servant. He grabbed Sarveali's shirt. In a voice as deafening as the thunder from the hills, Changiz Khan shouted, "Is this rhinoceros diarrhea? Take it away! It's as undrinkable as a whore's menses." Sarveali was responsible for the termination of yet another Oriental institution. The age-old art of winemaking died in that district, just as the Jew had predicted.

THE WINE PATRON DID NOT TURN SARVEALI into a good lover, either. Nonetheless, Yazgulu's employment under the Bibi as governess-in-charge of Virasb and Lohrasb, the twins, delighted her, and slowly diffused her unhappiness.

And Sarveali did not mind when Yazgulu decided to separate their mattresses and continued to refuse his pitiful attempts at lovemaking. Each night, despite their physical distance, Yazgulu began to whisper stories to Sarveali about the twins, the Bibi, and Changiz Khan before they fell asleep. Once Yazgulu leaned over and whispered, "The Bibi told her cousin that the Khan has been sleeping with some singer in Tehran." Sarveali immediately felt a sensual excitement, imagining the copulating Changiz Khan as Teimour Khan. Sarveali took Yazgulu's hand and placed it on his stiffening member. But his wife was too involved in her own tales of the mistress and master and scarcely seemed to notice.

Yazgulu confided later that the woman the Bibi had mentioned was Madame Mehr, a famous singer in Tehran whose husband was a master *santoor* player and professor of musicology at Pahlavi University. "Oh, and there's this other woman, a non-Muslim widow. She has been seen in the Khan's Jeep in Shiraz." This time, Sarveali imagined Teimour Khan making fierce love to the widow, the grunts and groans similar to the ones he heard from outside his master's room in the brothel. And when Yazgulu whispered to Sarveali in the darkness, "And there is another woman— the green-eyed wife of an army colonel in Solomanabad," Sarveali imagined the woman wearing the colonel's military hat while Teimour Khan made love to her.

As Yazgulu's anecdotes continued, so did Sarveali's futile erections. Once Sarveali awoke in the middle of the night and noticed Yazgulu rubbing herself underneath the sheets. She began to tremble as if she were going through a seizure. When Yazgulu started to moan, Sarveali determined his wife must have just experienced an orgasm. That night, he also masturbated with utter joy, conjuring up Teimour Khan's face and body. Thus the couple continued to bring themselves to orgasm without each other's cooperation. Neither complained about these untraditional sexual practices—tales related by Yazgulu followed by quiet periods of masturbation.

THE BIBI HAD CHOSEN TO IGNORE her husband's multiple adulteries. She sublimated her passion by indulging her obsession with medicinal remedies. Sarveali first heard of the Bibi's new love from Yazgulu. "The Bibi told me today that she loves to treat the sick. The girl who came here last week had something called anthrax. The Bibi put this medicine on her made of yellow thorn and goat yogurt." The following night, Yazgulu asked Sarveali, "Did you see the rug weaver's daughter wheezing all the time? The Bibi told me she had asthma and gave her some medicine made from quince seeds. I helped her mix it together. The Bibi told me that quince seed medicine will cure everything."

Sarveali was thrown into a deep pond of thought. *I bet the potion could get rid of my disease! I'll teach 'em all; I'll father nine children. And if that redhead, cat-eyed wife of mine keeps refusing me, I'll just divorce her and marry a city woman, and we'll produce son after son. Everyone will say, "That Sarveali is really a man now."*

Fantasizing happily, Sarveali no longer heard his wife's whispers, but his reverie was interrupted by a loud giggle. "You know the Bibi's cousin, Bibi Sonbol Khanom's daughter? She has the winds. The Bibi told me, 'I used fennel seeds. I was the only one who could cure that fat girl's farts.'" Sarveali, aggravated by the abortion of his fantasy, cried out, "Shut up, you blasphemous woman! Don't talk about the bibis like that!" But his wife's words stayed with him. He turned his attention to a new dilemma: *Could the daughter of tribal nobility really develop intractable flatulence?*

THE NEXT NIGHT, SARVEALI PAID CLOSE ATTENTION to his wife's stories, hoping to learn more about the quince seed potion. "The Bibi shouted, 'Yazgulu! Fetch me that little jar of quince seeds, and bring me the jar of London Rocket and the jar of starch on the same shelf.' We mixed the London Rocket with cooled-down boiled water, and added some sugar. And then I gave the children the London Rocket and the quince seed potion myself."

For a moment, Sarveali was filled with pride for his blue-eyed wife. She had become so important to the Bibi. But his concentration shifted back to the quince seed potion and he forced himself to imagine his small, ugly body enlarging into a virile hero. Still, his penis remained flaccid.

"The Bibi also told me that London Rocket cures most anything," Yazgulu whispered away. He was familiar with London Rocket and knew the tiny granulated seeds cured both diarrhea and constipation. But it was the quince seed potion he wanted to experiment with. He still agonized over his unconsummated marriage. *But how could I even do it to her? She acts as if she's got no vagina!* Sarveali consoled himself. He reconsidered. *She's a woman; she must have one.*

Over time, he began to notice the overt stares his beautiful wife received from strange *and* familiar men. The stares filled him with jealousy, making him feel even more helpless about his marriage. Whenever Yazgulu went to the bazaar for the Bibi, Sarveali entered the bitter world of paranoia. Which merchant's establishment did his wife frequent this time? What if she started to enjoy the company of the virile, thick-mustachioed butcher? He had heard once that women, especially beautiful women, seek pleasure elsewhere if they do not receive it at home. Deep in his small body, he knew instinctively that his wife would eventually betray him, but not when or how. He prayed he could find a quince seed potion that would magically give him the ability to penetrate his wife's vagina so they could finally become a normal couple.

SARVEALI'S NUPTIAL LIFE CONTINUED to be fallow for over two years, but the same period brought unmatched prosperity for Changiz Khan. Wheat and cotton prices soared. Yazgulu noted that Changiz Khan's enormous prosperity had enhanced the Casanova in him; he was more often away than at home. "The Bibi said, 'The only thing these women want is his money.'" Sarveali also felt that wealth was the best fuel for a lecherous engine, frustrated that as months passed by he was often unable to imagine a scene between Teimour Khan and any of "these women." He frequently turned away from Yazgulu, ignoring her as he stroked his penis, hoping for an erection.

One of these nights, in the early spring of 1949, Sarveali dreamed of Teimour Khan riding a white horse and holding a hyacinth as blue as Yazgulu's eyes; he entered an illuminated courtyard that reminded him of the Kamab estate before the raid.

The next morning, Changiz Khan pointed to a foreign postal envelope as Sarveali served him his Turkish coffee. "Teimour Khan has finally decided to come home." Sarveali's eyes shone, remembering his dream the night before. Forgetting his "unnatural" malady, he imagined resuming his duties as he served his repatriating master once again. He thought again of the day in the brothel when he held his master's cologne-scented clothes to his face and listened outside the door as Teimour Khan copulated with the prostitute. The memory of his master's scent still excited him, and the thought of attending to him once more pushed his recent fantasies of siring nine children far back in his mind.

Chapter 12

Teimour Khan's Pan American flight from Switzerland landed at Tehran Mehrabad Airport on a midspring day in 1949. In the lobby, Sarveali, who had driven from Shiraz with the chauffeur in the new Buick Roadmaster, was shocked to find a well-coiffed, chic and beautiful woman—the infamous Madame Mehr—accompanying Changiz Khan. The master had spent a few days in Tehran before his brother's arrival. Although Sarveali felt that flaunting one's mistress in such a public manner was unacceptable for commoners, for a great khan like his master such infidelities were limitless. Sarveali felt a mixed sense of pride and envy. It was his khan, after all, who was accompanied by such an overt token of masculinity, a famous singer and the wife of a prominent professor. Again he wished Teimour Khan were escorting such a woman instead of his older brother.

When the plane landed, Sarveali felt a divine being had just descended from the heavens. His heart pounded convulsively as Teimour Khan waved and smiled slightly. *Now that my old master is back, I'll prove to everyone, even to Sheikhak's spirit, that I'll always be Teimour Khan's faithful servant.*

Teimour Khan now stood taller than his older brother, and head and shoulders above his old servant. Doffing his fedora to Madame Mehr, Teimour Khan bowed, revealing dark brown hair combed up in a stylish pompadour. He was dapper in his white linen suit and turquoise shirt and striped tie, and his smile showed full, sensual lips. Sarveali ran toward his master, who was looking at Madame Mehr as if enchanted with his brother's mistress. Sarveali knelt and kissed Teimour Khan's right hand, forgetting it was the instrument of childhood beatings. He gazed down at the master's brown-and-white spectator shoes he happily imagined he would soon be polishing. He was so absorbed in his adoration of Teimour Khan that he did not notice his joyful greeting was reciprocated by only the briefest of glances.

Teimour Khan brushed Sarveali away and strode off with Changiz Khan and Madame Mehr. Sarveali and the chauffeur followed with several heavy suitcases. Teimour Khan talked eagerly to Madame Mehr as Changiz Khan frowned. As Madame Mehr's laughter rose, it became obvious that the flirtation would soon end in her seduction. Sarveali was pleased his wish would soon be granted.

Madame Mehr jumped into a new Thunderbird with the two khans and Sarveali and the chauffeur followed them to the Semiramis Hotel. When they arrived, dozens of porters ran about collecting luggage and Sarveali was bidden to wait outside on the street. He waited obediently in the midspring Tehran sun as the chauffeur left to purchase *kababs* and bread.

When Madame Mehr and the two khans emerged from the hotel, Madame Mehr was talking gaily. "The elevation there is 1,700 meters and that's where the Alborz foothills begin. It's next to Sa'adabad, the Shah's summer palace. From here, we can even see such prominent mounts as Damavand . . ." They approached Sarveali standing in front of the two cars. He heard the young Khan whisper an aside. "I'd like to see *her* mounts," as Madame Mehr continued to chat about the Darband Hotel Restaurant atop a northern Tehran mountain. She and the two brothers were planning to dine there, and Changiz Khan, grimacing, abruptly ordered Sarveali to wait where he was for their return.

At midnight, the Buick finally returned to the hotel. Sarveali hurried to make himself available. Ten minutes later, Teimour Khan and Madame Mehr reappeared hand in hand. Teimour Khan, in a loud, alcoholic voice, shouted, "My lovely singer, I'd love to see your *chambre Persienne*. I'm longing for a haremesque Oriental setting."

"We shouldn't do this," Madame Mehr whispered quietly.

"Why ever not, my dear? Someone, whose name I can't recall now, as the Shiraz wine has suffocated my brain cells, once said 'Adultery is the foundation of society,' especially *this* society, the 'reverse-café society,' where all delicious things happen behind closed doors . . ."

The sight of his master and the woman disappearing in her Thunderbird gave Sarveali an erotic thrill. *My wish has been granted*, he thought. *He will have her tonight.*

THREE DAYS LATER CHANGIZ KHAN ORDERED Sarveali and the chauffeur to prepare the car for the drive back to Shiraz, nearly an eight-hundred-kilometer journey. Sarveali had not seen Teimour Khan since the night he and Madame Mehr left the hotel together. As he, the chauffeur, and Sarveali fit Teimour Khan's suitcases into the trunk and the cargo compartment above the Buick, Teimour Khan suddenly appeared. He took a seat in the back of the car and waited for his brother to join him.

When the chauffeur opened the door for Changiz Khan, he sat next to his brother without a word. As soon as Sarveali and the chauffeur arranged themselves in the car, Teimour Khan shouted out, "Is there a colony of dead rats in here?"

Sarveali was horrified. He had bathed as best he could in the basin of his lowly inn. He lowered his face to smell his armpits, but before he could apologize, Teimour Khan sprayed the interior of the car with his own cologne, Creed, a French brand he had loved since adolescence. The aroma seemed a curative remedy as the car passed through the southern gate of Tehran, and everyone but the chauffeur fell asleep.

When Sarveali awoke, he heard Changiz Khan scolding Teimour Khan. "You've always been fascinated with this silly intellectual and eccentric life, bizarre film festivals, those leeches you call artists and writers . . ." The servant fell asleep again, unwilling to hear his old master scolded or an argument erupt between the brothers.

They spent the night in Isfahan. At the public bathhouse, Sarveali tried to cleanse the stench from his body. Teimour Khan said nothing the next day about body odor and instead lectured the occupants of the car. "Being an immigrant is like being eternally thirsty, suspended between two futile and impotent water springs sourced by nostalgia. When one drinks from one spring and fails to satisfy thirst, it's only inevitable that he begins to lust for the water of the other spring . . ." Even though he didn't understand his master, Sarveali listened happily, paying close attention to his stories about literature, the arts, and his problems with pharmacology. He could not help noticing that Changiz Khan did not seem to find the stories as fascinating as he did and fell asleep halfway through his brother's recitation of his meeting with the literary glitterati of Tehran.

The rest of the family was meeting the khans at the ruins of Persepolis, sixty kilometers north of Shiraz. As soon as Teimour Khan saw the sign marked "Persepolis 100 km," he took a silver flask from his pocket and took a big swallow. He sprayed the interior of the car again. The mixed scent of alcohol and cologne reminded Sarveali of his humiliation. *I swear to God I bathed at the public bathhouse,* he thought, a wave of self-hatred falling over him again. He looked back and noticed that Changiz Khan was still sleeping. "Soon we'll see Persepolis, a simultaneous symbol of old glory and our nation's emasculation. You know, we've always been fascinated with the dead of the past." Teimour Khan continued to lecture his sleeping brother and servants until the ruins of Persepolis and its tall columns appeared in front of him. He shouted, "Sarveali, turn around." Teimour Khan sprayed his servant, covering his arms, chest, and forehead in clouds of Creed cologne.

THIS TIME, THE COLOGNE WAS SO AROMATIC that it didn't produce somnolence but made Sarveali feel he could lift even the tall columns in front of him. When he saw the entourage of more than twenty automobiles waiting to greet them, the stimulant effect of the cologne compounded his excitement. As he witnessed his young master being kissed and welcomed by the crowd, he imagined the adulation was for him as well. *After all, was he not Teimour Khan's servant and protector?*

The Bibi had arranged for the cook and the owner of a *kabab* house in Shiraz to assemble a picnic. Filled with mountainous energy, Sarveali directed the cook and other hired staff to set up makeshift braziers and heat pre-cooked dishes. Meat and disemboweled poultry were skewered and grilled. When Sarveali thought there might not be enough meat to feed everyone, he purchased two lambs from a shepherd, watching the multitude of foreign automobiles come in, as stupefied as if one of the wonders of the world had landed.

On several long tables placed side by side and sur-rounded by wooden folding chairs, numerous jugs of wine (the last of émigré Ishaq Shamoun's Vintner's Reserve 1939); raisin *aragh*, a local brew; Russian vodka; Hennessy cognac; and champagne were lined up like an army of sol-diers. Soon *kababs*, grilled chicken, gizzards, livers, yogurt-cucumber dips, and other accompaniments joined the bottles of liquor.

In the midst of the picnic, Sarveali finally noticed his wife among the welcoming party. The contrast of power-ful males at the table and Yazgulu carrying melons to the creek to cool gave Sarveali a shiver.

My master has brought heaven. Sarveali lowered his nose to his chest and took a deep breath of his Creed-impregnated shirt. He again looked toward his wife. Yazgulu was kneel-ing daintily next to the creek, immersing each melon in the freezing waters.

Teimour Khan and Changiz Khan walked toward the creek. Sarveali felt acquisitive pride at the possibility that his young master might have noticed his bride. Without re-alizing it, Sarveali began to follow them, trying to muster all his ability to hear what the khans were saying. He hoped they would talk about his new wife, his extension of himself.

Teimour Khan asked his brother, "So, tell me, who is *this* Rita Hayworth?"

Changiz Khan whispered in his brother's ear and then looked back at the inquisitive servant. "Sarveali, are you sure we have enough meat for everyone?"

"Yes, sir." He heard Yazgulu say coquettishly, "*Salam,* Changiz Khan and Teimour Khan." She raised her eyes to stare at the two khans. *A bit too daring,* thought her husband.

The khans nodded to Yazgulu without speaking and turned back to the picnic tables. Sarveali noticed a string of sweaty pearls fall from Yazgulu's eyes into the melons she was slicing.

"Are you sick?"

"Yes, umm . . . no. I mean I'm just hot. But I'm fine."

SOON AFTER THEY RETURNED TO THE MANSION, Teimour Khan began to drive off in his brother's Buick every night, not returning home until the early hours of the next morning. When he was in residence, the young khan rarely spoke to Sarveali except to give him orders. Sarveali eavesdropped on Teimour Khan's telephone conversations to learn his master's plans. "I kissed her passionately and caressed her engorged nipples. She was a good fuck, but now I have to get rid of her. Her father criticized Nima Youshij so harshly . . ." The father of his latest mistress, a journalist, had attacked the avant-garde Persian poet. Teimour Khan placed literature above all things—even his own sexual desires.

Meanwhile, Yazgulu was as quiet and reclusive as ever during the day, overly talkative at night. "What does Teimour Khan like to eat? Who was that city girl who visited the other day? Does he have a fiancée?" Sarveali, pleased by his wife's curiosity about his master, eagerly answered her questions and even added some information of his own.

One afternoon, Sarveali served tea to Teimour Khan and a gray-haired guest. "My fear of intimacy used to be only applicable to European women. But now I've concluded that my phobia is not geography specific. I hate the women in Shiraz as well." *Perhaps my handsome khan would wish for a beautiful Madavani girl?* Sarveali wondered hopefully, plunging into another erotic fantasy. He continued to listen to his master's conversation.

"Since the aroma of urine, menses, ejaculate, and sweat are the same globally, the brothels in Shiraz smell the same as in France, Switzerland, and Morocco."

That night Sarveali told Yazgulu his old master hated Shirazi women. "But perhaps he prefers women from Kamab." Yazgulu made a noise in the back of her throat and said to herself in a playful, secretive voice: "He's been here nearly three months now and still found no woman to marry! I'm sure when it's kismet, God will bring him a worthy one."

The next day, Sarveali heard Teimour Khan speed in through the mansion gate, narrowly missing the rejuvenated jasmine tree. He followed Teimour Khan to his room immediately, where he was struggling to open a bottle of wine. "If you would permit me, I could open that . . ."

"No you *cannot* . . . this is Mouton Rothschild 1944, and the painting on the label is by a friend of mine, Jean Carzoux . . ." Sarveali bowed and stood next to Teimour Khan for a moment, expecting an angel or a butterfly to fly out of the magic bottle. No such miracle occurred, but as his master sipped the wine from a Cartier glass, Sarveali observed the similar ruby of Teimour Khan's lips and the ruby of the wine. He stared in delight at his master's appreciation of the wine, remembering Ishaq Shamoun and his own winemaking failures.

"My heart is glazed with this ruby red," Teimour Khan murmured as Sarveali left the room, his heart aching at his ignorance and incomprehension of everything that mattered. Sadly he prepared for his master a tray of cold cuts, cucumber-yogurt dip, and grilled eggplants, then summoned Yazgulu.

"Take this to Teimour Khan," he directed.

Yazgulu's face glowed as if it were the moon. She even stopped to sprinkle rose water on her hands and cheeks.

Later that hot summer night, Sarveali observed Yazgulu lying in bed inhaling something sweet lingering on her fingers. The familiar, intoxicating scent of Teimour Khan's Creed cologne crossed the impassable valley that had grown between the two mattresses. *Thank God,* Sarveali thought, *it seems my wish that Yazgulu would attract my master has come to pass.* Thoughts of his master copulating with his wife elevated Sarveali to such ecstasy that he and Yazgulu simultaneously experienced erotic relief, both stimulated separately by the scent associated with their mutual lord.

The following day, Sarveali and Yazgulu waited impatiently for Teimour Khan to return home. At the sound his car, Yazgulu, who was sewing a patch on her husband's pajama trousers, reddened, and her face took on the shade of Teimour Khan's lips and the wine he had opened the previous night. When he called for another tray of food, Yazgulu took it to him without waiting for her husband's instructions and returned to her chamber nearly an hour later. This pattern continued through the autumn months. Teimour Khan would return home and ask for food, which Yazgulu would take to him. One night, Sarveali noticed his wife rubbing her belly. He assumed his wife was pregnant, musing to himself, *Finally I will become the father of my master's child.* But as autumn progressed to winter, Teimour Khan began asking for cold dinners only sporadically. And Yazgulu was not pregnant after all.

Changiz Khan and his family prepared to spend the winter and spring months at the Kamab estate. Sarveali and Yazgulu were both relieved to hear that after staying in Shiraz for nearly six months, Teimour Khan would shortly join them in Kamab. Each secretly wished that this change of atmosphere would somehow resurrect Teimour Khan's attraction to Yazgulu.

Chapter 13

Teimour Khan was no happier in Kamab than in Shiraz, even after the entire family returned to the estate and Sarveali spent his days and nights fetching *aragh* for his master. Once Teimour Khan asked for candles to light, and Sarveali accurately speculated that his master wished to illuminate the adjacent dark storeroom. A few days after his arrival, Teimour Khan and his brother engaged in a tumultuous argument. The younger brother complained to Changiz Khan that he had received only a fraction of the family funds while he was in Switzerland. Sarveali noted that Changiz Khan did not bother to defend his actions, and Teimour Khan finally gave up and said, "I no longer wish to remain in this cemetery of 'dung hills.'" His comment frightened Sarveali. Was his master planning to leave the family again—deserting his servant and the two nephews and niece, whom he seemed to cherish?

FOR SEVERAL MONTHS, TEIMOUR KHAN TRAVELED back and forth from Kamab to Shiraz, always restless. He communicated as little as possible with his brother. Then, one day in the autumn of 1950, the Bibi invited her brother-in-law to visit the quince orchard her father had planted for her, thirty minutes away.

"The fruits are beautifully ripe in early autumn." Sarveali heard the Bibi say. When Teimour Khan reluctantly accepted his sister-in-law's invitation, Sarveali immediately rushed to his quarters and changed from his rubber slippers into shoes more appropriate for accompanying his master to the orchard. *What if he gets thirsty and wishes for a glass of sherbet? Besides, I really want some of that quince seed thing, although the need is not so great now that my master is here.*

But by the time Sarveali arrived at the guardhouse, Teimour Khan's Jeep was nowhere to be found, so with the Bibi's permission, he joined her in Changiz Khan's Buick, and they drove toward the orchard. Sarveali would have been grateful to learn if the properties of the quince seed potion would cure his "unnatural" state. But since he did not wish to raise suspicions about his sexual interests, he concealed his curiosity and remained quiet in the backseat, sporadically glimpsing Teimour Khan's Jeep speeding ahead of them. At the orchard, hundreds of trees aligned themselves obliquely along the road; their intense ocher-colored fruits dotted the green of the leaves, producing an exotic landscape. A flock of doves, as if mistaking the orchard for paradise, flew over the two automobiles. When the cars stopped and the passengers exited, a pair of doves circumnavigated them and then crashed into the windshield of Teimour Khan's Jeep, dying instantly. Sarveali surveyed the crushed birds and the blood-stained windshield. *Is this an omen?* he wondered, observing a sort of smile on the faces of the doves, as if death had frozen them in a happy state. He took a white handkerchief out of his pocket to clean the bloodstains from the glass. *I could grill these birds for Teimour Khan,* he thought, and proceeded to pluck out the feathers as he followed the Bibi and his master on their tour.

The Bibi immediately began to lecture Teimour Khan about the pharmacological properties of quince. Sarveali, walking deferentially behind, hoped the Bibi would say something informative about the fruit's properties.

"Have you ever benefited from the infusion of quince blossoms? Or quince fuzz? Do you know why the sour quince has antitussive properties?" the Bibi asked as Sarveali, listening attentively, observed the ambivalence on his master's face.

"I have no idea," Teimour Khan replied.

"Did you know the fuzz on the skin of a sweet quince is less potent in its expectorant property than the fuzz covering a sour one?" the Bibi inquired. *When is she going to talk about the seeds?* Sarveali fretted.

"I did not know that any damn fuzz existed," Teimour Khan retorted. Even though Sarveali noted that Teimour Khan's ignorance on a subject within his academic field seemed to embarrass him, Sarveali resented the Bibi's pedantry toward her brother-in-law and attributed it to the animosity between Teimour Khan and her husband.

"And do you understand about their blossoms, dear Teimour?" the Bibi loftily asked.

"I have never shown any interest in anybody's or anything's blossom," Teimour Khan replied in a tone that suggested the Bibi was boring him silly. *Maybe now she will switch to the seeds,* Sarveali hoped. However, before the subject could change, Teimour Khan abruptly charged away toward his Jeep. "I just remembered that I need to get back to Kamab," he said, not bothering to bow farewell to the Bibi. Sarveali dropped the fully plucked doves on the ground as he ran after his master, who reluctantly let him into the Jeep.

Teimour Khan drove fast and carelessly along the gravel road, sending stones flying in all directions. He veered onto a bare plain carpeted with yellowish soil that ended in a range of rocky hills. A lone conifer tree stood next to a small shrine, and Teimour Khan, at full speed, drove directly toward it. Sarveali gasped at the recklessness of his obviously unhappy master.

When Teimour Khan came to an abrupt stop less than a meter from the conifer, he and Sarveali noticed a huge eagle owl that had landed on a small tamarisk bush next to the conifer. The owl's feathers ruffled and its eyes glowed like flame.

"Oh my master, may Allah, the prophet, and the imams save us, this owl is a bad omen," Sarveali said as he looked at the small shrine, surprised that he remembered to cite the divine figures in the shrine. He felt a bit of pride also in his knowledge that in Iran owls are thought to be harbingers of doom.

Teimour Khan gave his servant a blank stare, put the Jeep in gear, and started driving as recklessly as before toward home. During the rough ride Sarveali jolted up and down, feeling as if his ribs were lancing his throat. A sharp turn nearly threw him out of the car. The young Khan did not utter a word to Sarveali until they reached the gate of the estate. "Ask the kitchen to get me some food . . . and ask my brother for some gin," he said after honking the horn several times, as if to awaken the entire household from their siestas. When Sarveali took the gin to Teimour Khan, he noticed the picture on the bottle was almost identical to the conifer they had seen earlier. He was considering this coincidence when Yazgulu passed him carrying his master cold meats and fruits.

That night, once again, Sarveali smelled Teimour Khan's Creed cologne on his wife's body and hoped that Yazgulu had mitigated his master's unhappiness. Indeed, the ménage à trois resumed and might have continued indefinitely if not for the cook, an obsessive voyeur and gossip. Within weeks, he had witnessed enough incriminating evidence against Teimour Khan and the servant's wife to report the matter to Changiz Khan.

One morning, as the cook was serving the midmorning Darjeeling tea to the master, he gleefully served his sexual observations as well. Changiz Khan placed a red 10-touman note in the cook's callused palm and ordered him to secrecy. "I know how hard it is for your tongue to keep quiet but I'll forgive you if you don't tell another soul of this, not even that nosy wife of yours!"

The next day, Sarveali overheard a loud squabble coming from Teimour Khan's room. Sarveali silently let himself into the storeroom off the bedroom and placed his ear against the bedroom door.

"You should be ashamed of yourself, Teimour!" Changiz Khan yelled.

"For what?" Teimour Khan asked in a weak postslumber voice.

"For fucking Sarveali's wife!"

"Don't you believe in *droit du seigneur*?" The foreign phrase was unknown to Sarveali.

"Stop it!"

"Well, fucking a servant's wife is not as bad as fucking your good friend's wife, is it? Like Madame Mehr—the wife of the music professor?" Sarveali felt a peculiar pride that he and his wife were the cause of an aristocratic quarrel. They were just as important in this case as Professor and Madame Mehr. But Sarveali's pride soon turned to torment. Changiz Khan said, "Why don't you sell your portion of the inheritance and move permanently abroad? Perhaps that will make you happy. You say you hate it here, anyway." Sarveali tiptoed from the storeroom, too saddened at the thought of Teimour Khan leaving him again to rebut the cook, who whispered "Sarveali, the Cuckold" to the chauffeur as Sarveali passed.

"That cat-eyed bitch wife of his likes the khanly dick between her legs," the cook went on, not noticing Sarveali walking downcast through the courtyard. "I was the first to see her with the young khan and told Changiz Khan. He gave me hush money. You're the *only* one I'm telling," the cook said to the chauffeur, laughing.

Sarveali knew the word "cuckold." The cook's remarks reverberated in his head and attacked him like a venomous snake. He froze. He was now emasculated, a public cuckold, his only source of sensuality now public knowledge, and the joyous nature of his master's adultery lost forever.

As life seemed to drain from him, a colloidal mass in his gut moved toward his throat and mouth. He vomited quietly into a nearby sink where three heads of lettuce waited to be washed. The spasms and twirling of his stomach continued to twine into a knot. When he thought the knot was just about to break, he ran to the latrine and emptied the rest of the poison from his body. He went back to the sink, picked up the heads of lettuce, and washed them of his own vomit.

Drenched in the cold sweat of shame, he realized later that night that he had an antidote for his affliction, something he had kept secret for some time.

A month earlier, Hashem Heidarloo had been hired to operate Changiz Khan's new combine. Sarveali had taken an unrequited interest in the handsome, muscular young man. But he noticed that Heidarloo had become attracted to the cook's son, whose effeminate behavior had intensified with puberty. The cook was enormously disturbed and ashamed of his son's reputation as a homosexual, but he had no idea of the pederasty that took place in a donkey trough of an abandoned barn.

The morning after the cook revealed Sarveali's secret to the chauffeur, Sarveali decided to expose the son's relationship with the combine operator to the cook. A few days later, knowing the combine operator and his young lover were meeting for a tryst, he woke the cook from his siesta.

"I have some business to speak with you about," Sarveali announced gleefully, insinuating that another scandal was about to be exposed. The cook followed Sarveali eagerly to the barn next to the donkey trough. There, the handsome Heidarloo, his trousers dropped to his ankles, was ferociously sodomizing the naked youth.

The cook's face paled and he fell toward the trough in a gesture of genuflection. As he knelt near the operator's splashed ejaculate, Sarveali thumped his quivering shoulders. "What's worse? Being a cuckold or having a faggot son?"

The incident tore the cook's gossiping tongue to bits. His innuendos against Sarveali stopped immediately and the name "Sarveali, the Cuckold" dropped from the household like mosquitoes sprayed with insecticide.

WHILE TEIMOUR KHAN TRAVELED back and forth from the mansion to the estate, Changiz Khan spent the last weeks of the winter conducting several meetings with a group headed by a man carrying a parchment-colored briefcase. The meeting resulted in an offer to buy Teimour Khan's properties. A few days later, Teimour Khan accepted the offer and agreed to the terms and conditions of the transaction. Sarveali's hope that Teimour Khan might change his mind about leaving the country vanished when he overheard him saying on the phone to a friend, "a beautiful apartment in St. Germain de Près in Paris and a huge villa in the Côte d'Azur." Sarveali knew those places were not in Iran, and that his master would again leave his country and his devoted servant.

That early winter night, when the lilac sunset turned somber and the chants of the muezzin announced the evening prayer, Sarveali and Yazgulu—for the first time in emotional unity—lamented Teimour Khan's impending departure. Leaving them both forever was the desired master and lover, the only one who satisfied both their needs at the same time.

On the first day of Bahman (January 23), 1951, the day of Teimour Khan's departure, Sarveali helped his master dress. He tied his master's boots in the manner he had loved since childhood: the knots resembled butterflies about to ascend. The young khan gave the knots a look of disdain and silently untied and tied his shoes again. Sarveali bowed his head. *The master is an adult now. I am living in the past.*

The Bibi ordered Sarveali to prepare Teimour Khan's farewell ritual. He arranged as neatly as possible several objects atop a round silver tray covered with gold and silk woven brocade. The tray held a miniature brass brazier containing molten-red charcoals burning clusters of wild rue. The Bibi placed red rose and narcissus petals in a small bowl next to four baklavas and a miniature leather-bound Koran. The ensemble, in traditional fashion, would dispel bad omens from Teimour Khan on his journey. The Bibi maintained a perpetual smile, seemingly quite pleased with the imminent departure.

Teimour Khan frowned as he clumsily kissed the Koran, as if it were a stale corpse. After the Bibi lifted the tray over his head and read verses from the Koran, he picked the most geometrically perfect cube of baklava and stuffed it in his mouth. Avoiding eye contact with Yazgulu and Sarveali as he got into the Buick, he shook hands coolly with his brother. The Bibi shed no tears as she poured the contents of the water bowl on the ground where Teimour Khan had stood. Apparently the two servants were the only members of the household to regret the young Khan's departure.

Chapter 14

Soon after Teimour Khan's departure, Yazgulu began having recurring nightmares. Every night she would cry out in her sleep, "Massih! Massih! What have I done?" When Sarveali reached through the space between their mattresses to comfort her and perhaps try to make love to her, his first touch immediately triggered the vaginismus that had begun in their nuptial chamber. The result was sexual inaction for both husband and wife, but finally Sarveali understood her rejection of him. She, like himself, desired someone else.

However, he was pleased to learn that his wife, while resisting his advances, had become invaluable to the Bibi. Yazgulu had been placed in charge of the estate's bakery, and was planning especially festive delights for the upcoming Iranian New Year, Norooz, which begins on the first day of the first month of spring, Farvardin (March 21). The top baker of Kamab had taught Yazgulu the fundamentals of operating the baking room and the Bibi even had an oven, a *tanoor*, built for her use.

After Norooz was over, a group of men in khaki uniforms came to inspect the estate. Sarveali learned they were exterminators, and they carried spray tanks and guns to eliminate malaria-carrying pests.

The men immediately started their task. Whenever a worker sprayed a room for quality control measures, the leader wrote on the wall: *De. De. Te.* in Persian and *D.D.T.* in English. Sarveali asked the cook, who had a few years of schooling, to translate. "Let me see . . . umm, 'da . . . da . . . t.'" The cook could not decipher anything coherent.

The leader, as if expecting the question, started his formal speech. "As per His Majesty's imperial *firman* and his edict, we are spraying this area so the subjects of His Imperial Majesty won't become inflicted with malaria, the pestilence from backwards Arab and African lands. Under the reign of His Majesty, the shadow of God on earth, we must remain healthy in order to take this nation into the gate of the great civilization . . ." The leader sounded as if he were reading from a memorized text.

Sarveali and the other staff were so impressed by the speech that they all agreed to permit the exterminators to fumigate the entire estate. This permission gave the leader, whose duties required him to visit each chamber, easy access to all corners of the property.

The following day, the exterminator and his team left. A malodorous chemical smell that reminded the household of wild-boar manure lingered. That night, Yazgulu slipped into a deep, delicious sleep. Three days later, the exterminator and his team knocked on the gate again. The leader claimed that the Ministry of Health demanded they exterminate again. Sarveali, still fearful from his previous speech, permitted entrance. That night Sarveali again noticed the intense aroma of wild-boar manure on his wife's body.

Three days later, Sarveali heard a loud commotion as he was preparing breakfast. The Bibi's silver collection had been stolen. She asked her husband to line up the servants, beat them, and interrogate them to elicit a confession. In a hurry to get to Shiraz, Changiz Khan refused. "What's a few silly dishes?"

"Your mother commissioned them in Mozzafar-uddin Shah's era!" the Bibi wailed.

"It's probably a rumor that worthless bibis concocted! My late mother had no interest in such frivolities!" Changiz Khan left his wife silent, her mouth agape, as he strode away to his Buick.

"Dear Bibi, I swear to God, I had nothing to do with it," Sarveali pled.

"I'm not worried about you or your wife, you know that," the Bibi comforted Sarveali. But the silver thief was never found.

A month later, Sarveali dreamed he was tying Teimour Khan's shoes into butterflies. At the same time, he could smell his master's Creed scent on his wife lying next to him. In the midst of dream and reality, the scent aroused him and he reached for Yazgulu. Immediately, her vagina clenched shut, and she pushed his hand away as if it were a fetid rodent. Sarveali slipped back into his dreamy, fragrance-filled state—one much more comforting than his reality.

Serving tea the next evening, Sarveali noticed that one of Changiz Khan's cousins who had come to seek agricultural advice was also wearing Creed, the same cologne as Teimour Khan. When he smelled mild kerosene and engine oil on Yazgulu a few nights later, Sarveali consoled himself that his wife must have used gasoline to ignite her baking oven. Preferring that his wife's body was only Teimour Khan's, he put aside his other suspicions.

God's Cocktail

Empire of Iran
1953–1969

Chapter 15

Nearly two years later, the great drought struck Kamab, as well as a devastating grasshopper plague. Together, the two disasters killed most of the wheat and barley crops of the Shirlu khans, leaving little grain for Changiz Khan to harvest in late spring. At the same time, Iran was experiencing more political turmoil. That summer, uprisings by the communist Tudeh Party, the Islamic extremists, and the National Front intensified, forcing Mohammad Reza Shah to leave the country. Flying his own plane, the monarch fled, only to return three days later, preceded by a coup d'état. In 1951 the Shah appointed Mohammad Mossadegh prime minister. Mossadegh was the man responsible for nationalizing Iranian oil, which Great Britain and Iran had owned since 1909 as the Anglo-Persian Oil Company. The prime minister's familial origin—the Qajar dynasty that had preceded the Pahlavi—and his strong popularity threatened the Shah and the monarchy.

On the morning of the coup, the twenty-eighth day of Mordad (August 19), 1953, Sarveali heard a clamor in the

111

streets while he was buying bread at the market. "Long live Mossadegh! Death to the Shah!" That same afternoon, at the butcher's, he heard the same people chanting, "Death to Mossadegh! Long live the Shah!" Curious about such a contradiction, Sarveali listened intently to Changiz Khan that evening. "Politics is a bastard child that should never be trusted, especially in this nation of hypocrites and idol manufacturers," the master pronounced.

Sarveali found it quite easy to memorize this statement word for word, but he tried in vain to unlock its meaning. The proclamation remained as incomprehensible to him as Shamoun's formula for making red ruby wine. He mourned, as he often did, his lack of education, and even went so far as to request the identity of this "Mohammad Mossadegh" from Changiz Khan. The "degh" in the man's name, which means "hectic fever," confused Sarveali even further.

"He was our premier!" replied the master. "But now that the Shah has returned, thank God, there's no more Mossadegh. He became our hero when he nationalized our oil, but under his weak leadership, only the pests of society rose to power. But who knows if this new regime will last. Wherever the wind blows, the so-called new middle class—the merchants, the intellectuals, and the clergy—will follow. One morning they chant 'pro' and the same afternoon, 'anti.'"

Two weeks after the coup, while Sarveali was still reflecting on Changiz Khan's metaphor—the pests of society—word came from Madavan that his uncle Barat-Ali had died of a heart attack. Yazgulu's ambivalent response, manifested by a few crocodile tears, a fraction of those shed on the day of Teimour Khan's departure, surprised Sarveali. Although it was customary to cry vehemently after the loss

of a relative—no matter how much of a scoundrel—
Sarveali could not produce a single tear. Yazgulu left for
Madavan the following day to attend her father's funeral,
without the companionship of her husband. She returned
to the Kamab estate after the seventh day of mourning.

A MONTH LATER, in the month of Aban (early October),
politics, like Barat-Ali's death, was forgotten as the Bibi
ordered the servants to prepare for her annual quince rit- •
uals, which involved washing and peeling the fruit, baking
quince, preparing quince jams, and extracting and pul-
verizing quince seeds.

"Each quince must be sliced into six pieces," the Bibi
said, "then boiled in heavy syrup." As Sarveali stirred, the
syrup burbled in the pots. He enjoyed the sweet scent. His
face saturated with the vapor, he prayed he could be bold
enough this time to ask the Bibi about the properties of
the quince seed potion and if it was possible for him to
have some. A droplet of syrup flew into his mouth as he
stirred, reminding him of the cone-shaped sweet sugar
loaves at his wedding. His mouth watered. Would the
quince seed potion taste that good? Could it turn his bitter marriage into a sweet one at last? Dare he ask? But his
opportunity to question the Bibi did not arrive.

After the maids finished cooking and bottling the
quince jam, the Bibi excused them. She then began to
transfer the seeds to various jars to prepare some of the
potion for herself and her children.

"Sarveali, go to the storeroom and fetch me some starch
and tragacanth. I want to make some quince seed potions
for the crown princes." Sarveali's heart pounded. The
magical moment had arrived. This was his chance to ask.
"What is the potion good for, dear Bibi?"

"Everything! It's a panacea! It can cure any unnatural malady, like diphtheria, pneumonia, and intractable coughs. People discover the benefits of medicines like these through serendipity. You'll never know if it will cure your particular malady unless you try it. But now I just want the twins to use it as a cough suppressant."

Although he did not know what diphtheria and pneumonia were, Sarveali understood enough about the word "malady" to be certain he had one. Terrorized by cowardice, he was hesitant to pursue the subject further, for if he did, he would also be admitting to the Bibi his failing marriage. But a magical stimulus liberated his tongue. "Forgive me, dear Bibi, but may I be so rude as to ask for some of your remarkable potion?" If the potion could suppress coughs and other unnatural problems, surely it could help him mate properly and father a child.

"Yes, by all means. Now get the starch and tragacanth."

At the storeroom door, the keyhole's geometric shape—a circle on top of a triangle—fascinated Sarveali. He lifted the key ring toward the ceiling, as the sun shone through the aperture and illuminated the correct key. But before he could adjust it in the keyhole, fragments of familiar moans and whispers flowed sluggishly through. Sarveali's heart hammered against his chest. He inhaled sharply, knelt down, and observed two heads superimposed on the keyhole. The henna-colored clusters of his wife's hair framed the black locks of the combine operator. Mounted on the beautiful Yazgulu, the man's naked buttocks moved with enginelike thrusts. Sarveali's hands trembled and his insides spun. Dread of impending doom settled onto him.

Finally, his suspicions had been confirmed. Yazgulu was an unholy traitor of his former master, and she also cared nothing for her husband's reputation. If the blabbing cook discovered *this* secret, "Sarveali, the Cuckold" would turn into a term even more ignominious.

I must kill her, he thought at once, his rage peaking. *She is a demon.* Then he remembered he must fetch the traga- canth as the Bibi had ordered. *Duty must come before vengeance, at least for now.*

He found the rarely used staircase at the back of the storeroom, enabling him to fetch the starch and tragacanth and deliver them to the Bibi. He concealed his agitation so well that the Bibi reprimanded him for his tardiness.

"What took you so long? I didn't ask for pistachio oil from Rafsanjan, duck intestines from China, or parrot beaks from India! Where did you disappear to? What hap- pened?" Then, noticing his face, "Why are you so pale? Maybe you have jaundice? Or is it your uncle's death?" Sarveali did not respond. He placed the jars on the table, but when he attempted to bow to the Bibi, his knees buck- led and, with difficulty, he fled.

"Where are you going? Did you not want some of the potion, the panacea?" the Bibi yelled after him.

AFTER HIS KEYHOLE OBSERVATION, SARVEALI CRIED in soli- tude in some ruins near the Kamab Cemetery. His des- tiny now seemed filled with unrequited love and loyalty to his master, a loveless marriage, and repeated cuck- oldry. Contemplating these afflictions, he walked through the graves, staring at the epitaphs carved into the rectangular tombstones. He could not read the words inscribed on the stones, but he noticed the pitiful condition of the burial grounds. Some graves seemed to have been molested by either rogue humans or animals. There were deep pits. *What if I fell into one of these? Would*

I die? If they were as deep as a well, I'd throw myself in and finish myself off right now.

Avoiding the holes, Sarveali walked toward the wall adjacent to the orchard. There, outside the orchard's territory, a lone persimmon tree splayed its leafless branches over the clay wall. Two shiny red fruits and a few leaves that resisted descent ornamented the branches, which were dancing in the autumn breeze. The sun shone upon his face. Sarveali raised his hand, and one of the last heart-shaped persimmon leaves fell into his palm. Its veins matched the fissures, lines, and calluses on Sarveali's hand.

Examining the leaf, he remembered what the gypsy had told him. "Someone close to you will wed you to a girl whose beauty will make you suffer for the remainder of your life." He also remembered bits and pieces of his conversation with Ishaq Shamoun. He specifically remembered what he had said about courage and alcohol. "You could kill your worst enemy."

On the way home, Sarveali purchased two bottles of *aragh* from Khalil the Distiller. Once back at the estate, he retrieved a hatchet from the barn and placed it, along with the bottles of *aragh*, in a kilim-lined satchel. Without looking directly at Yazgulu, suddenly despising her henna-haired beauty, Sarveali told his wife she must accompany him to Madavan the following day.

"But we still have a few days . . . three days, until my father's fortieth day of mourning," Yazgulu protested.

"Your father's seventh, fourteenth, or fortieth means nothing to me! Pack up, now!" He bit his lip to prevent himself from calling her a whore. His wife's rubicund face paled as if admitting to her own guilt and shame. Although Sarveali could not have guessed her mood, Sarveali's command was so unlike him that Yazgulu felt if he were to touch her now, her vaginal clenching would not return.

But she only obeyed without question. "Yes, sir."

Sarveali went to the Bibi immediately to seek permission to leave for Madavan for the day under the guise of attending to his uncle's mourning family.

"You are still very pale. You're taking your uncle's death very badly, it seems. Probably because you chose not to go to the funeral. But you can go now. And take Yazgulu with you," the Bibi replied.

Changiz Khan's tractor-trailer was hauling sugar beets to Madavan the next morning, and Sarveali requested that he and Yazgulu be taken on the trip. The couple did not exchange a single word during the journey. On reaching the Bahadoran Bridge, built to carry the dusty road across a rivulet of the same name, Sarveali asked Yazgulu if she was thirsty. Yazgulu nodded. Sarveali asked the driver to stop. "We'll get off here! When are you going back to town?"

"Later today."

"We'll meet you then."

Sarveali and Yazgulu dismounted and walked toward the rivulet beneath the bridge. Sarveali opened the mouth of his satchel where the two bottles of *aragh* embraced the hatchet. Leaving Yazgulu by the stream, Sarveali said in his newly found tone, "Stay here by the water. Don't move. And don't wander off." He walked toward the ruins of the two-centuries-old Bahadoran Citadel that once belonged to Changiz Khan's great-grandfather.

Sarveali warily observed the ruins of the square-shaped clay citadel. Four phallic towers that had not crumbled gave testament to a bygone glory. Sheikhak had once told him the citadel had walls a meter and a half thick where horses could tread. Its current dilapidated condition—crumbling walls, termite-infested wooden door, and ruined vestibule—was the result of an inheritance dispute among the Shirlu khans of generations past. *All it needed was a periodic besmearing with hay and clay to seal the rooftop.* Sarveali felt as sad and ruined as the crumbling monument.

As he walked, avoiding scorpions and rodents, he opened the first bottle and took a large gulp of the caustic liquid, impatiently anticipating the moment he would no longer feel any emotions at all. As the main salon's ruins came into view, he quickly swallowed the rest of the bottle. The marbled chimney with its engraved Persian writings had survived years of neglect. *I too have survived neglect and disrepair. Pity I'm not made of marble.* Soon he felt the alcoholic fire within his head. He opened the second bottle. From where he stood, he could see his wife washing her vermillion red scarf in the stream. His intoxicated mind clumsily traveled back as far as possible, but he could not remember when she purchased the scarf.

Who gave that scarf to my wife? he wondered, his agitation growing.

What man gave that scarf to my whore wife?

Despite his numbness from the *aragh*, the rage inside him began to build steadily and Sarveali began to weep. "I am nothing but a wife-whore cuckold. The combine operator or the exterminator leader bought her that scarf, no doubt! I'm going to kill her and then I'll get both of them. Only my master can have her . . . only my m-m-master!" Hiccupping violently, he noticed he had already finished the second bottle. He tipped it against his lips and licked the last few drops. Disgusted that he was still not drunk enough, he threw the bottle against the marbled chimney. It only clattered and dropped heavily to the ground.

"I can't even break a glass bottle," he moaned, opening his satchel and grabbing the hatchet. His hair stringy from perspiration and his face contorted, Sarveali deserted the citadel and ran toward his wife who was sitting placidly, looking at the stream, her head scarf covering her henna hair, her thoughts far away.

As Sarveali came to an abrupt halt behind Yazgulu, he saw the image of his face floating above hers in the water. He tried one last time to decipher some love in the blue of her eyes as she turned toward him, but his inability to enjoy her beauty impelled him into a final drunken rage. He lifted his hatchet. "Don't do it, cousin!" she screamed. Her voice, as it echoed against the clay walls of the destroyed citadel, vibrated in his eardrums.

Chapter 16

Out of his mind with guilt and drunkenness, Sarveali forgot his appointment with the tractor driver and ran all the way from the Bahadoran Bridge to the outskirts of Madavan, near Changiz Khan's sugar beet farm. His shirt and pants dripped with the blood of his wife's head, which he had cleaved in two. Yazgulu lay facedown in the rivulet where she had dreamily washed her head scarf only an hour before. The intense red of her flowing blood overpowered the scarf's vermillion. In spite of his horror, his intoxication caused him to feel little remorse for his dead wife. It was as if a massive tumor of shame had been excised from him. As soon as Sarveali saw the sugar beet tractor, he attempted to board it but slipped to his knees on the pebbles. Finally, to the wide-eyed stare of the tractor driver, he settled on the fender next to his empty satchel and commanded, "Return to Kamab and take me to the police!"

As the driver charged down the road, the tractor complaining with flatulent noises and cloudlets of diesel smoke, Sarveali became calmer. His stomach roiled but his mind began to clear. "The devil has gotten under my skin," he said to the fearful driver, who gave him wild gazes as he steered the tractor in the direction of Kamab. The tractor's kinetic tempo seemed to increase at Sarveali's words. "Take me to municipal police headquarters," Sarveali continued. "I must confess."

Past the National Garden and meters before reaching police headquarters, Sarveali, still holding his empty satchel, jumped from the tractor and ran past a guard with a harelip. The guard, dozing, did not notice Sarveali's pale complexion, disheveled hair, and blood-stiffened clothes. He waved his hand in an involuntary, ritualistic salute. Sarveali entered the first office, which was occupied by a uniformed official of Herculean proportions. The sergeant's nostrils flared at Sarveali's odoriferous state and he jumped from his seat to confront the little man.

"I demand to speak to the head of the troops!" Sarveali shouted.

The Herculean sergeant came from behind his desk and dealt Sarveali a blow on his right cheek that knocked him onto the cement floor. His eyes snapped shut, and sparkles mixed with red, tulip-shaped globules whirled into blackness. From far away, Sarveali heard, "Mother-fucker! Do you think this is your mama's house? Marching in and showing disrespect to my office? What the fuck is your problem?"

Sarveali rose dizzily from his prone position on the floor. "I am the head servant of Changiz Khan Shirlu, and I just killed my wife," he said. Chaos followed. The officer yelled at two youthful policemen: "Arrest him!"

Sarveali found himself grabbed by the ankles and dragged up the stairs to the second floor. His head, battered by alcohol and collisions with the cement, had swelled to the size of a watermelon by the time the police officers unlocked and opened a rusted steel door. They dropped him to the floor and threw the empty satchel after him. When he regained his senses, he realized he was not alone. A dozen men stared at him in wonder. Sarveali thought he recognized some of them, but he was in such pain that he crawled to a corner of his cell and, exhausted by remorse, fell asleep.

WHEN CHANGIZ KHAN WAS INFORMED of Sarveali's crime, he was filled with anger. Not because the stupid servant had butchered his slut of a wife, but because now he would have to train a new factotum. Even though he had repeatedly stated that "true feelings of humanity manifest themselves within the circle of the suppressed minorities," what he really regretted, as in the case of Shamoun returning to Israel, was the disappearance of a consistent source of Khollar Shiraz wine—ruby red, pungent, and robust, with an aroma and flavor that infused heaven into his taste buds. While Sarveali's winemaking was nowhere as good as Shamoun's and might even taste like a "whore's menses," it was better than nothing. He decided to plan meticulously for Sarveali's freedom. Otherwise, who would tie his shoes every morning? Who would know exactly how he wished his eggs and Turkish coffee prepared for breakfast?

When Sarveali awoke in prison the following morning, he tried to fight off his alcoholic amnesia and sore head so he could remember what had happened the day before. Scenes slowly came to him in pieces. The hatchet in midair and tulip-shaped globules of blood floating in the stream appeared in his mind like a scene in a painting. He knew in an instant that he was a drunken murderer and that he was doomed. Soon he would be either hanged or executed by a firing squad. It was not unlikely that an executioner would strangle him to death with his bare hands.

Sarveali surveyed his cell in despair. Ugly fellows sat around the cell's sole source of heat—a brazier in the middle of the room. The walls were blackened with dirt, graffiti, and charcoal smoke. Besides the ripped kilim and two straw-woven blankets, the cement floor was bare. The room had no windows, but Sarveali noticed a locked door that he would later learn opened to the female chamber of the section.

During the day, he gradually learned the crimes of each occupant. A shepherd had beaten the local butcher, accusing him of short-weighting his slaughtered goats, and a peasant had attacked someone with a hatchet over a few square meters of land on which he had already built a hut. "I didn't kill him, though," the peasant said, grinning at Sarveali out of the corner of his eye.

Sarveali's crime was the most reprehensible; he was the only murderer. "If that peasant beat the butcher and was jailed, God only knows what they'll do to a man who killed his wife!" the guard with the harelip said gleefully.

For four days, Sarveali sat in the corner of his cell, sure his name would be called any moment and he would be hanged, shot, strangled, or even beheaded. He puzzled over his dreadful deed. *Was it worth it? I should've divorced her, but divorcing a whore would make me look like more of a cuckold; killing her made me a man. At least now I'll be respected, no matter what happens.* He continued to concoct heroic rationalizations. *If I'm put to death, people will remember me as a man of honor and courage, whose honor would not be compromised.* Simultaneously consoled and aroused by his thoughts, he again pictured the murder scene:

tulip-shaped globules of blood floating in the water, the head scarf awash in red.

He closed his moist eyes and imagined his hanging ceremony. The hangman was laughing and preparing his knot as if he were fixing a swing for a child. Sarveali imagined the slip noose breaking his neck while the whole town watched him swing. A demanding voice ended his reverie. "Jokar! Jokar! Sarveali Jokar! Come with me! Bring your belongings!" It was the Herculean sergeant.

They've come to take me off to purgatory, without a doubt! Sarveali thought. In a minute, death would show its face. *God forgive me! In the name of Allah, the Merciful and the Compassionate!*

The officer took him down the hall, opened a wooden door, and pushed Sarveali inside another room.

"You'll be here for a while."

"You aren't going to hang me?"

"Where in the devil did you come from, you yokel! You bumpkin! First, you rush in here drunk and tell everyone you've killed your wife. Now you're asking me to hang you? This is what I get for working on the dark side of the moon, in this filthy town, dealing with you peasants! Believe me, if you are to be hanged, I will not soil my hands with hanging a dumb fuck like you."

The enormous officer stormed away, slamming the door behind him.

So it was that four days after his wife's murder, Sarveali was transferred to the "deluxe" section of the prison, thanks to his master and his connections.

Chapter 17

The "deluxe" section of police headquarters was filled with prisoners of a different type. There was the local school vice principal, arrested for communist leanings, the bookstore owner jailed for his outlawed National Front affiliation, and a corpulent gentleman covered by a white ankle-length shirt who proved to be an opium smuggler from Baluchestan. Each of these men had special social status.

I thought I was being taken to the hangman's post, but I've come to this nice guesthouse instead. It's practically a hotel. Sarveali almost forgot his heinous crime as he looked around his new accommodations. Of course it was Changiz Khan who had paid not only for the new quarters but also for the fine cuisine—basmati rice mixed with walnuts and raisins or stew of eggplant and split peas—that was delivered to him each day. Sarveali ate better than he ever had at home.

But within a week, all this culinary attention came to an end when Changiz Khan's cook told him that the Bibi had forbidden more treats. "That wife killer needs to be hanged. The twins have been crying for days, and Bibi Naz refuses to eat. They miss Yazgulu to no end! How could someone kill such a beautiful creature?"

Sarveali contemplated the importance of the Bibi's harsh criticism. *She* was unlikely to help him avoid the hangman. But he cheered a little when the bookseller announced, "While we are both here, I would like to teach you the alphabet. I believe the entire nation should become literate, one by one."

"Alphabet?"

"Yes, Alefba."

"Alphabet: *Alef, be, pe, te, se* . . ." the bookseller clarified by repeating the Persian alphabet, noting that Sarveali might be difficult to teach. But unlike winemaking, Sarveali took to the fundamentals of the alphabet readily. Little by little, as the stains of Yazgulu's blood washed away from his mind and the pain in his head subsided, he occupied himself with more positive endeavors. *When they hang me, they will be hanging a literate man.* The former vice principal, impressed with the little peasant's labors, added his bit. "Godless communist though I am, I'll teach you some verses from the Koran."

Soon Sarveali completed the first lesson in the primary school's first grade book. He learned to write his name. The first time he wrote "Sarveali Jokar," the letters turned into a baby chick lifting its beak at him. Sarveali found he enjoyed reading and writing. Soon two months had passed, if not happily, at least with some purpose.

He learned the Koran by repetition, chanting verses and praying in the Shiite Muslim manner. He began to love the sound of the Arabic verses, but he still had problems with comprehension.

126

"'Allah-oooo-Akbar' means 'Allah is the Greatest,' the preface to any Koranic manifesto," the vice principal lectured. "Nakeer and Monker, the death angels, visit the dead on the first night of the deceased's entombment . . ." Sarveali confused the word "Nakeer," the Arabic name for the death angel, with the Persian word, where "na" means "no" and "keer" means "penis," or "penis-less." *Poor Yazgulu, "na-keer" I was in life. Now this man tells me another "na-keer" will visit her in the afterlife too.* He thought about his dead wife from time to time as he learned to read and write, slowly replacing the ghastly image of her death with happier visions of her striking henna hair and bright blue eyes.

As the months passed and it became obvious that, while he would not hang, he might be imprisoned for life, he continued with his lessons. Sarveali was delighted when the bookseller said, "Sarveali, let's start on a new lesson about a shepherd who cried wolf," fondly remembering his own shepherding days and his favorite pearl goat.

Meanwhile, the opium smuggler from Baluchestan became Sarveali's closest friend. "Hey, Mr. Jokar! Sarveali! How did you get moved in here? You're just a servant. What's your story?" With pride, Sarveali told the smuggler of his connection with the Shirlus. He told him all sorts of stories about Changiz Khan, leaving out only the murder he had committed and the fact that Changiz Khan had not communicated with him since his incarceration. As a storyteller, Sarveali was so convincing that the opium smuggler immediately saw a potential opium backer in the great Shirlu.

"Do any of the khans in your master's family indulge in opium?"

"Not really. Except for a couple of old ladies," Sarveali replied, feeling guilty at revealing negative secrets about his master's dynasty.

"You know, Sarveali, when you take 'brown gold,' you feel like the king of the universe, like an eagle feared by the avian world." The Baluchestani could see that not only would Sarveali make a fine apprentice of opium smoking, but in the future, whether he was released from jail or imprisoned for life, a splendid practitioner.

He immediately began to describe opium and its cultivation, pharmacology, and heavenly euphoria. The agricultural and medicinal aspects of opium confused Sarveali, but he listened carefully to what the smuggler said: "It'll make you so powerful you could excavate a mountain with your eyelashes; you'll become the biggest eagle in the Zagros Mountains . . . It allows you to perform whatever you want to do in life perfectly!" He taught Sarveali how to smoke by sketching the phallic-shaped pipe and demonstrating where to place the opium. "Soon I'll get small pieces you can take like tablets. It won't be like smoking it, but you will still feel like you're in heaven."

Sarveali listened carefully to what the opium smuggler taught him. Perhaps the opium could help him become a better servant, compensating for the shame he had brought his master, if he were ever freed from prison. He discovered all too soon that he was a natural for the soothing drug—his nature, as always, helplessly tempted by endeavors others imposed on him.

Chapter 18

Two months after Sarveali's imprisonment, in November 1953, Changiz Khan finally implemented a plan to win his factotum's freedom. In his new Willys, he drove to the late Barat-Ali's house.

Changiz Khan's mission was to speak to the fat and flaccid Gholi, Sarveali's cousin and brother-in-law, now the head of his late father's household. In order to win Changiz Khan's pity, the entire household had prolonged their mourning, and was indulging in forced, exaggerated weeping. Screams ricocheted from the house and echoed against the alley's mud walls. As Changiz Khan drove up, Gholi, Kokab, and other relatives began to beat their breasts, exclaiming over the death of their husband and father, and the murder of Yazgulu. Like the ravens on the ground before him, Changiz Khan was oblivious to such demonstrations of mourning. He was only concerned with convincing Gholi Jokar, the new heir of Barat-Ali, to issue unconditional clemency to Sarveali for his sister's murder. After Gholi received a few slaps and promise of a financial settlement, he agreed to all the terms Changiz Khan suggested.

TWO DAYS LATER, CHANGIZ KHAN APPEARED at the prison for the first time, followed by a familiar man with a briefcase.

"This is your lawyer," Changiz Khan announced.

Sarveali's fellow inmates stared, their curiosity piqued by Changiz Khan. The prisoners could tell by the handlebar mustache, black-striped suit, starched white shirt, solid gold cufflinks, and Hermes tie that the man before them held a superior position in life.

"You're a lucky man, Jokar!" the lawyer said, walking toward Sarveali. "Your master, His Eminence, has convinced your brother-in-law to issue you clemency for what happened to his sister—your wife—I mean . . . I mean, your murdered wife, umm . . . your former wife!"

"Praise of God upon my master! I'm nothing but the dust he walks on!" Sarveali rushed from his usual cross-legged position on the floor to Changiz Khan, bent over, and kissed the great man's hand. Still holding his hand, Sarveali began to weep. His whiskered face and straggly hair rested on his master's jeweled fingers.

"Sarveali, don't make a scene!" Changiz Khan tried to pull away from his servant's grip, but Sarveali gripped his fingers tight, continuing to kiss his hand.

"We're getting clemency!" the lawyer announced. "Gholi Jokar forgives you! All he wanted was blood money, which your master generously took care of."

"May you live more than 120 years!" Sarveali exclaimed to Changiz Khan.

THAT NIGHT SARVEALI DREAMED the lawyer was soaring through the air on a gigantic *qalam*, a reed pen carved from bamboo stems and used for calligraphy and writing. He descended toward a blood-red basin the shape of a tulip to immerse the nib. He soared into the air again, directing the pen like a rocket as he wrote a sentence next to the "D.D.T." scribbles on the estate walls. The cook suddenly appeared. "Sarveali! Your lawyer just wrote 'Free the Nakeer!'" Sarveali thought again of the Arabic name for the death angel, the Persian word for "no penis."

He awoke in a cold sweat. His dream was yet another reminder of his impotence. First, he had been certain he would be hanged. Then, as surely as Allah reigned supreme, he knew he would be imprisoned for life. After all, his crime was the most horrendous in the prison. *What an obligation he owed to his masters. His life and salvation.* But lurking somewhere in his unconscious, something nagged him. *I am a wife murderer!* He thought of the smuggler and his stories of the power-engendering opium. *I don't need to excavate a mountain with my eyelashes. I just need to free myself from my own weak mind.* He slowly drifted back to sleep.

EVEN AFTER GHOLI'S ISSUANCE OF CLEMENCY, it still took time to extricate Sarveali from prison. The judge had to be bribed. "Your master was very generous. After delivering countless toumans, partridges, tangerines, and shaddocks, he's finally willing to set you free," the lawyer told him.

"But your cousin is getting very greedy," he continued. "He wants five hectares of land in Madavan, twelve square meters of rugs, and fifty goats. His wishes grow as he gets fatter and fatter." But now Sarveali was not so concerned with his freedom, even less concerned with his title of murderer, and not at all concerned with his stunted mind. Only a few days earlier, he had found the smuggler lying on his cot, resting from a siesta. As embarrassed as the time he asked the Bibi for the quince seed potion, Sarveali had to muster his courage again to ask the Baluchestani for opium. "Have you any of the thing that you say can turn someone into an eagle?"

"Yes, I do. I received a shipment yesterday, in fact." The corpulent man, having waited patiently for Sarveali to approach him, removed a box from beneath his cot. In the box were four golden-brown sticks, each wrapped in grease-proof paper and tied together with cotton twine. He cut a pea-sized piece from the tip of one of the sticks and put it in his mouth. Closing his eyes, he whispered into Sarveali's right ear, "Can you believe that *this* is the best grade from Yazd, the purest of them all?"

Without waiting for a response, he opened his eyes slowly and took a small jar from the box. "This powder contains nutmeg, cardamom, cinnamon, saffron, and ambergris. Take a small bite of the golden beauty and follow it with a spoonful of the powder." When Sarveali put a small piece of the acrid substance in his mouth, he grimaced in disgust. "Is this bitter thing snake's poison?"

"Have patience, my dear sir! As the poet says, 'Sour grapes will eventually become sweet raisins.' And the more bitter the grape, the sweeter the raisin."

Sarveali attempted to neutralize the unpalatable taste of the opium with the powder's sweet amalgam. He took a sip of sweetened hot tea and swallowed the mixture. Relaxation came over him, and he felt light enough to levitate. He forgot his prison sentence and the murder of his wife. His hallucination transformed the prison cell into a structural vastness greater than the Khan's entire estate. He heard the voice of the bookseller reading poetry of the most delicate nature. He gently let himself down onto the rug next to the smuggler's cot

and fell into a lovely little dream where colors intensified and deepened.

At dawn, two days later, Sarveali took another dose of
opium, afraid the lawyer would bring more ominous news
about his sentence. But he did not come and the next day
Sarveali experienced severe vertigo and nausea. His head
spinning, he vomited into the prison latrine. Sarveali suffered from intractable nausea the entire day, as well as
painful constipation. When the lawyer returned to inform
him that His Honor, the judge, wanted more cash to help
make the down payment for a house for his mother-in-law,
he watched Sarveali's bouts of nausea with disapproval.

A few days later, the lawyer visited Sarveali again. "I've
interviewed Gholi again," he said, pleased that Sarveali's
nausea seemed to have subsided. "After three rounds of
rebuttals, we're finally close to an agreement. Now he
wants seven hectares of land. He's also asking for 80 percent of your salary. But in return, I made him sign a contract that states he will provide retirement care for you
when you're old, may Allah bestow upon you 120 years of
longevity."

As the lawyer said "seven hectares of land," Sarveali vi-
sualized a colossal mountain range sitting on a vast plain.
And "may Allah bestow upon you 120 years," seemed to
suggest time travel.

"Is this arrangement suitable, Sarveali? We need to send
the case to the high courts in Shiraz immediately. I hope
they also agree."

In spite of frequent hallucinations, Sarveali's opium use
seemed to miraculously accelerate his learning the Persian alphabet and his memory of the Koran's verses. Like
most addicts, he began to convince himself that taking the
drug was harmless and that the side effects, nausea and

constipation, were only an occasional nuisance. As Sarveali continued to take "God's cocktail," the smuggler's term for the intoxicating drug, his present reality, the recurring visions of the murder, and constant negotiation of his prison terms became as insubstantial as the soft breeze caressing the date palms of the estate. He spent his nights in phantasmagoric dreams, days learning the alphabet and the Koran.

His fellow inmates, however, were not as happy with their lives. The communist vice principal and Koran instructor announced his repentance. He no longer hated the imperial government and began to carry a portrait of His Imperial Majesty, Shah Mohammad Reza Pahlavi, the Light of Aryans, next to his chest. On the first day of his transformation into a red-blooded monarchist, he commanded Sarveali to bow in front of the portrait of His Imperial Majesty to pay his respects.

"His Imperial what?" Sarveali noticed that the glints from the Shah's crown jewels darted beams into his eyes.

"Majesty. Yes, H.I.M., Mohammad Reza Shah Pahlavi, Shahanshah, the King of Kings, the Light of Aryans, Commander in Chief, Shadow of God on Earth," the former communist announced as he straightened his neatly tied ascot.

Sarveali did what he was told, submitting to a crouch in front of the portrait. Like his master, he was obediently pro-Shah, imagining Teimour Khan sitting on the Peacock Throne one day.

The nationalist bookseller did not repent his politics but sank into a perilous period of melancholy, accusing his former party comrades of being traitors. Most of them had fled abroad or had been offered an official contrition to remove them from prison. Now only the bookseller's decrepit mother, whose medical condition forced her to bend forward at a 45-degree angle, always gazing at the ground, visited him.

Sarveali empathized with the woman, hoping he could someday offer her a potent dose of opium to cure her ailment. He would observe her during the long visits, dressed in her black chador, begging her son to repent and apologize for his past antimonarchy activities. And as more and more of the former enemies of the Shah were released once they aligned their ideologies with those of the present government, the communist and nationalist prisoners were released too. Sarveali and Sistani, the Baluchestani opium smuggler, became the sole occupants of the "deluxe" section of the prison.

"This is a city filled with affluent potential consumers for 'God's cocktail.'" Sistani held an unused stick of opium between his fingers. "And the land at the bottom of the Zagros Mountains is very fertile. My master would do anything to partner with someone who owns such land. In fact, my cohorts have discovered that your master owns the best land. It's just outside Eram Pass." The smuggler fortified his appeals to Sarveali with daily treats of "God's cocktail." And with each dose of opium, Sarveali forgot his desire to be released, until one afternoon when his ex-teacher, the bookseller, paid him a visit.

"Remember, if you wish to play with elephants," he said disapprovingly, "you need an estate grand enough to house them."

"What? Who's an elephant?" Sarveali asked.

"You're about to get yourself into a filthy business meant only for big men," the bookseller insisted.

But unlike Sistani's gift, which left him in a perpetual state of happiness, the bookseller's wisdom gave Sarveali no meaning or comfort.

ON THE THIRTIETH DAY OF ESPAND (March 20), 1954, the last day of winter, the lawyer arrived with the clemency agreement and informed Sarveali that he needed to prepare for his release. As Sarveali proudly signed his name, he again noticed how his scrawl resembled a baby chicken's.

He could not believe such a miracle had finally happened. He had entered the penitentiary a criminal expecting execution and was leaving cleansed of the shame of cuckoldry and exposed to a new delight that gave him almost as much joy as his love for his old master.

When Sistani heard of Sarveali's impending freedom, he approached him greedily. "Remember, you promised to introduce me and my people to your master?"

Sarveali knew he could not live without the drug that gave him such courage and happiness. *With "God's cocktail," I will become the finest servant ever. And my master is grander than any khan!*

"So will you arrange a meeting?"

"I will do my best."

Yet again, Sarveali left behind one horrendous ordeal only to take up another.

IN APRIL 1954, SARVEALI WAS FINALLY RELEASED from prison accompanied by a stash of opium Sistani provided him. His Baluchestani friend was to be released a week later. Three weeks after the Baluchestani was freed, the smugglers arrived in Kamab, where Sarveali had arranged for them to stay with Khalil the Distiller at his hostel. After three months of taking opium by mouth, Sarveali was to graduate to an opium pipe. Sistani was finally going to show him how to smoke "God's cocktail."

Chapter 19

Sarveali is the imperial-booted eagle of the Zagros Mountains. He penetrates the indigo sky, darting through its limpid, frosty clouds, charging toward the sun.

The entire universe, every millimeter under his microscopic eye, worships him—the peacocks of India, the scarlet-beaked parrots of Africa, naked Afghan boys, his new European wife. He is the omnipresent and omnipotent emperor. The eternal god of virility, he has fathered numerous blue-eyed, henna-haired children. They chant their loyalty to him in a foreign tongue.

Now he imprisons two crimson-breasted, long-tailed tits in his talon grasp. They play with his penis among flutters of soft-feathered wings. Virile and potent, monumentally manifested by his priapism, Sarveali declares himself Sultan Sarveali Shah, pivot of the universe, his erect penis the flagstaff of his imperial canton.

The world is now under his reign. He ascends again and sees the pinnacle of the tallest peak of the Zagros. He punctures its apex with his beak. Thousands of swallows exit the orifice and become his army of disciples. He nestles in the body of a fig tree.

Suddenly the eagle feels a sharp pain. He sees he has been deeply penetrated by an arrow. Then he sees his own feathers at the end of the deadly missile's shaft, his peril directed by his own quills.

LYING IN THE HOSTEL hours after his first indulgence of opium smoking, an agonizing pain seized Sarveali as he emerged from his hallucination. The last cluster of morphine had metabolized and purged itself from his body. He struggled for sleep, for a remnant of hallucination to sprinkle over his thirsty body. But time had detoxified him of every bit of the brown tablet he had consumed.

Suffering from severe withdrawal, Sarveali's bliss transformed into an inferno of sobriety and the familiar horror of murder and impotency. In anguish, he stared at the pipe and the burnt tablet's blackening corpse, the tiny opium box with its cut cubes. He resolved that his skull must always harbor the ambrosia of the opium smoke, and banish his ugly visions forever.

SARVEALI CONTINUED TO BE AMAZED at the extraordinary experience of smoking opium. As long as he could smoke a *mesghal* (five grams) a day, he could perform limitless tasks. He felt he could pick all the citrus fruits off the trees, cook a meal for six hundred, run to Shiraz for an errand, and serve his master the most mystic Turkish coffee all at the same time. However, over time, as he continued smoking opium at the hostel with the help of his former inmate, his intense hallucinations were followed by deep valleys of sobriety and despair. As a result, Sistani was forced to constantly adjust the dosage. He needed Sarveali to find the courage and ambition to ask his master to meet with the Baluchestanis.

How could I, Sarveali the Cuckold, dare wheedle Changiz Khan Shirlu into talking to these people? he thought. But as the molecules of "God's cocktail" began to penetrate the deepest crevices of his brain, Sarveali gained the courage. He decided to ask Changiz Khan as he assisted him with his morning shave. As he held the art deco chrome-framed mirror in front of his master's face, the words finally formed in his quivering mouth.

"My former fellow prison inmate and his master are begging for an audience with you. Would Your Eminence give them the honor of your presence?" Changiz Khan applied shaving cream to his face, surprised at Sarveali's eloquent request.

"Who is this inmate?" Changiz Khan inquired, focusing his attention on his right sideburn. "The National Front bookseller? Or that communist with the dressing gown and ascot?"

"No, Your Eminence, the Baluchestani," his voice quivered.

"Oh . . . that pregnant white cow," Changiz Khan sneered.

"Yes, sir," Sarveali replied sheepishly, admitting to himself Sistani's resemblance to a pregnant heifer.

"What does he want? And who is his master?"

"He did not tell me. He said they need to discuss a private matter with you."

"Oh, they said that, did they?" He kept his gaze focused on his reflection. Sarveali hid behind the mirror so Changiz Khan could not see his deceitful face.

"Tell them to come tomorrow." Changiz Khan wiped his shaven face with a white towel Sarveali handed him, then applied aromatic cologne and lotion. Sarveali inhaled his master's musk, the scent of his own sweet victory.

The next day, Sistani and his master, accompanied by a servant with a cyst in the center of his forehead, arrived at the gates of the estate in a 1930 Dodge truck with mismatched fenders and headlights that wheezed like a geriatric on his last breath. The visitors swayed back and forth on wooden chairs mounted to the bed of the truck.

Changiz Khan found the guests hideous. As if the Baluchestani khan's gold front tooth, halitosis, and obsequiousness were not bad enough, their general body odor and the deformed servant's smelly feet made Changiz Khan's eyes water. Later he said the encounter was "as radioactive as Hiroshima."

The Baluchestanis brought him a rifle as a present, claiming it had been handmade by their gunsmith on the Pakistani side of Baluchestan. However, Changiz Khan could see the English words "Royal British Army, Ceylon Division" etched on the side.

"It is such an honor to be in the presence of His Eminence, the Great Khan of the Shirlus." The Baluchestani khan immediately launched into a presentation on opium and its potential economic impact for Kamab.

The financial aspect of their proposal and the promise of the drug nearby captivated Sarveali, but he quickly noticed his master's appalled reaction. "My father, grandfather, and ancestors were warriors," Changiz Khan said with pride. "They were men of war, freedom, and chivalry. After the 1907 treaty when the Russians and the Brits split our country in half, my ancestors resisted the British attacks in the south. If it were not for them and other southern tribes in the province, our monarchy would have been threatened. Our nation would have been balkanized and disintegrated. It is not in our culture to enslave the vulnerable youth of our nation with the filth of opium." He looked down his nose at the interlopers. Stunned that Changiz Khan had rejected their lucrative offer to provide them a parcel of his land in exchange for their capital, cultivation, and distribution, the Baluchestanis departed. Humiliated, Sistani glared at Sarveali. But before they left Kamab, the men did manage to persuade Khalil the Distiller to convert part of his establishment into an opium den. They told the naive owner, "This will be a very lucrative business. As you know, Islam has not forbidden opium."

The opium peddlers left a good supply and a pipe with the hostel owner for Sarveali, hoping to persuade him not to forget his role in their mission. Ashamed that he had offended his master, he spent the night at the opium den. After his night smoke, he dreamed he was the only virile white goat in a black herd. The other black goats pulled his intestines out through his rectum and publicly hanged him by his entrails. He was choking when he woke up, sputtering from the cold water the two servants sent to find him had poured over his face. Still upset over the smugglers' visit, Changiz Khan had sent for Sarveali when he was nowhere to be found.

Changiz Khan, still in his martyrdom mode, decided not to punish Sarveali for his absence. "Similar incidents in my father's epoch would have involved fifty whip lashes on the culprit's bare back," he shouted at the cowering servant. "Some servants were hanged by their ankles, suspended for days. You're lucky to live in this modern age." Ashamed, Sarveali remained quiet, deciding to plead for his master's forgiveness when he served him his breakfast.

The issue of Sarveali's substance abuse still remained. Changiz Khan was mildly concerned about his servant's new habit but lacked the vigor to lecture him. As long as he performed his duties, Sarveali was forgiven his weaknesses.

That evening, Changiz Khan read that the 1953 Paris Protocol sought to limit world production of opium to medical and scientific use. Since Iran was one of seven countries licensed by the United Nations to oversee poppy production, he began to rethink his position.

While Sarveali brewed Turkish coffee for Changiz Khan the next morning, he noticed that even the swirling brown liquid reminded him of opium. Now was the time to plead to Changiz Khan for forgiveness. He fell to his knees, throwing his face on his master's feet. "I eat shit! I eat shit!" He could taste the salt of his tears mixed with the polish on Changiz Khan's hunting boots.

In his mind, Changiz Khan had already forgiven his servant, and was more concerned with his coffee getting cold than with Sarveali's need for repentance. "Get up! You are making a fool of yourself. You are forgiven, anyway," he said, quite kindly. "Now pour me a cup of coffee." As Sarveali turned back to his duty, Changiz Khan said, "And remind me about those Baluchestani contrabandists. Tell me again, which of my farms did they visit?"

Chapter 20

Sarveali rolls on his pistachio-green blanket. The blanket darkens to jade and lengthens. Meter by meter, Sarveali rotates along the length of the narrow covering, as if on a vast green plain whose fertile soil advances the indiscriminate growth of poppies. The blanket becomes longer and metamorphoses into a road connecting the township of Kamab to the city of Shiraz. Now a serpent, the road entraps Sarveali as it coils forward.

He passes the turquoise water of Baharlu Lake, where tiny wavelets transform into monstrous waves rushing toward him. The waves hurl insults at the Shirlus. In a rage, Sarveali declares war against the lake and plunges into it. At his side, a blue-eyed mermaid with henna-colored hair and red, shiny lips begins to cry red goldfish tears.

GASPING FOR AIR, SARVEALI OPENED HIS EYES. A cloud of fumes rose from the molten charcoal in the brazier; an opium pipe rested on the embers like a caliph in his rouge-cloaked harem.

He hacked at the massive smoke invading his eyes, nostrils, and chest. "I can't breathe," he gasped, and staggered outside. He found himself on the front porch of the now popular opium den, where the moon's luminous rays met him. Devouring the clean air, trying desperately to replenish his oxygen-deprived lungs, he splashed cold water from the basin on his face. He imagined he had caught a goldfish from the water and felt it wiggle on his cheek. The sensation startled him. He rubbed his cheek, scraping off not a goldfish but a cluster of tadpoles and a glob of green algae. He tossed the mess on the ground and collapsed. "Devil opium," he shrieked as he fell.

He woke the next morning on the cold stones of the courtyard, remembering a promise he had made to Changiz Khan to retrieve truffles for his dinner omelet. A local shepherd had a special technique for locating them after they mysteriously formed near piles of cow dung during thunderstorms. Ashamed and plagued by anxiety, Sarveali staggered off to meet the shepherd. After obtaining the truffles, Sarveali cooked an exotic omelet for Changiz Khan's breakfast. Changiz Khan enjoyed the omelet so much that he forgot to whip his servant for his absence the night before.

IN THE LATE SUMMER OF 1954, as Changiz Khan was having his morning coffee, he told Sarveali the latest news. "The United Nations' Narcotic Program deputy director engineer—a former classmate of mine from Zagros—and his team are coming from Tehran to inspect our poppy farm."

"Yes, my patriarch." The farm they had planted three months earlier would soon enhance his dwindling supply. And it was he and his Baluchestani friends who had inspired Changiz Khan to sow the farm. *If only Teimour Khan were here to enjoy the fruits with me.*

A week later, the estate gate opened, and three white Land Rovers emblazoned with the official emblem of the lion and sun arrived. The director engineer and Changiz Khan kissed cheeks, then sat down to a sumptuous dinner of basmati rice infused with pomegranate sauce, stuffed partridge, and the cook's specialty—*kabab-e-mast*—doe meat macerated in yogurt, lemon juice, saffron, and other mysterious concoctions, skewered through a freshly carved fig branch, and grilled on willow-wood charcoal.

After dinner, they discussed Changiz Khan's latest cash crop. "What made you decide on opium farming, Changiz?" the director engineer asked in a dialect so academic it was incomprehensible to the lurking Sarveali, who spoke only elementary Persian.

"One of my servants was approached by a group of ridiculous Baluchestanis. One looked like a cross between a pregnant frog and a pregnant cow! They had apparently visited my field and found it fertile ground for poppy farming."

"Those Baluchestanis know opium farming better than many agricultural engineers," the director engineer said.

"My dear engineer! Are you saying I should've gone to them instead? At least you smell better. Is that Aramis you're wearing? It reminds me of someone. Not the Baluchestanis, that's for sure! They wore a special scent made from an amalgam of rhinoceros shit and Bedouin armpit concentrate. I told my cousin their fetid aroma was most likely radioactive!" Changiz Khan burst into laughter.

"Actually, it's not Aramis, it's Creed . . ."

The series of artificial coughs Sarveali gave to announce his entrance masked the rest of the engineer's sentence.

Sarveali carried a tray with a cognac bottle and two snifters symmetrically placed on either side.

"We have fifty-five hectares currently under cultivation," Changiz Khan said after his first sip of cognac. He held the snifter by the stem instead of under the bowl. "And you should see the young girls who work the farm." Changiz Khan winked at the director.

"Nymphets wandering among poppy flowers! How romantic!" As the director engineer readjusted his position in the armchair, Sarveali smelled his cologne. Heaven and hell engulfed him as he remembered; it was Creed, the scent he had detected on Yazgulu after she had been with his master. Once more, he was torn by guilt, remorse, and shame over his murderous act.

As his emotions resurfaced, so did his memories of Teimour Khan's glorious physique and beauty. The reverie instantly erased anything adverse within him as he glanced at the director engineer, who was nearly as handsome and rosy-cheeked as his old master.

The next day, Sarveali rode in the Jeep's backseat to the poppy fields. He paid particular attention to the crowds that formed along the main streets of Kamab, watching the cavalcade leave the township. He felt his familiar pride at being the factotum of Changiz Khan, the wealthiest and most powerful dignitary in his part of the province. He made up comments about the locals' jealousy.

Look at that Haji Moshrefi, the charlatan bazaar merchant, Sarveali thought as the merchant spoke to his assistant. *That bastard with the gold tooth is clearly envious of my master.*

And see that turban-headed stomach worshiper? I saw that mullah mutter at the Jeep. Curses, no doubt. Is he a man of God or of envy?

His negative thoughts seemed an ominous augury, and his inability to preserve fleeting moments of optimism toppled Sarveali from his pride. *Happiness is like a cattle's fart—mild in odor and never lasts long,* he mused. He did not realize his prescience; already the mullahs were becoming increasingly outraged by the secularism of the nation, especially by families like the Shirlus now at the peak of their financial power. It was time for an opiate release. "Dear God, just one puff! Perhaps two!" he prayed.

"AFTER ROSTAM KILLED HIS SON, Sohrab, all of Iran's white poppies turned red from his blood," the director engineer said, surveying the vast, colorful field. The others in the Jeep—Changiz Khan, Sarveali, and the director engineer's colleagues—silently observed the brilliant blanket of poppies covering the field, some in anticipation of psychic relief, some of financial gain.

"And after six thousand years, it is our great Changiz Khan Shirlu who has resurrected the white, the pink, the purple, and the reddish orange."

Sarveali remembered a film he had once seen with Teimour Khan that depicted the tragedy of the mythological hero who killed his son without realizing he was his own flesh and blood. Sarveali's longing for his master suddenly grew so strong that he could barely remember the story, but he did remember how Teimour Khan had ridiculed him for returning to the film several nights in a row hoping Rostam would somehow discover that the young lad was his son and spare his life. Sarveali's eyes moistened. Teimour Khan may have considered him naive and stupid for mistaking cinema for reality, but no one had ever touched him like his former master. Not even the great Changiz Khan, who was being lauded for bringing poppy farming into twentieth-century Iran, could replace Teimour Khan.

Changiz Khan's poppy field appeared perfect. The director engineer examined the soil and evaluated the climate, humidity, and ecology of the terrain the way a falcon observes his domain before nesting.

"Changiz, this is a crop-science miracle!" he said. "An agricultural utopia!"

"Yes, a utopia full of houris," Changiz Khan pointed to an adolescent girl in a group carrying pots of water on their heads. "Look at that one! Her rosy cheeks match the red flower where the blood of Sohrab splashed 60,000 years ago!"

"How can they carry those pots and walk with such ease?"

"Because they learned choreography at the prestigious National Ballet Company at the Kamab School of Fine Arts, of course," Changiz Khan said, sarcastic as usual. "You should observe their motions in bed; perhaps they learned *those* from the clergy."

The director engineer was silent. He hastily changed the subject. "Changiz, this area is a utopia indeed. The fertile soil at the footsteps of the Zagros Mountains . . . the sparse rainfall and low humidity . . ."

"Oh, you forgot the pigeon shit. The millions of white pigeons and doves that witnessed Rostam kill his own son mourned the loss by defecating on these fields." He imitated his friend's scientific cadence as he took his flask out of its leather case and had his third swallow of whiskey.

"Did you sow five hundred grams of seed per half a hectare?"

"My dear engineer, don't ask me. How would I know?"

"Look at this one's peduncle. Look at these tillers," the director engineer continued.

"I would rather look at that beauty's peduncle." Changiz Khan gestured with his flask at the girl carrying the pot. Sarveali was shocked at the sexual innuendo and vulgar language. *But I suppose someone as powerful as my master can say whatever his tongue wishes.* "Changiz, the next thirty days are crucial. Any horticulturist will tell you. The growth cycle for *Papaver somniferum* is 120 days. I believe three months have already gone by," the engineer broke in.

"As Allahhhhhhh wishes, we leave everything to kismet," Changiz Khan replied, well lubricated and carefree.

"Changiz," his friend said, a didactic tone creeping into his speech, "if this crop is harvested properly, you will be the top opium grower in the nation. Perhaps even win first prize among the seven nations! The United Nations is taking this project quite seriously!"

Changiz Khan, far from serious now, pointed to the girls again. "Do you think those nymphets consider me number one?" he inquired as Sarveali detected discomfort in the engineer's face. Sarveali ignored Changiz Khan's comments, instead relishing the scent of Creed cologne on the director engineer and noticing how tightly his buttocks fit into his khaki trousers.

Chapter 21

Nearly a month later, in autumn of 1954, Changiz Khan ordered Sarveali to prepare for another trip to the opium farm. This time, officers of the U.N. Narcotics Program were coming to supervise and audit the harvesting process.

"We should expect eighty milligrams per pod and between eight and fifteen kilograms of raw opium per hectare," said an official with round spectacles, whose lenses resembled the bottom of small tea glasses. His observation pleased Sarveali because he hoped to obtain more of the fine brown substance for his personal use, and visiting officials were less likely to notice a diversion.

In prison, the Baluchestani had told Sarveali that the best way to smuggle opium was to insert opium tubes in cucumber-shaped containers and place them in the rectums of donkeys or camels. Sarveali decided to mastermind a plan involving a herd of stray donkeys that lived on the outskirts of Eram. He privately discussed his contraband plan with Changiz Khan. To his delight, his master was pleased, as he wished to give his premium-grade opium to business and political associates as gifts.

"I know you smoke opium, but I will allow your plan as long as you don't become so addicted that you humiliate me."

It was at that moment that Sarveali considered surrendering his devotion to Changiz Khan. In his mind, his master's permission to indulge in "God's cocktail" was as efficacious as converting an infidel into a pious Muslim. Could his opium habit be so potent he would consider changing allegiances? That evening, however, after another pipe, Sarveali's devotion for Teimour Khan returned. Changiz Khan would never replace his long-lost master.

Changiz Khan and Sarveali were not the only two caught in opium's grip. The Bibi made a special request. "Tell the peasants to gather all the dead peduncles, roots and stems, of the poppy plants, and sack them up for our goats to eat. I will make their milk into fine yogurt, cheese, and cream." The Bibi had heard that milk, yogurt, and cheese from goats that fed on the remains of poppy plantations had interesting medicinal properties.

Later that evening, Sarveali and several peasants inserted fifty cucumber-shaped tubes filled with opium into the lubricated rectums of the herd of donkeys. The moon at its apogee provided the clandestine team the necessary light to complete its project. As if cognizant of the conspiracy, the donkeys, led by a young shepherd, quietly trudged the graveled terrain toward the mountain. In the morning, shepherd and team would wait at a village in the northern hills for other smugglers who would return the herd to Changiz Khan's date palm groves in the village of Zeerab.

As Sarveali walked back to the poppy farm after overseeing the caravan's start, hoping for the mission's success, he heard whispers behind a wild tamarisk tree. "My dear, do you enjoy my embrace under these ancient stars, next to this poppy farm that will hallucinate half the world?" It was Changiz Khan. A closer look revealed that the woman in his arms was Madame Pamchal, the wife of the local police chief. Sarveali stood by in the moonlight, both perturbed and delighted at his master's happiness.

"Your left eye is blue and your right is green. I am not sure which I should love more!" Silence took over the vast terrain and the moon disappeared as a nimbus covered it. The sky became completely black.

"With you at my side, I feel I'm no longer on the dark side of the moon, my sweet Changiz Khan," the female voice said, her voice delicate even to the misogynist servant.

"My love, I will illuminate the whole world for your enlightenment with the lightning of my phallus." Sarveali compared his master's "lightning" with his own penis and, at that moment, felt a peculiar sense of inferiority. His phallus seemed no more than a lantern. He tiptoed away, uncertain whether he had been discovered.

The following morning, Changiz Khan began to bellow at Sarveali as he entered his master's tent. "You son of a bitch! What were you doing lurking near me and my companion last night?"

Sarveali presented his carefully thought-out defense. "My master patriarch, I was only trying to protect you. I believe the whole town wants your downfall. Please forgive me, but the township is full of envious people. May syphilis and gonorrhea fall upon the bastard *bazaaris* and mullahs!" Sarveali surprised himself by his assertive words and kissed Changiz Khan's hand before he could make a move.

"My master, my patriarch! I pray for your . . . umm . . . your empire's . . . eternal prosperity!" he declaimed. "And master, fifty-two donkeys full of opium departed for Zeerab last night. Most likely they have just arrived, Your Eminence."

"Oh! Good job! So that's why you were out at night, you scoundrel! Not protecting *me!*" Changiz Khan gave out a loud laugh.

But later, when one of the donkeys was found with no opium, Changiz Khan called to his servant again. "Come here, you Don Juan of the asses!" When Sarveali worriedly appeared, Changiz Khan's laughter instantly relieved him. "That's what happens when you use donkeys as transporters. When the tube ruptured, the opium must have been released into the donkey's bloodstream, giving her unimaginable hallucinations. At the same time the donkey must have chewed the opium with her cud, which I'm sure gave her a magical breath." Sarveali was pleased with Changiz Khan's teasing and relieved to learn that Changiz Khan forgave him for the missing opium.

THE FIRST OPIUM HARVEST CONTRIBUTED GREATLY to Changiz Khan's prosperity. But as his financial state grew, so did the covetousness of others. Sarveali learned second-, third-, and sometimes fourthhand through his primitive news service of the jealousy of the bazaar merchants, the mullahs, and other sundry townspeople in Kamab. The weak suffered the most envy, which Sarveali hoped would eventually die off on its own, particularly the clergy's. It was the mullahs' large appetite for fine foods, according to Mullah Abolfazl, the Stomach Worshiper—the most prominent cleric of Kamab—that caused the greatest enmity. Sarveali overheard him criticize the Shirlus for being "too secular to throw monthly religious feasts."

Sarveali heard from the local baker that the mullah said, "All Shirlu khans are impious, and their women only become religious later in life. Their tithes are too low, and in the rare occasions they do throw a religious feast, they only serve *gheimeh* and never *ghormeh sabzi.*" Sarveali didn't understand the term "tithes" but knew quite well the difference between the dishes. "*Ghormeh sabzi* is the mullah's favorite, not *gheimeh!*" the baker clarified.

Sarveali's own joy in life, however, grew. His new stash made him forget even the most envious maledictions against the Shirlus. His ugly nightmares plummeted in number, while the melodramatic hallucinations—like the one where Yazgulu turned into a mermaid beneath an indigo-colored ocean—came more often. He enjoyed smoking his premium-grade opium at the den, where he could smoke in peace, far from the torments of murder, prison, and addiction. Even his visions of being a fish thrown onto shore, flopping to death on the ground, vanished after a few puffs. As long as he had access to the substance, his life was filled with bliss and erotic dreams. And he still refused to believe that his addiction caused his work to suffer.

At times, opium helped Sarveali analyze himself with unprecedented depth. *Does any cuckold reach contentment? Does one in a happy marriage commit adultery?* He never received a suitable answer. But he remembered that Changiz Khan had pointed out to the director engineer, "Lord Byron says love is as sweet as wine, but if kept in the container of marriage long enough, it turns sour like vinegar." For Sarveali, the word "Byron" translated as "Bahram," a legendary Persian king. He began to imag-

154

ine how brilliant and intellectual the Persian kings must have been.

SIX MONTHS LATER, IN THE SUMMER OF 1955, Changiz Khan took the Bibi to the Ramsar Resort by the Caspian Sea. He also invited Madame Pamchal, the mistress he had romanced at the opium farm. Sarveali heard Changiz Khan state to the Bibi, "The poor woman's husband is away from the province on duty." As Sarveali watched the three of them leave, he knew the trip would be disastrous. Until now, the Bibi's altruism and interest in medicine had permitted her to ignore her husband's infidelities. This time, she would not be able to forgive him.

Sarveali's intuition proved right. When the couple returned to Kamab, the Bibi became melancholy, quiet, and disinterested in anything, even the children and her de facto patients.

When Sarveali subsequently served tea to the Bibi and her guests, he realized he had entered a gossip session about powerful husbands with incessant sexual curiosity.

"He was carrying the whore over his shoulder, and they were walking toward the horizon through the waves. I was left behind with the maid," the Bibi said. Sarveali lingered at the door with the tray of tea to hear the rest of the story. Astonished voices filled the room, most of them false. Sarveali surmised that all the women had their own problems, and to be a khan's wife was to have an unfaithful husband.

As Sarveali returned with refreshments and more hot tea, the elegant ladies had switched their chatter. With the servant silently moving among them, they turned to rumors that Empress Soraya, after four years of marriage, had still not produced an heir for the monarch.

Chapter 22

Nearly two years later, on an early evening in May, Sarveali was bringing a bottle of whiskey and a container of ice to Changiz Khan in his private quarters. The khan had just returned from visiting a cousin and was lounging in his favorite leather club chair. Sarveali knew Changiz Khan enjoyed these moments of solitude, especially when his wife and children were away in Shiraz. The master was not wearing his usual farm attire but was still dressed in his street clothes: an eggshell suit and dark gray shirt, both made of linen, and black-and-white spectator shoes. As Changiz Khan gulped down his first glass of whiskey and began to pour another, Sarveali left to get a pitcher of water. Exiting the room, Sarveali caught a glimpse of himself in the lobby mirror. Although he was only twenty-nine years old, several years Changiz Khan's junior, Sarveali looked much older. He scrutinized the gray strands sprouting from his scalp and sideburns, his three-day beard that was far removed from the peach fuzz of a young boy. Even his skin, carpeted with fissures shaped like worms, had darkened since his youth. Beneath his eyes, two purple, semicircular splotches, manifestations of the chronic constipation caused by his opium habit, colored his rough skin further. As Sarveali gradually lowered his scrutiny to his torso, he saw the misaligned buttons on his khaki shirt handed down from Changiz Khan, the belt fastened two holes tighter to keep his trousers, also hand-me-downs, from dropping to his rubber-soled cotton shoes. Sarveali was two heads shorter than Changiz Khan and had to turn up the cuffs of his trousers so he would not trip. *I've become so ugly I would terrify a helpless baby! If one were placed before me, I'm certain it would burrow its head in its mother's bosom to hide,* Sarveali lamented.

The screech of the telephone disrupted his self-pity, its metallic cacophony shattering his thoughts into a thousand shards. As Sarveali picked up the wall-mounted phone, he continued to inspect himself in the mirror. "Sir, Changiz Khan, it's the mayor!" Sarveali shouted at the closed door as he inspected his liver-colored lips.

"Tell him I'm not at home!" Changiz Khan shouted back. "I only speak to the governor and those above him. I don't speak to his rank. He needs to wait until morning to call on me for bribes!" Sarveali left the telephone only to observe his master chuckle, revealing full red lips, the distinguishing physical trait of the Shirlus. Sarveali pleaded, "But it's urgent! He says he's received a telegraph and it's a matter of life and death!"

Changiz Khan left his lounge chair and drink, and approached the large telephone, its receiver dangling where Sarveali dropped it. "Yes, sir? What telegraph could be so urgent that it's a matter of life and death?" he shouted into the mouthpiece. "You must mean the zebras and not the citizenry of your own constituency, eh?" Changiz Khan chuckled again. When Sarveali heard him say the word "zebras," he thought he must have misheard and began to listen more attentively. "Yes. All right then. I will contact the office of His Excellency first thing tomorrow. Good-bye." Changiz Khan guffawed loudly as he finished his dismissal. He dropped the handset with a crash, denting the wall plaster, which fell to the floor in a dust storm. "*Mister Mayor* has no doubt soiled his pants by now. You could smell that coward's shit all the way through the telephone line!"

Sarveali asked himself if smells that fetid could really travel through telephone wire. But Changiz Khan was only berating the official for being a lackey of the governor in Shiraz, the one who had sent the telegraph.

That afternoon, Changiz Khan gathered his entire staff to relay the telegraph message: the royal family was planning to visit. "The second cousin of the husband of one of the princesses' nieces—not even blood relation—read in a textbook that zebras roam the Yazd-e-Khast Plains, which, of course, is adjacent to my Roumeh Pass groves. It's true. As a child, I often went on expeditions with zebra tamers. Of course, no one really hunts zebras. The real sport is in taming them. To tame a zebra, the tamer chases it on horseback, catches up to it, and then jumps off the horse onto the wild zebra. Then the tamer has to beat the wild ass on the head or yank its ears until it stops. It's a silly sport, really, but apparently this so-called prince wants to see it. So, at the governor's request, I've decided to throw an outdoor party for the guests. Countless numbers are coming with this 'royal entourage.' The government has even arranged to install an electric generator for outdoor lighting."

That night, thoughts of the impending visit and the mystique of zebra taming bombarded Sarveali. *Will the prince be as handsome as Teimour Khan? What dishes will they like? Will the servants be allowed to observe the taming up close? Are zebras vicious? Do they bite?* Two hours later he was still awake, wracked with anxiety, so he left his bed and headed for the opium den.

An hour past midnight, pleasant hallucinations saturated him as he made his way back to the estate. When he looked up, he saw the image of the Shah in the face of the moon. *I announce to the entire nation that Mr. Sarveali Jokar has cooked and served the best* ghormeh sabzi *that we, the commander in chief of this ancient civilization, have ever had—better than that of the best chefs of the imperial courts.* As Sarveali's gaze at the moon intensified, the imperial image became a striped circle. A zebra emerged and charged toward an image of himself, who punched the wild animal in the forehead with his steel fist. Millions of people cheered: *Long live Sarveali, the only man in the world to knock down a zebra with a single blow.* By the time he heard the crowd's adulation, he had reached the gate of the estate and was finally ready for a deep sleep.

A WEEK LATER, CHANGIZ KHAN HAD DEPLOYED the necessary supplies for the gathering at Roumeh Pass. Sarveali would not be able to smoke opium in the open air of the camp, so he brought along several doses to take by mouth. He also brought a bottle of sweet cherry sherbet, just in case he needed to mask the bitterness.

The cook commissioned a builder to construct makeshift brick stoves and *kabab* grills, and he and Sarveali arranged for a ten-ton Mercedes-Benz truck to transport the equipment needed for outdoor cooking: cookware, pots and pans, silver and china, Yazd silk tablecloths, long rectangular tables, and numerous wooden chairs.

The cows, calves, goats, lambs, and poultry arrived from Changiz Khan's dairy farm in a caged trailer hauled by a tractor. As the livestock arrived, Sarveali recognized the driver as the one who had delivered him to the police station after Yazgulu's murder. A younger man sat on the same fender Sarveali had occupied on the way to prison. Images of the citadel, the bridge, and the blood of his wife splashing in the rivulet suddenly engulfed him. Quickly he surrendered to his anguish. Taking a bottle of sherbet and a pea-sized cube of opium from a small box, Sarveali walked behind a tall walnut tree and took his first dose. He leaned against the tree trunk and waited for the drug to penetrate his body. When he felt sufficiently lifted, he headed for the makeshift kitchen.

As the cook babbled on about his brother, one of the zebra tamers coming for the royal visit, Sarveali thought to himself: *If he doesn't shut up, I'll grind his tongue into ground lamb. Let's see if he can mouth one more word about his stupid zebra-tamer brother then.*

The camp was adjacent to the Roumeh Pass Cascade, the running springs at the top of the snowcapped Zagros Mountains, and the source of many reservoirs and waterfalls. After the rushing, icy water made its serpentine descent, it purled in streams and shoals toward the groves and plains. Sarveali followed one with his eyes. A strange peace filled him. *I wish my master were here to enjoy this with me—my glorious Teimour Khan!* His joy ended as the tulip-shaped globs of blood resurfaced in his mind. His eyes fluttered open. An iridescent rainbow with seven prisms of light hovered over the waterfall.

Uncertain if what he had just observed was real or imagined, Sarveali turned his attention to the Ministry of Energy workers installing the small generator. He greeted the bar staff setting up the alfresco bar. In the midst of all the preparations, Changiz Khan finally arrived. He was wearing a safari-style suit with a white linen shirt, riding boots, and a brown fedora. He immediately headed for the bar, disregarding the greetings of his staff and even ignoring the zebra tamers.

"My dear Armenian companions, what a nice bar!" Changiz Khan ran his hands along the bright red vinyl siding and chrome-plated barware ornamented with Bakelite handles, and eyed the cut-crystal glassware and ice buckets, the art deco accessories. "This is straight out of a scene from *Casablanca!*" he said. "Fit for royalty, even for His Majesty, the Shah."

With the day's first drink firmly in hand, Changiz Khan addressed the zebra tamers. The first one, the cook's brother, had a handlebar mustache. The second one genuflected until his aquiline nose touched the ground. The third was a massive muscular man who applied kohl to his eyelashes. Although they claimed to be avid zebra tamers, no one had ever seen them at work. "Will you be ready when the royals come?" Changiz Khan asked, suspicious of their skill.

"I will punch them in the head so hard they will forget whether they are zebras, asses, or foxes!" the cook's brother boasted.

"With one stroke, I'll force my hand down their throats and remove their gallbladders. I'll offer them to you as amulets to bring you health and prosperity!" The aquiline nose revealed his quince-yellow teeth.

Then a bellowing voice disrupted the show of bravado. "After *I'm* done, they'll dance to the tunes of Ashogh Behyar's *Kamancheh!*" said the one with kohl eyes. His laughter roared, and kohl-saturated tears smeared his flaxen cheeks.

161

"Well, before we endanger the whole species, let's have a drink," Changiz Khan said, turning to the bar. Sarveali and the zebra tamers followed.

After his third "senatorial martini," Changiz Khan was suddenly struck with generosity. He searched his pockets for *baksheesh* to offer his guests. When he ran out of cash, he took out a Swiss West End watch from his jacket pocket. Sarveali remembered the watch from the days before the twins were born. But when Changiz Khan reached out and handed him the watch, he was astounded. He had never owned a watch and could not even tell time; nonetheless, the idea of being given a timepiece once worn by a noble khan seemed to him the highest token of servitude. Changiz Khan, who had intended to give the watch to the cook's brother, laughed at the servant's bewilderment and pride.

After Sarveali and the cook assembled Changiz Khan's umbrella-shaped white pavilion and set up a *charpoy* inside the tent for their master to sleep on, they set up their own bell tents outside. The electric generator lulled all of them to sleep, even Sarveali, who slept on a blanket spread on the ground. His excitement at owning a watch erased all of his anxiety about the zebra taming. Instead, he gazed at the waxing moon. This time he imagined he saw the luminous face of his new watch in the lunar circle. Even the moon could not compete with the beauty of his timepiece. *Look at the circle of my moon. It's perfect, not like that thing in the sky that looks like a round bread ripped by a dog.* Before he fell asleep, he wished again that he could show his new gift to Teimour Khan. "I'm sure he would teach me how to decipher it," he murmured to himself, drifting off into dreams.

THE NEXT AFTERNOON, Changiz Khan and his entourage left the camp to explore the zebra terrain, returning five hours later. They could barely contain their excitement, for the party had indeed spotted a sizable herd of zebras.

The next morning, a company of soldiers led by a colonel arrived to set up camp for the visitors. The governor of Shiraz, his deputy, and their entourage followed. Changiz Khan greeted them all, offering food and drink.

Two hours later, the national anthem—followed by chants of "Long live the Shah! Long live the Monarchy!"—blared from the distance, heralding the arrival of the "third grade prince," His Highness Kamyar Ardeshirkia. The royal party had just come from a tiger hunt in the Kerman province; the creature's glorious corpse lay mounted on an oversized Land Rover.

Sarveali stayed busy. Using a pewter ladle, he stirred the pot of *ghormeh sabzi* stew—a lovely batch. The recipe was his pride. A magical, aromatic steam rose from the pot, clouding Sarveali's face. It reminded him of the image of the monarch in the moon admiring the dish. But before he could drift into another fantasy, the chauffeur, followed by two military personnel and four officials in black suits and sunglasses, notified the barmen to prepare the royal beverage service.

As the flow of aristocrats approached the bar, Sarveali's knees trembled. Accompanied by the entourage, Changiz Khan ignored Sarveali and his stew and headed straight for the bar, where the bartender presented the men with the "imperial martini," his newest creation. Changiz Khan sent the kitchen staff word that they need not worry about serving lunch; the guests had already eaten. Dejected, Sarveali packed up his sixty-person vat. His stew was too good for the servants, but perhaps he could serve it after the royals returned from their zebra taming.

After the party had exhausted the "imperial martinis," Changiz Khan recommended that they drive to the plains where the zebras roamed—beyond the waterfalls, past the walnut groves, through Roumeh Pass. Before departing, the chauffeur gave the barmen advice. "The Khan wants you to follow us with some bottles of liquor, ice, and . . ." Out of breath, he pointed at Sarveali and the cook. "Oh, and don't forget, take his servant and the cook with you! And bring some food in case the guests want a snack."

Sarveali and the cook packed up a sealed container of chilled caviar, a pot of opium goat yogurt, several baskets of fruit, bread, grilled eggplants and *kababs,* and soon caught up with the zebra cavalcade. After driving for nearly half an hour, they finally stopped in the middle of the Yazd-e-Khast Plains.

The head bartender stopped his conveyance at a distance from the entourage. "There's a nice herd over there by those hills . . . and the cars are going to chase them this way." Changiz Khan's Jeep and two army vehicles charged at high speed to the north of the plains, where they would divert the zebras toward the entourage.

"Gentlemen, come on top of our station wagon, so you can watch with my binoculars." Sarveali was pleased by the head bartender's invitation and accepted the glasses. But as soon as the tamers mounted their horses, the cook yanked the binoculars from Sarveali's hands.

"Let me watch! Look, there's my hero brother and that idiot who calls himself a tamer." Before Sarveali could scold the cook and cast maledictions on his brother, a cheer arose. The vehicles had successfully chased the zebras in the tamers' direction. The bartender took his binoculars from the cook and, like a sportscaster, began describing the scene.

"The kohl-eyed big man just fell off his horse! I guess no zebra is going to play the *kamancheh* today!"

"That serves him right for trying to imitate my brother!" the cook yelled. At a distance of almost five kilometers, Sarveali could barely see the cloud of dust surrounding some animals he assumed were the zebras.

"Now the two horsemen and the zebras are approaching each other." Sarveali grimaced, squinting his eyes to distinguish the horsemen from the herd.

"Now the man with the big nose has jumped from his horse on top of a large zebra . . . he's beating its head, but . . . oh no . . . wait . . . the zebra just shook him off. The tamer has fallen to the ground!"

"I hope his nose breaks in half! We won't get any gall-bladder amulets with his lack of skill!" the cook yelled, and grabbed the binoculars from the bartender. "Pardon me, but it's time for my brother to tame the herd." Sarveali felt covetous about not having a brother of his own. *The cook's brother can't win! If he wins, I'll hear about this for the rest of my life!*

"Wow! My brother just mounted a gigantic zebra! The animal stopped right in his tracks as if he were my brother's slave." The bartender took the binoculars back. "He's right. The animal is not even moving. Your brother must have really tamed it."

As the cook ran toward the crowd, Sarveali was relieved; he could not tolerate another word of the cook's adulation of his brother. Excited and full of comments about zebra taming, the guests ignored their drinks and exotic snacks, and then climbed into their automobiles to head back to the campsite. Following the entourage, Sarveali tried to ignore the cook's bragging. *Since when was zebra taming more important than caviar and whiskey?*

The colonel and a group of army officials examined the tamed animals secured in a caged trailer. Changiz Khan followed his guests, finding the zebra lying limp in the corner of the cage. Upon closer examination, the onlookers discovered that the animal had passed much worm-infested dung before death engulfed it.

"The zebra was captured diseased and looks like it's been dead for decades!" the army colonel professed as he poked his baton into the cluster of the wriggling mass. Changiz Khan was furious at the failure of his tamers. When the prince was informed of the news, he whispered in his aide-de-camp's ears. As Changiz Khan and his servants looked on, the colonel continued to rant. "Apparently these parasitic worms tamed the poor ass before the professionals had a chance!" The prince's aide-de-camp approached Changiz Khan.

"His Highness has enjoyed the zebra taming and is very grateful for your hospitality," he said to Changiz Khan, barely hiding a smile. "But His Highness must depart within the hour." The khan frowned. "As His Highness wishes," he said, barely restraining his own annoyance and embarrassment.

The minute the royal entourage had departed, Changiz Khan asked for whiskey to soothe his rage. The servants understood that the khan had been insulted by the miniroyals and that they, by association, had been insulted as well. After Changiz Khan was adequately comforted by his bottle, he took his annoyance out on them. He yelled to the barmen to pack up and to Sarveali he cried, "No food at all for those so-called zebra tamers, unless they like dung worms!"

THE NEXT MORNING Changiz Khan emerged from his tent feeling somewhat more charitable and ordered the staff to donate the vats of unconsumed food to nearby villagers. In exchange, he arranged for another day of hunting with two local men. This adventure proved a much greater success than the one the day before. When Changiz Khan returned, he was in high spirits and so were the local hunters. They had come upon two mountain rams of a breed with males known for ferociously mounting each other. The Khan immediately began to recount to his awed servants a tale of how he had managed to shoot both rams with a single bullet. "I have never seen rams, or any male animals for that matter, mount with such primal exuberance. And there were so many of them."

"Well, there are faggots among all of God's creatures," the kohl-eyed zebra tamer added. Sarveali and the cook nervously shifted their weight, avoiding each other's stare.

"At least these rams could mount better than the likes of you. You call yourselves tamers. One couldn't ride a horse, another unable to mount a zebra, and the third could only catch a deathly sick ass whose belly was filled with flesh-eating worms!" Changiz Khan laughed at his ridicule, the success of his ram hunt freeing him of his former embarrassment. Sarveali looked at the silent cook, his brother, and the other tamers, pleased he had escaped the moment's ridicule.

"In any case," Changiz Khan continued, "same-sex relations aren't natural. They're just abnormal and disgusting . . . regardless whether it's among rams or Arab sheikhs." Changiz Khan sneered. "Whoever exhibits this behavior should make a visit to Dr. Ravani's mental sanitarium!"

Sarveali had failed again. *I hope His Eminence never learns of my "disgusting behavior." May God bring a cure for this illness!*

May He purge the poison from my body! He was reminded again of his aborted plan to get the quince seed potion from the Bibi to cure his condition, but he consoled himself with another large piece of opium.

The Bibi was not pleased with the tale of the zebra adventure, either. At home she confronted Changiz Khan. "The twins have cried since the day you left them behind. Did you forget you have a daughter and two sons? Do you want them to make themselves bleed to win your attention?" Her bubble of patience had burst, since she had discovered a satchel with a small amount of *kuknar*, an amalgam of poppy seeds perfumed with ambergris of sperm wale and deer musk. The Bibi knew only too well about the aphrodisiac's ability to enhance a man's sexual prowess. As always, Changiz Khan offered his wife no response. Instead, he called Sarveali to attend to him at the estate slaughterhouse. The corpses of the copulating rams hung by the hooves of their back legs, their curved horns intertwined in a seeming embrace. Changiz Khan examined the number of rings around the shaft of each pair of horns to calculate their ages.

"The passive one was four years younger than the ram that mounted him. I guess this old one found himself a nice young lad to play with!" Sarveali's face reddened. He was no better than these defiled mountain rams. But nothing remedied shame better than smoking an opium pipe. He could hardly wait for evening at the inn's drug parlor.

Chapter 23

In 1960 the United Nations discontinued its opium program. An oversupply of the narcotic had led to uncontrolled drug-diversion schemes that profited only smugglers. That same year, the cold winter froze Changiz Khan's seventy-five-hectare citrus orchard, and grasshoppers plagued his wheat harvest for the second time. When Sarveali overheard the accountant inform his master of his dire financial position, he feared for his own future.

Changiz Khan immediately left the accountant and gestured for Sarveali to follow him. He drove aimlessly through the countryside as Sarveali sat quietly next to him, forbidding his tongue to say a word. They passed the Bibi's quince orchard and crossed a plain that Sarveali thought looked very familiar. When Changiz Khan slowed to a stop next to a white plaster shrine where a single conifer tree stood, Sarveali clearly remembered that he had accompanied Teimour Khan here. Changiz Khan entered the shrine, something Teimour Khan had avoided, telling Sarveali to wait. The brilliant green of the conifer stood out starkly against the dull plaster.

With his new watch and some help from the cook, Sarveali had taught himself to tell time. He was able to calculate that Changiz Khan emerged from the shrine thirty-five minutes after he had entered. His eyes were moist, and Sarveali even noticed a tear on his master's cheek. As he made his way back to the Jeep, Changiz Khan pronounced:

> *Since I've no friend in this dead, faithless time*
> *Who doesn't prove to be my enemy,*
> *I choose to be alone—*there's *happiness;*
> *From this point on it's me and only me!*

Apparently the poem was from an epitaph inscribed in the shrine. Sarveali felt more than ever that his master's unhappiness was sure to lead to his own.

Master and servant made their way back to the Jeep and found an eagle owl perched on the hood. *I swear that is the same owl that frightened me and Teimour Khan!* As they came closer, the owl, resembling a dark gray feather emerging from a white hat, did not fly away. It continued to perch on the car's hood, blinking its huge yellow eyes with such melancholy that both men felt instant premonition and alarm.

Changiz Khan took his loaded Browning shotgun from the back of the Jeep and discharged it twice into the air. The sound of the shots ricocheted off the nearby mountain.

"I just want to scare the bird off. It's a bad omen to shoot an owl," Changiz Khan whispered. The owl opened its wings and ascended gracefully into the air, giving Sarveali and Changiz Khan one final paralyzing gaze.

Back at the Kamab estate, a gloomy autumn sunset greeted the two men, exacerbating their anxiety. The muezzin's prayer-time chant rose over them and a gray haze hovered over the tangerine sun, soiling the orb as it disappeared. Sarveali's gloom increased with the darkness.

As he served Changiz Khan his evening cognac and both men reflected on the afternoon's events, a vehicle clamored its way through the estate's front gate. It belonged to Changiz Khan's cousin, who was greeted with the remark, "What an ominous day this has been."

The cousin stopped short and gazed at Changiz Khan in sympathy. "Can you believe this country? We are in the atomic age, an age when we should be moving the nation toward progress in technology. Instead we behave like Bedouin Arabs of fourteen hundred years ago."

The cousin went on. "Talks of land reform have intensified in the capital. The politicians are jealous of *our* prosperity, of the tribal khans, that's for sure! Even President Kennedy is spreading ideas within the royal palace for some sort of land reform." The cousin spoke so fast that some parts of his speech were incomprehensible even to his own ears.

Sarveali continued to fill the cognac snifters like a nurse administering painkillers.

"We will soon become cash-poor khans with only reminiscence as our glory, reduced to bragging about the rotten bones of our dead!" The cousin kicked a nearby stool as if it were the politician approving land reform.

The men's ruckus sparked the Bibi's attention as she passed by them with her children.

"What is wrong? Are you two quarreling over some mistress again?" she asked sarcastically. Sarveali felt a twinge of embarrassment.

The cousin repeated his diatribe, magnifying its threatening nature. "I knew that misery was imminent!" the Bibi cried out in response. "Thanks to you, dear husband, you and your sinful acts—your women and your part in the suicide of the poor music professor . . ." Sarveali listened intently. He had not heard about the suicide of Madame Mehr's husband. The Bibi continued. "Now we will *all* face misery and poverty, innocent and guilty alike. My sons will be forced to beg on the streets when they should be remembering their benevolent ancestors, the Khans of Shirlu!" Her daughter held her arm comfortingly as the Bibi left the room. The twin boys, Virasb and Lohrasb, stayed behind, hoping for more ranting and cursing. Sarveali could only remember the mournful eagle owl.

Changiz Khan called for bourbon. He looked at the bottle in disgust. "That ungrateful Kennedy! We even drink *his* whiskey! It's a Kentucky bourbon! We drive *his* Jeeps, Buicks, and Cadillacs; use *his* John Deere tractors and combines; wear *his* Brooks Brothers suits . . ." He noticed his sons eagerly listening for new curse words.

"What are you boys doing here? Go do your homework."

"We're not children! We're fifteen now and we want to know what will happen to *us! We* want to know why *our* lands are being seized. Will we have to revolt like our ancestors revolted against the British?" Lohrasb asked. For the first time, Sarveali saw the youthful image of Teimour Khan in the twins, the same cadence in their speech and excited tone as their uncle's.

"Boys, nobody is going to revolt. Our allegiance to the Shah and the court will continue as long as His Majesty does not interfere with centuries of tribal customs." Changiz Khan lifted the bottle of Woodford Reserve and gulped one-third down straight.

Soon his intoxication reached a point that included verbal or physical violence. Sarveali hoped he would not be the immediate victim of his master's abuse, but Changiz Khan's worries exploded like a burst abscess. "You midget Sarv-e-Shit-Ali," he began, enunciating each syllable slowly, "how many times have I told you to bathe and wash your socks every day?"

"Calm down! Our problems are more urgent than a servant's socks!" His cousin poured himself a large glass of Woodford Reserve. He picked up three ice cubes and dropped them into his glass, where the warm whiskey took over. "Do you see how that ice melted and disappeared? We will melt the same way, you'll see!" Changiz Khan responded, finishing another glass of whiskey in three gulps.

His disappointment infected everyone and ominous thoughts spread like pestilence. "What do I have left . . . thirty years at most, maybe?" he asked the room. "Even if they take 40 percent of my land, I'll still be left with 2,000 hectares . . . is that correct? I'll be fine . . . fuck the next generation! Did I do anything to prevent that air-injecting prison doctor from murdering my father? No. All I did was cause him anguish, which is exactly what my own twins will do to me." Changiz Khan collapsed into his armchair as if he had fainted. Sarveali looked at his master, his hair standing on end, his eyelids fluttering; his cheeks took the color of his red lips, which began to twitch like a fugitive lizard. The scene frightened him. The twins left the room in disgust. But the master did not stir. "All I need is a slant-roof shack with a whore at my side and a satchel full of *koknar* potion." His slurred speech was barely audible. "We men of nobility can fuck for seventy-two hours straight with only two handfuls."

Sarveali had heard horrid phrases fall from his master's lips before, but it was the first time he had seen Changiz Khan raving drunk, hiccupping loud enough to shake the house. "And my potion—my virility potion, the sperm whale from the Persian Gulf—will soon disappear too. Those fucking Arabs are about to separate our Persian Gulf island of Bahrain from Iran, and it won't be long before those sheikhs form their own nation. No more *koknar!*" He let out a donkey bray and began to weep. "The U.N. dropped its dope project and now we're facing land confiscation; it's a grandiose conspiracy . . ."

The master turned to Sarveali, who feared he would be kicked like the stool. "Why are you still standing here, you dope addict?! You raccoon! Just look at him, he looks like a deviated pickle! I'm sure now that your stash is diminishing, you'll join the rest who are lining up to take our land!" Changiz Khan laughed maniacally, falling out of his armchair onto the floor.

A tremendous headache suddenly plagued Sarveali; his mouth became as dry as the Salt Desert and his abdominal pain reminded him he had not had a bowel movement in days. He fled the room, pausing in the hall to scrutinize himself in the same wall mirror he always used. He *did* look like a raccoon with his pointed nose and the black splotches around his eyes. He bent over, turning himself laterally to see if he resembled a deviated pickle also. He craved "God's cocktail." He knew opium would transform him from a raccoon into a powerful eagle and straighten his stooped posture into an erect one. But a sense of duty kept him where he was. He waited outside the door until the sound of loud snores signaled him to tiptoe into the master's chamber and spread blankets over both khans, imploring God to help them find a solution to their problems.

Chapter 24

Like a household sentinel, Sarveali had been standing watch on the front porch of the estate since early morning, despite his late tryst with "God's cocktail." When he saw the Bibi, he expressed his morning salutations, but the sight of her tears resurrected the ugly scene of the night before.

The hazy sunrise matched the Bibi's mood—as if a stubborn painter had brushed shades of indigo and gray over the tangerine sun. The Bibi was still in tears when Sarveali brought her breakfast tray—a plate of eggs, a small bowl of quince jam, bread, a pot of tea, and a tiny teacup sitting on a saucer ornamented with the face of Soraya, the former empress. The Bibi poured tea into her cup and then into the saucer, expanding the surface area so it would cool faster. She screamed as if in pain.

"Oh, I have burned her! I burned the empress with my hot tea! That's why the Shah divorced her!" She wailed and pushed her eggs away. Sarveali felt helpless. He understood the depth of her melancholy, but how could he comfort her? She had lost her reason. This turn of events frightened Sarveali more than being called a raccoon or a deviated pickle. The Bibi's sudden madness seemed the worst disaster yet to fall on the house of the Shirlus.

IN JANUARY 1963, fourteen months after Changiz Khan and his cousin had drunkenly ranted about their future, the state-run media announced the implementation of land reform. Landowners in the whole country were ordered to give up or sell two hectares of their property to any willing peasant at a highly discounted rate, and no landowner was permitted to own the agricultural lands of any village in its entirety. Given the high density of the peasant population in their area, the reform would come at an astronomical cost to the Shirlus. In addition, the khans would soon lose their entire labor force.

The Bibi, whose mental health had steadily declined, still enjoyed daily rides into the countryside. One day, as they drove in the Land Rover with the twins next to the chauffeur and Sarveali in the very back, she sighted a crowd in the road ahead. They were the new "landowners," and until recently, some of her servants. The new property owners barricaded the road in front of them and, tattered as ever, shouted, "Death to feudalism!" "Death to khans!" "Long live the Shah!"

The Bibi recognized them. Her rage rose. "My family has always been pro-Shah!" She looked ready to tear her hair out. "See that man in the blue shirt? That shirt used to belong to my husband. I cared for his mother when she was sick with diphtheria. And him! I took care of his daughter's anthrax," she cried out, pointing to a former gardener. She began to gesture wildly at the crowd.

The young Bibi Naz Khanom tried to comfort her. Sarveali worried the mob would attack the Land Rover any minute. As he considered telling the chauffeur to turn around, the twins burst into laughter. Their laughter reminded Sarveali of Teimour Khan, but he quickly became concerned when he heard Lohrasb speak. "These stupid peasants pronounce everything wrong. They say 'Jobedin Shah' instead of 'Javeed Shah' and 'Feed the Shah with barley.' They can't even get simple words right."

"*Khanzadehs*! Keep quiet! You are bothering the Bibi!" Sarveali pleaded.

"Stop the car now, you cowardly chauffeur," Virasb shouted as the chauffeur began to back up.

"We'll finish these fools off right now!" Lohrasb followed.

The chauffeur had barely stopped the car when the twins leaped out with blowguns they had recently purchased for shooting sparrows. Sarveali could tell that the Bibi, in spite of herself, felt immense pride in her sons' courage. Like the heroes in their favorite John Wayne movies, the twins lined up in front of the Land Rover and commanded the group to disperse.

"Leave now, you lowlifes! And if you don't, we will make sure you clear the road!" Virasb warned in his best gunslinger voice.

"Out now! Or the biggest remaining piece of your flesh will be your earlobes!" Lohrasb added.

It took little to disconcert the protestors. At the sight of the two strong boys, they fled as fast as they could from instruments that could barely kill a bird. Meanwhile, Sarveali—who had waited his whole life to prove his loyalty to Changiz Khan's family—froze with fear, crouching in the Land Rover with his head tucked in his chest.

The twins hoisted themselves back into the auto, overflowing with postpubescent testosterone. They shrieked in unison. "Gentlemen, clean your trousers in case you've soiled them!" And the Bibi, momentarily forgetting her charitable persona, laughed sarcastically at Sarveali and the chauffeur. "It seems there are some who can easily attack defenseless women with a hatchet, but when it comes to showing real courage . . ."

Sarveali longed for death, the only thing that would erase his humiliation. He sank further into his seat, remembering Sheikhak and his anecdotes of brave servants who always protected their masters. But now, when his chance appeared right before him, he had failed the test. For the rest of the road trip, Sarveali remained silent, wallowing in shame. The chauffeur also remained quiet. The twins, however, laughed all the way back to the estate, satisfied with their adventure.

LATER, SARVEALI SERVED TEA as the Bibi recounted to her husband the incident and her first taste of the consequences of land reform. Changiz Khan dropped his head in his hands. It was clear to Sarveali that his master needed to portray the situation as tragically as possible, hoping to gain the upper hand over his long-suffering wife.

"Just wait until they realize that no family can support itself on two hectares of land," he groaned theatrically. "And in a couple of years, when the program fails, the government will see how they've killed off our country's agriculture. We'll have to survive by importing cotton, wheat, and barley from America. Yes, my dearest, we are definitely in harm's way." Sarveali couldn't recall the last time he had heard Changiz Khan address his wife with such endearment.

The Bibi's sobs continued, finally annoying Changiz Khan. He continued his saga of gloom. "Yes, we will be ruined! Completely ruined! Forget your love of money, your Persian rugs, your gold. Forget sending the twins abroad. Forget your quince orchard and silly curative rubbish. There won't be any patients to treat or a quince orchard to cure them with."

"What? My orchard? What would anyone possibly want with that? No . . . No! They cannot touch my quince orchard! I will die; I will kill myself before they touch a single leaf of my beautiful orchard." As the Bibi screamed, she tore at her hair, little tufts falling like dust to the floor.

Much to Sarveali's relief, the muddled Bibi did not mention his cowardice. In return, he resolved to refuse any lands the reform offered him. *I may be a coward, a raccoon, and a bent pickle, but I'm not disloyal,* he thought.

Sarveali suffered severe insomnia that night, despite the "God's cocktail" he had smoked earlier. He thought of the Bibi he had known all these years—a bride, a mother, an altruistic healer, and now a woman on the brink of madness. A dream emerged: Hundreds of warriors on horseback galloped over the ramparts of Eram Castle, the home of the Bibi's ancestors. From behind the castle's moat, a disturbance rose from the thousands of peasants cutting down the cactus trees that sprang up beside the water. The tongue of a peasant turned into a cactus with deadly thorns.

Sarveali awoke troubled and served the Bibi a very early breakfast, making sure her saucer did not have Empress Soraya's picture on it.

The Bibi refused to eat. "Tell Davoodi to get the car ready. I wish to visit the Eram Citadel," she ordered.

The Bibi refused to bring the children with her, despite the twins' pleas. "We want to play 'Remember the Alamo!' this time!" But she enlisted Sarveali to join her, despite his disgrace the day before.

An aging woman opened the heavy gate to the ancient citadel a few centimeters. Sarveali and the chauffeur forced it open a bit more, and the party entered below the brick gatehouse, through the dark vestibule and into the inner courtyard of the desolate ruins. Although her face was damaged by geriatric fissures, the old servant's eyesight was surprisingly intact. She bowed to the Bibi, peering at Sarveali and the chauffeur with a mixture of wonder and doubt.

"Maryam, you look like a fourteen-year-old bride today!" the Bibi said. Sarveali and the chauffeur chuckled under their breath.

While the tea was brewing, the Bibi walked the citadel with Sarveali at her side. Frogs leaped out of the dilapidated bathhouse. The Bibi screamed as two semitranslucent lizards flopped on the ground in front of them.

"Look at these tadpoles swimming in this filthy algae," she said in a sad voice, staring around her. "See, Sarveali? I've abandoned the legacy of my ancestors. And now I can't even provide for my children. All I can expect now is doom." Sarveali could see this visit was not wise and searched for some way to comfort her.

The wizened servant called out to them. "Sarveali, tell the Bibi to be careful. I had to kill a rattlesnake on the grounds a few months ago." The Bibi was already walking toward the tower. "My Bibi, the tea will be ready in a few minutes." The voice could barely be heard from a distance.

The Bibi ignored Maryam's announcement and proceeded to climb the stairs of the tower where the emblems of the khans had once flown. Sarveali followed the Bibi up a crumbling stone stairway that spiraled to the roof. The sound of scampering rodents distracted them. The Bibi tripped on the broken riser of the third step, but she brushed off Sarveali's aid. "Wait for me here," she said. Two black ravens cawed and flew out of the room, flapping against the stairwell wall before flying away to the roof. Sarveali fell back in dismay as the Bibi mounted the stairway alone. The servant noticed hundreds of cards at his feet half-eaten by termites and picked one off the floor. He read slowly. "Membership cards of the Shirlu tribe, peasant class, issued by Bahador Khan Shirlu, the Ilkhan."

He could hear the Bibi walking above him and crept after her, trying to stifle his fear. She was climbing toward the roof and Sarveali, hearing the footsteps, was reminded of his dream. The unhappy Bibi was probably standing on the edge of the watchtower roof. *Now that she was on the ramparts, was she haunted by the ghostly images of horse-riding warriors charging around the thickness of the wall?*

For once unafraid of his mistress's wrath, Sarveali now took the stairway two steps at a time. He reached the roof just as the Bibi faltered on the precipice and stepped off the ledge into space. In horror, Sarveali watched the cactus trees below engulf her. The morning breeze wafted past her skin, her hair, her outstretched hands. He heard a mournful scream from his mistress, then silence. Sarveali had no strength to speak or cry out. He just stared at the lifeless body impaled on the cactus.

Seconds later, the chauffeur was standing beside him. Mute, they both stared blankly at the cactus trees. The chauffeur finally found his voice.

"Sarveali! You miserable peasant! Your Bibi is dead! The Khan will kill us! There is no God but Allah! Oh God, please give us mercy!"

The Bibi's crumpled corpse, submerged in a green sea of cactus branches and leaves, reminded Sarveali of his wife's dead body, the blue water of the stream ornamented by her blood. Why had he become so close to such tortured women?

"Oh . . . my Bibi, you didn't burn the empress!" Sarveali moaned. The chauffeur gave him a look of confusion as they rushed down the tower's stairwell, almost knocking over the ancient servant who was humming to herself and tenderly carrying the Bibi's tea tray up the four long flights to the roof.

FOR THE NEXT TWO YEARS, visits and telephone calls to Changiz Khan from governors and other officials gradually dwindled to nothing. Signs of the family's diminished political influence were followed by even more contention between Changiz Khan and his accountant. "You love to give me bad news!" Changiz Khan yelled again and again. He had quickly become indebted to the usurious bazaar merchants, just as Sarveali had predicted on the way to the opium farm.

During the third year of land reform, the landowning peasants found themselves facing their own heavy financial burdens. By the end of 1965, these small landowners discovered that, indeed, two hectares of land were not adequate to provide for a family. Many were forced to leave their meager farms and migrate to the cities. Now the khans were left just as Changiz Khan had prophesied— with neither servants nor labor force to work the land they still cultivated.

Because drastic measures were required to accommodate Changiz Khan's diminishing affluence, all the servants except for Sarveali and the chauffeur were terminated. Sarveali became the cook, the maid, and the gardener. He labored from dawn until Changiz Khan went to bed and, as he promised, refused his right to any of the Khan's land. When the cook left the estate, the two servants mourned the end of a long, mutual legacy.

The downsizing of the estate continued. Changiz Khan ordered the Bibi's quarters, the upstairs bedrooms, and the storerooms boarded and sealed. Changiz Khan's quarters and his children's bedchambers were the only rooms kept open. He ordered Sarveali to close the baking room and scale back the size of the kitchen. Sarveali sectioned off the scullery and the slaughterhouse and removed the outdoor coal-burning stoves and ovens and huge man-sized vats. He equipped the new kitchen, now only large enough to serve a family of six, with a primus stove and other small gadgets. Finally only a ghost of the previous estate house remained. Sarveali watched helplessly as the beautiful place dwindled into dust like the Bibi's ancestral citadel. *The estate will take us with it when it tumbles to the ground,* Sarveali thought, deep in another opium reverie.

In 1966 Changiz Khan sold his Shiraz mansion, using it as collateral for a usurious loan. From the remaining proceeds, he bought a modest four-bedroom house on Ferdowsi Avenue. Bibi Naz Khanom, now twenty-one years old, and the twins, twenty, moved to the house.

Sarveali was paid only erratically, his small salary dwindling continuously. When Gholi demanded six months' worth of outstanding payments on Sarveali's prison clemency settlement, Changiz Khan ordered the accountant to issue him the money immediately. Opium had hitherto freed Sarveali from his own torments. While he did not have access to a limitless supply of the drug as he had during Changiz Khan's opium-farming days, sometimes a small amount would suddenly appear from nowhere. More often he would buy the drug from the den owner with what little money he had left.

In the autumn of 1967, the Shah and Empress Farah celebrated their coronation ceremony on the monarch's birthday, October 26. The streets in Shiraz were festooned with lights, and portraits of the Shah and Empress Farah hung from every building. Crowds wedged into the streets to participate in the celebration. Changiz Khan and his cousin decided this was an auspicious moment to negotiate another loan from a Shirazi bazaar merchant. Desperate for cash, they had decided to sell their shotgun collections.

As Changiz Khan's wealth and power declined, the two cousins grew closer. Often they would discuss their mutual miseries over drink. "We'll go to that Armenian's café. Perhaps *he* will still consider us royalty!" Changiz Khan said, as they set out for Shiraz. The trip to Shiraz was uneventful, until they reached the outskirts of the city. The chauffeur brought the Land Rover to a sudden stop. A crowd blocked the street.

"Bunch of testicle lickers!" Changiz Khan said. "Look at these brownnosers!" his cousin added. Changiz Khan pointed at Sarveali. "Go disperse them." Hoping this would be his moment of glory, Sarveali stepped out of the Land Rover. "Move! The Khan's car needs to pass!" he yelled, waving his arms at the crowd. Someone tapped him on his right shoulder. When Sarveali turned, a man in uniform struck a blow to his jaw so fierce that Sarveali felt it had been detached from his face. He fell to the asphalt. He tried to lift himself off the ground but everything in his surroundings—the crowd, the buildings, his master's auto—began to rotate around him. He collapsed again.

Changiz Khan rushed to the officer. "Sergeant, why did you strike him? My servant did not commit an illegal act."

"Servant? Haven't you noticed? Feudalism is dead! You can no longer delegate your shit work," the officer answered arrogantly.

"You motherfucker, I will challenge generals ten ranks above you!" Changiz Khan said, his eyes sparking with rage. Sarveali, still on the ground, looked up at his master and the officer. Changiz Khan, head and shoulders taller than the sergeant, was much more muscular. But the anger in his face had more to do with his frustration at his dwindling power than with his injured servant.

"Sir, I hope you are aware that you are insulting a ranked officer . . ." The sergeant gulped. ". . . badgering a uniformed official of His Majesty's Imperial Army." He backed away from Changiz Khan and returned his efforts to the crowd.

Changiz Khan looked at his servant lying on the pavement. "Get up! Be a man! Do you see the political damage you could have cost me?" Sarveali slowly regained his equilibrium and rose, his jaw bruised and aching.

Changiz Khan announced to all who were listening, "The minute those peasants came to this city and put on a uniform, they forgot the people who were once their protectors. Who fed them? Who cured their illnesses?"

Sarveali tried to conceal his anguish at having failed his master again. At thirty-nine, he felt as emasculated as a child. As they neared the café, Sarveali prepared himself for the ridicule he knew he was about to face. To keep himself from bursting into tears, he daydreamed that Changiz Khan was praising him instead. *The moment the Brigadier General Tahamtan expressed the slightest gesture of rudeness to me, Sarveali shot him in the forehead with a revolver.*

AT THE CAFÉ, AFTER A FEW DRINKS of the local *aragh*, Changiz Khan and his cousin seemed to forget the street incident. The master ordered Sarveali to give the café owner the fresh wild boar meat and pistachios he had brought. For years, Changiz Khan had helped the Christian owner of the café make *mortadella,* a sausage with garlic and pistachio nuts. Changiz Khan loved this dish with such intensity that not even the Islamic prohibition against swine could prevent him from indulging. He mockingly called himself a "gastronomic Christian," since ham and alcohol—both prohibited delicacies—were among his favorites.

"I hunted those boars myself," he bragged to the café owner. "They were frightening our female cotton pickers. Yes, we have *female* workers now! Since their men have gone to the cities or the sheikhdoms of the Persian Gulf, only their women are left to work our fields. That's right. Cotton farming . . . I don't even know where to start." Changiz Khan paused. "Now we have an influx of weevils plaguing the cotton bolls," he continued. "Another conspiracy against agriculture in this country. Most of our lands have been taken from us and now our cottonseeds are contaminated! There was a time we could feed the entire nation without the need of imports. We fed the Allies in the second war and later the Americans . . ."

His cousin interrupted, trying to diffuse Changiz Khan's moroseness. "Yes, that's right. Hitler was quite angry, too, seeing as how the wheat we gave the Allies was the sole reason for his downfall."

"You will always be Grand Khan! Dear Changiz Khan, please be more hopeful!" The café owner tried not to chuckle at the cousin's sarcasm.

Despite Changiz Khan's denunciation of present government policies, he, his cousin, and the entire café cheered when the Imperial Army marched by. In their decorated uniforms, the military personnel marched in perfect unison while countless tanks, carriers, and weaponry passed behind them. Sarveali hoped there would be fireworks. But the parade eventually passed on, and Changiz Khan returned to his troubles.

"So I chased them in my car," Changiz Khan continued, "and killed the pair and their three cubs." His voice filled with anguish. "A *pair* of boars with three cubs . . ."

They all fell silent. "Let's celebrate the coronation and your successful hunt with a new delicacy I've imported from Armenia," the owner broke in. Changiz Khan's spirits rose when he took a sip of the cold, exotic *shalakh*, an apricot spirit. He made a toast. "Long live the past and long live this bottle which will become my dead boars' companion."

He finished his third glass. "What do you think? Will we end up like those poor boars, the last I'll ever shoot? Didn't I tell you? I have to sell my prized gun collection. Apparently, under the protection of His Majesty, no one needs guns in our society anymore!"

Just then the chauffeur spoke up. "My Khan, this is as good a time as any to inform you. I must leave you and the estate. I've been offered a position with the Ministry of Handicrafts. The salary is higher and they can afford to pay me on time. I hate to leave your royal offices, but I must support my family. I tried to tell you be-before but I c-c-c-couldn't." The chauffeur rose to his feet. He placed the car key on the Khan's table. "Your Eminence, here is the key. I respectfully resign."

Sarveali waited for his master's outrage. Perhaps he would shoot the chauffeur with one of the rifles he was about to sell. But Sarveali only heard Changiz Khan's familiar inebriated laughter as he yelled, "Go ahead! Leave me, you ungrateful castrated jackal! You don't know the first thing about loyalty! I took pity on you and hired you when you could barely ride a donkey! I brought you up. I taught you how to handle modern machinery! This is how you repay me?" The chauffeur did not say a word but took two steps back and bowed before exiting through the café door.

I'm the only one left now, Sarveali thought as the chauffeur tipped his hat and, after twenty years of service, left his employment and all their lives.

Part III

Rapture and Decay
Empire of Iran
Islamic Republic of Iran
1969–1981

Chapter 25

Three years later, in the early months of autumn 1970, Sarveali woke before dawn. Throughout the night intermittent incubi, visions of his past and forebodings of impending adversity, assaulted his skull as they struggled to escape. Such was the pain that when Sarveali tried to get out of bed, his joints and muscles screamed in agony. But Sarveali, as always, forced himself to remember that duty must take precedence over pain, over lassitude, over the horrid symptoms of opiate withdrawal. Eventually freeing himself from the purgatory of his bedcovers, Sarveali put his trousers on over his pajama pants and left for the kitchen, still wearing a nightcap on his head, painfully aware of his slow, heavy movements, his monotonous groans.

Finally reaching the kitchen, he lit the primus stove, filled a kettle with water, and put it on the burner to boil. He dropped a tablespoonful of grade three Indian tea into one of the few fine china teapots that had managed to survive the family's vicissitudes. Was it the same pot that served the Bibi "Empress Soraya" tea just a few days before her suicide? He could still remember the Bibi's screams, how she had cried out, afraid she had "burned" the empress painted on the small saucer.

The kettle screeched and Sarveali poured the steaming water into the pot. As he perched on a short-footed stool waiting for the tea to brew, his headache ripped once more against his skull. He drank four cups of tea, hoping he could deceive his body into quiet and his mind into ease. The painful waves of opium withdrawal attacked him much more often now. On occasion the drug turned up through someone's death or a friend's hoarded supply, but it was always a meager amount, never enough to satisfy his years of addiction. All of his small salary—the 20 percent he kept before surrendering the rest to Gholi—was spent on the drug. He *had* to have the magic potion; it was the only thing that kept him from madness.

Waiting for Changiz Khan to awake, Sarveali distracted himself by slowly walking to the citrus orchard. He passed the barn, its roof crumbling onto the old stables. Sarveali berated himself for being such a negligent servant. "That roof desperately needs to be besmeared. I'll do it as soon as possible." As the only remaining servant at the estate, Sarveali's jobs now encompassed the work of twenty. He performed tasks he had never performed in his life—ironing clothes and baking sweets, irrigating the citrus orchard, keeping Changiz Khan's Jeep in good condition, painting doors and windows. Now, as he surveyed the disintegrated barn roof, he realized that fixing it was a mere fantasy. Without opium, he could barely perform his existing duties, much less this arduous task.

Reflecting on those constant duties reminded Sarveali that he needed to obtain another supply of his drug as soon as possible. Mulling the possibilities of finding his next supply, he spied his favorite tangerine tree. Despite its withered state, a few late autumn leaves danced gracefully, showing off the tree's last two fruits, which had grown so high they were inaccessible to the fruit pickers. Before the fruit had even ripened, Changiz Khan had sold the crop to the fruit brokers. Because the Khan needed constant cash to maintain a fraction of his former living standards, he sold his citrus at such a low price that the brokers were, in fact, controlling his destiny.

"Oh, 'bride of the orchard,' you look so sick. Old age and loneliness have us both in their grip. I am only forty-two, but I feel as though I'm living in the body of a seventy-year-old." A sob escaped Sarveali as suddenly as sparrows darting from their nest, so involuntary that he could not even decipher what provoked it. Was it his dead uncle's abuse, his wife's adultery, Teimour Khan's abandonment, guilt from murdering his wife, his opium addition, or loneliness? Or did he simply desire "God's cocktail" to such an extent that he was like a spoiled child crying for baklava? His thoughts meandered three decades back to his first baklava from Sheikhak and he sobbed again, wallowing in self-pity.

He lay on the grass next to the tangerine tree, its crown between him and the turquoise sky and limpid clouds. As he lay there, overwhelming loneliness caused Sarveali to imagine the shovel was a lover. He embraced the rod and kissed its metallic head, as he sank into an unhappy doze.

When Sarveali opened his eyes, the full morning sun shone on his face; black silhouettes circled above him under the solar flare—buzzards. He shook his fist. "You fuckers," he cried. "I'm not dead yet!"

When his equilibrium was somewhat restored, Sarveali returned to the house and his master. Changiz Khan now had gray hair that he regularly dyed black. As he sat in an armchair on the porch waiting for his daily Turkish coffee, he fondled his handlebar mustache, also dyed, deep in his daily ritual of contemplation and reminiscence. He was dressed in the pajamas and dressing gown he had worn since the Bibi had committed suicide, both faded and threadbare.

As Sarveali prepared Changiz Khan's coffee, he struggled to manage his own pain. He was conscious that he had not bathed or washed his garments in weeks. As he bent down to offer Changiz Khan the coffee, his hand trembled, the tray flew out of his hand, and the hot beverage poured onto Changiz Khan's crotch.

"You just burned my rusty member, you fool, whatever was left of it! What's wrong with you?! And you smell fetid, like a dead boar rotting for a year!"

The following morning Changiz Khan told Sarveali to pack for Shiraz. "I'm going to cure you of this filthy addiction once and for all," he said. "Who knows, you might try to kill me one day if you think I have opium in my pockets. Not that I ever will."

Half a day later, Sarveali was admitted to a substance abuse clinic. The clinic director, Dr. Ravani, claimed he had discovered a new substance unknown to any other hospital—what he called his "magic laudanum." Changiz Khan and Sarveali met privately with the doctor before Sarveali's treatment commenced. "So, my dear Ravani, tell me about your 'magic laudanum,'" Changiz Khan invited the doctor.

"It's called methadone. Besides me, only one other doctor in Tehran currently uses it for curing opium addiction. But please keep this in this room, my dearest khan. You know this nation is like a herd of sheep. I don't want everyone to know about my potion." Changiz Khan laughed and said, "I agree with you completely, my dear lunatic doctor."

The doctor continued, "So, what's wrong with this man you've brought to me?" He looked at Sarveali, who realized he had not had any opium for three days. Or was it four? His headache pounded his forehead, searching for a way out. The pain was intensified by his nausea and an embarrassing realization that his constant diarrhea was about to attack him again.

"He is my only servant now, but he is a pitiful opium addict who can't get the substance these days. Without the drug, he's become worthless!"

"A grand khan without a servant? I can't imagine. It's like Priapus without a penis! Don't worry! I will clean him up for you." Dr. Ravani reassured Changiz Kahn, glancing at Sarveali who was trying not to vomit.

Just as Sarveali was preparing to reach for the director's waste basket, the doctor inquired about Teimour Kahn. Sarveali's spirits lifted a bit, and his inner upheaval calmed.

"We have not heard from him in many years," Changiz Khan said. "He left before the coup in 1953, and according to my children, whom he corresponds with only sporadically, he mostly lives in Paris these days. He always was the smart one. But now that he's unloaded everything on me and fled, it's a wonder I don't take up opium myself."

Interpreting the doctor's silence as interest, Changiz Khan continued with his usual rant about his land. "It's cursed. Now agriculture is nothing more than running a whorehouse." Waves of nausea and diarrhea attacked Sarveali again; he eyed the waste basket a second time and reflexively constricted his sphincter.

"I'm only able to produce cotton saturated with wee-vils," Changiz Khan went on, "wheat that attracts grasshoppers, watermelons that rupture and wither before they even begin to redden. Every winter, my orange trees freeze. My late wife's quince orchard died overnight. I have no one to help me . . ." Changiz Khan paused and Sarveali shut his lips tight.

"Stop, Changiz Khan! Stop!" Dr. Ravani interrupted. "I hope you are aware that I no longer run a depression clinic. Besides, khans should never be afflicted with depression! Didn't your ancestors defecate gold? My dear khan, life in Iran today is about adapting to the political climate. Once I heard about the latest opium crackdown, I immediately turned my lunacy bin into a rehabilitation center." At that, Sarveali dashed from the room, shouting "Latrine! Latrine!"

FOR THE NEXT THREE MONTHS, SARVEALI SUFFERED every known torture of opiate withdrawal, but it was nothing he hadn't suffered before. Headaches, muscle spasms, diarrhea, fever, flu symptoms, and nausea gradually dissipated as painkillers and the "magic" methadone slowly gained control over his body.

Surprisingly, as his illness yielded to treatment, his old sexual longings returned. The son of a Royal Air Force general was going through detoxification in a room down the hall. Sarveali admired the lanky young man and took every opportunity to gaze at him from a distance. He followed the youth around the grounds. Whenever the lad returned Sarveali's stares, whether by intention or accident, Sarveali felt each hair on his body rise, unaware that "pilo-erection," a condition characterized by the body hair standing on end, was yet another autonomic symptom of opiate withdrawal.

Three months later, when Dr. Ravani released Sarveali from the clinic opiate-free, Sarveali realized he had never found the courage to approach his object of lust. He was also shocked to discover that Changiz Khan had employed a new servant to replace him in his absence. Disconsolate, Sarveali was transferred into the service of "Little" Bibi Naz Khanom in Shiraz. Sarveali's only comfort lay in knowing that he was still a factotum of the family. Finally rid of his addiction, he resolved to serve the Khan's daughter as loyally as he had served her father.

Bibi Naz Khanom, now in her mid-twenties, had married a pediatrician the year before Sarveali's detoxification. They lived alone in Changiz Khan's modest house in Shiraz, while the twins were at university in Tehran and Changiz Khan determined to die at his estate in Kamab.

Sarveali soon found his new appointment a relief from the despondent Changiz Khan. He enjoyed the lighter workload and living in the city he remembered so well from Teimour Khan's days at prep school. Now that he lived far away from the opium den in Kamab and had no more connections to opium dealers, he was no longer tempted by the habit. Bibi Naz Khanom welcomed him; she knew of Sarveali's recent detoxification and forgave him his many years of addiction.

Sarveali worked as hard for the Bibi as he had for her uncle and father. He kept away from her husband, who seemed aloof and mysterious, as much as possible. Dr. Darioushi divided his time between private pediatric practices at the Niazi Hospital and Medical Center, and the Pahlavi University Faculty of Medicine. At home he immersed himself in reading in his private library, which he secured with a padlock when he was out. The pediatrician, who knew about Yazgulu's murder, rarely spoke to Sarveali.

The little Bibi had her own problems. She tried in vain to win her husband's attention, feebly trying to persuade him to cut down on his work and reading. After eavesdropping on them through the bedroom walls, Sarveali worried that he was witnessing yet another unhappy marriage.

"But you work so hard, my dear. You deserve the rest," the Bibi would complain.

Only visits from the twins cheered up the married couple. When they were home from university, Lohrasb and Virasb spent most of their time teasing Sarveali. But now Sarveali suffered these humiliations in the service of his new masters without a thought. With his new life, he had enough leisure time to go to the cinema and cafés, and marvel at the products in the well-stocked boutiques. Best of all, the fortunes of the Shirlus seemed to have reached a plateau. Eight peaceful years passed.

Chapter 26

One beautiful June morning in 1978, Bibi Naz Khanom called Sarveali, now fifty years old, to her room.

"Will you please go to Mr. Abgir's shop behind the prison and buy two bottles each of mint, pussy willow, pennyroyal, and syrup of sour cherry?" Seven months pregnant after eight years of a childless marriage, Bibi Naz Khanom still spoke in the genteel manner that contrasted so sharply with her father's.

"Yes, the Shirlu crown prince or princess in me desires a bottle of mint water and sour cherry syrup right now."

Sarveali left the house carrying a vermillion-red plastic hamper. Swinging his hamper, he reached Ashraf Alley via its narrow opening. The alley resembled a twisted serpent, its vertebrae infested with lumps, cysts, and inflammations as the alley's width varied meter by meter, certain parts wide enough for a wedding procession, others so narrow even a thin man would be constricted passing through.

The ominous thoughts that had remained dormant for eight years suddenly erupted when Sarveali reached the

Karim Khan Zand Citadel at the end of the alley. The sight of the Citadel's towers reminded him of the two most dismal events in his life—when he murdered his wife next to the Bahadoran Citadel and when he watched helplessly as the Bibi committed suicide at Eram Citadel. The images of the towers rotated in front of him as he thought of his own implication in the two deaths.

The establishment where Sarveali had purchased bottles of aqua vitae of pussy willow, distilled rose water, lime juice, honey syrup, essence of mint, currant-colored amarelle, and other potions for years proved a good balm for his resurrected gloom. He loved to hold in his hands one of the hundreds of multicolored and tightly capped glass bottles, to feel the metal cap held in place by crimping its edge over the bottle's flange. A ceiling fan whirred above him, dispersing and intensifying the aromatic aerosols throughout the shop.

Mr. Abgir's knees creaked like rusted hinges as he rose from his chair to greet Sarveali. He was nearing seventy and suffered many symptoms of decrepitude, his curved spine forcing him to bend forward. He wheezed and coughed.

"God's grace, Mr. Abgir!"

"Oh, Sarveali the Great! What can I thank for the honor of your presence?" Mr. Abgir bowed. In Shiraz, Sarveali was not thought of as the son of Zolfali, the Blind Licker, but as a man to be honored.

"May God give you health and prosperity."

"Health? What health? Those days of youth are over. Now we must prepare for the exodus. Of course that son of mine, may God inflict him with diphtheria, is nowhere to be found, and *I* must do all the work."

"Don't say that, Mr. Abgir. You have a fine son." Sarveali remembered the boy's tall, slender physique.

"He's been a canker sore in my heart. These are difficult times, Sarveali. Girls revealing buttocks and breasts, boys like my son dressing like girls, shameless naked women dancing on television in the middle of the holy month of Moharram—all in the name of Westernization. No wonder there are . . ." Mr. Abgir lowered his voice, "demonstrations," he whispered. Sarveali was not sure what the proprietor was referring to but knew that "demonstrations" couldn't be anything good.

"We've had nearly thirty years of peace and quiet since the Second World War. Or at least twenty-some years since the coup of '53. People always insist on shaking things up every couple of decades as if they had restless worms up their asses."

Sarveali remained quiet, his meager knowledge of politics failing him.

Mr. Abgir abruptly changed the subject. "Forgive me for not offering you anything to drink! What would you like?"

"Nothing but your health."

"How about some aqua vitae of mint to soothe your worried soul?" Mr. Abgir peered at Sarveali. "You look a bit shaken up this morning.

"Here is the ambrosia of God for Sarveali the Great. Drink to the Shirlu family and to the great Changiz Khan." He placed a tall glass of aqua vitae with ice in front of Sarveali.

"May God return your kindness." Sarveali finished his drink quickly and left the store.

He walked along Zand Boulevard on his way home, admiring the upright stance of the sycamore trees lining the street. Once he had left the area surrounding the citadel, his feelings of ease returned, so when a violent blow assailed the back of his head, he was unprepared. A muscular middle-aged man with salt-and-pepper hair aimed a mace stick at Sarveali's head.

"I swear to all the sacred imams! There is no God but Allah!" Sarveali pleaded.

"Shut the fuck up, you wife killer!" the man screamed, wielding the mace at the servant's eyebrows. The attacker forced Sarveali's head down to meet his right knee. Sarveali could taste the salt of his own blood flowing from his nose and mouth. Another blow knocked him to the pavement.

As he fell, the attacker grabbed a bottle of sour cherry syrup from the hamper and smashed it against Sarveali's skull. The blood and fruit mixture covering his head dripped onto the sidewalk. Sarveali lay supine.

"You fucking coward! If you had real balls you'd get up and fight!" Sarveali suddenly detected the accent of his birth village, Madavan. "You wife killer! How could you kill her? How could you kill Yazgulu?"

Sarveali's mind screamed. *Why is he talking about Yazgulu? Who is he? And why does he sound like he's from Madavan?*

From across the street, a woman shouted. "Leave the poor man alone, or I will shoot you myself! You should fight someone your own size. Just wait until I get my shotgun, you stupid bumpkin!"

The salt-and-pepper-haired man stopped beating Sarveali, threw the pussy willow bottle on the sidewalk, and fled. As he raced away in his green Peykan, he rolled down the car window and spat at Sarveali. "I'm Massih Madavani, you wife murderer! I am the man who should've married Yazgulu, not some midget like you!"

An ambulance transported Sarveali to Niazi Hospital. In the infirmary bed, delirious from pain, Sarveali saw a phantasm of his dead wife. Yazgulu was in a gauzy white dress, holding a bleeding dove. She blotted the gown with the bird's blood. Barat-Ali suddenly appeared. "The family whores go to the family midgets!" he called out.

FOUR DAYS LATER, SARVEALI WAS DISCHARGED from the hospital with bandages covering his skull and twenty-five stitches in his head. His black eyes and bruised face prevented him from hiding his injuries. As he hailed a taxi, Sarveali could see his image in the window's reflection, the bandages, contusion, and bloodstains only worsening his ugliness. As Sarveali climbed into the taxi, the young driver stared at him with disgust.

As the taxi made its first turn onto Khayyam Street, Sarveali saw hundreds of youths carrying banners and chanting slogans blocking the road. He stared at their beauty and ignored their slogans. The taxi driver disrupted Sarveali's pleasure. "Were you beaten by these demonstrators, too?" Embarrassed, Sarveali remained quiet. *That word again. What did it mean?*

"Come on, tell me. Who did it? The soldiers or the demonstrators?" The driver made eye contact with Sarveali through the rearview mirror. "Old man, even the bloodstain on your bandage resembles the word 'Allah.'"

"What can I say? Who are these demonstrators, anyway?"

"Idiots. Crazy people. Look at them screaming. 'Death to this one,' 'Death to that.' Do you know how many statues of the Shah and his father and son they've destroyed? Yet these are the same fuckers who chanted, 'The Shah is God's Shadow,' 'God-Shah-Nation,' just a few days ago."

Sarveali was surprised to hear the cab driver talk so openly about politics. Only a decade ago, Changiz Khan had told him to avoid political discussions with anyone, merchants and mullahs alike. He hoped these demonstrators were not chanting antifeudal slogans again.

"Freedom now! We want freedom!" the demonstrators shouted.

A team of police officers appeared. An officer shouted over his microphone, "Children, disperse! Go home to your families. There will be no illegal acts committed here today. Don't let these agitators get to your simple young minds!" The officer lectured the young people like a school principal.

Sarveali and the driver watched as a youth of perhaps sixteen years approached a parked Vespa and opened its gas chamber. The boy lit a match and threw it inside the tank. The motorcycle ignited into an enormous blaze and exploded.

The taxi driver screamed, "Let's move!" As the taxi sped away and the crowds scattered in all directions, Sarveali watched as the boy who had dropped the match ran crazily in circles, twisting flames rising from his body.

The sight horrified Sarveali, but the taxi driver seemed unaffected as he went back to his complaining. "These bastard kids have no discipline. I tell you, they're all looking for death. There went the first one!" The sight of such pleasure crossing the driver's face as his prediction of death materialized and the boy fell to the street shocked Sarveali. A crowd leaving a mosque rushed to the street and formed another blockade.

"Our corrupt police have just killed six Muslim brothers," yelled a mustachioed man, running past the taxi toward the flames. An ambulance blasted past and sirens wailed around them. "You can let me off here. I'll make the rest of the way by foot," Sarveali cried.

"Long live the Shah!" called out a nearby woman with well-coiffed hair.

"Long live the Shah!" called out a man in a fedora.

"In the bazaar, they announced that the police killed sixteen youths," added a beautiful man with long sideburns and honey-colored eyes. Even though Sarveali knew his story was not true, he wanted to believe him.

"Lady, I tell you, you should not appear so well dressed when you're this close to the mosque, the believers' mosque." A bearded man who seemed to work for the mosque gestured at the woman's dress and uncovered hair.

"I will never wear that evil chador. The Shahanshah has bestowed on the women of Iran the privilege of dressing as we choose." The bearded man spat at the woman's feet and walked away.

Sarveali made his way home slowly. He had a great deal of news to convey to Bibi Naz Khanom. The closer he got to the house, the more his pain receded as the demonstration took center stage.

"I saw a demo . . . a 'demo-fica-tion'—a boy burned himself—but people say the police shot him and fifteen others."

"Yes, I know. Radio Iran just announced it. The boy died from third-degree burns. You mean you actually saw the dem-on-stra-tion? By the way, I talked to the twins last night. They said there is martial law in Tehran and Isfahan. They're leaving Tehran by car today or tomorrow."

Sarveali closed his eyes for a moment. He could see the young boy strike the match, then the explosion and the towering flames.

"Never mind, Sarveali. We mustn't worry. Just forget it and make me some licorice-root tea. I need a paregoric. You know, this whole affair reminds me of the adage of the forty crows." Sarveali listened intently. He still didn't understand the word *demonstration*, and knew nothing about forty crows.

"Someone saw one crow and told his friend," the Bibi started, "who told another guy that *he* saw six crows. He then told *someone else* he'd seen *twenty*. In the end, someone said he saw *forty* crows, when there was really only one crow in actuality, if there was one at all." The Bibi paused. "Now, the licorice-root tea, please," she asked, putting an end to talk of death.

Chapter 27

A week later, as Sarveali and the Bibi kept themselves informed of protests and carnage by listening to the radio, the television, and the public's exaggerated retellings of what happened in the streets, Virasb and Lohrasb, now thirty-three years old, arrived from Tehran. They had completed their two-year tenure as officers in the Imperial Army after receiving master's degrees in sociology.

"The Bibi told me you left Tehran last week, my master *khanzadehs*." Sarveali kissed the twins' hands one by one as they exited their canary-yellow Zhian auto, the Iranian counterpart of a Citroën.

"We had to maneuver through eight hundred kilometers of barricaded roads in the midst of this martial law," Virasb said.

"Well, didn't the troops know that you are the *khanzadehs* of Shirlus *and* former army officers?" Sarveali asked.

"Those two titles are just liabilities nowadays. Nobody today is too fond of a khan or an officer. Our generation is doomed. And by the way, I like your head scarf! Nice fashion statement! But now I need a nap," Virasb said.

Lohrasb continued, "Yes, very nicely tied head scarf indeed, Mr. Jokar. As for being officers, thank God after a two-year tour of duty, we're no longer in the army."

Later that evening, after Bibi Naz Khanom returned from her visit to the obstetrician, they all sat down to dinner.

"Is there any liquor in the house?" Virasb asked.

"Well, my husband doesn't drink. But I keep a few bottles in case Father visits."

"Father's liver could metabolize a Caspian Sea full of whiskey." Virasb poured himself and his brother two glasses of whiskey before the national TV newscast began.

"Today, the seventh of Shahrivar, 2537, Imperial Year . . . umm, my apologies, I mean Islamic Year 1357, August 28, 1978 . . . As if the carnage of burning four hundred people alive at Cinema Rex in Abadan were not enough, Casino Monte Carlo was destroyed. Terrorists and provocateurs attacked the Bank Melli Iran, Pahlavi Avenue branch. Shams Brewery was burned. The Museum of Modern Arts was attacked, but the security guards were able to diffuse the attackers."

"Wow! So much destruction all in one day," Virasb said. "We love to destroy things. If the Greeks, Arabs, Muguls, Afghans don't do it, then we just do it ourselves."

"Well, the clergy *is* known for not being fond of modern cinema and the arts." Lohrasb finished his whiskey. "They only like to issue fatwa after fatwa so people will burn each other—pyromaniacs!"

"Is there an equivalency ratio for a burned restaurant and a burned cinema in terms of pyro-satisfaction?" Lohrasb asked.

"Stop that! You never take anything seriously," Bibi Naz Khanom protested. "I'm frightened."

"Pour me some more whiskey, my dear gravid, gestate, fecundated, and inseminated sister. If they keep attacking the liquor stores . . . oh, then this bottle of Johnnie Walker Red could be our last." He made a show of savoring the scotch.

"We're going to Kamab tomorrow, that famous center of civilization and fine arts," Lohrasb said. "We hope to start the Kamab Ballet Company. Perhaps the head mullah and the muezzin could do a pas de deux."

"I'm going to bed," his sister said. "Everything is always a game with you two."

As the guardian of Sarveali's tender feelings left the room, the twins began their never-ending ridicule of him. "Do you still sleep with your hatchet under your pillow? I guess you didn't have that when you got beaten up by your compatriot, did you?"

"Never mind the hatchet. With your height, have you ever entertained the idea of professional basketball? And with that head scarf, you could be a fashion model!" The twins burst into laughter.

Deciding that discretion was the better part of valor, Sarveali stood silently, observing his young masters. Teimour Khan shone from the twins' faces and figures and filled Sarveali with memories. *Where has my master gone? I wish to God I could serve him one last time*, Sarveali thought as he admired the two replicates of Teimour Khan. Although they were in their thirties, the boys looked younger, with shoulder-length dark brown hair; honey-colored eyes; full, ruby lips; and fair skin. Each twin wore a black, long-collared shirt beneath a wide-lapelled denim suit. Sarveali looked down at their elastic-gusseted and leather-strapped boots with regret. There were no laces to tie into butterflies.

The twins finished their whiskey bottle and danced to Gogoosh, the Iranian pop diva. "Irrigate me, I'm the desert," she sang on the stereo as the twins threw the empty bottle out the kitchen window, where it smashed into pieces. The sound of shattered glass reminded Sarveali of his beating from Massih. The pain in his head returned as he touched the swollen spot where the assailant had struck him with the bottle of cherry syrup.

A FEW WEEKS AFTER THE TWINS LEFT FOR KAMAB, the first day of Mehr (September 23), 1978, Bibi Naz Khanom gave birth to a son she named Nima, after her uncle Teimour Khan's favorite poet, Nima Youshij. Sarveali had his stitches removed when he visited the hospital.

On that same day, what the Bibi termed "disastrous autumn" began. Sarveali watched on the television more demonstrations, burnings, killings, and mass prayers. He also learned a new term: "revolution." After Nima's birth, martial law was enacted.

But it was not until three months later that the Bibi and Sarveali watched the old regime's coup de grâce. The Shah fled, and thirty-seven days later Ayatollah Ruhullah Khomeini arrived from France to institute the Islamic Republic. Khomeini, an outspoken cleric whom the Shah had exiled for criticizing his secular and progressive Westernization reforms, was to lead the new republic.

Six months after the revolution, Bibi Naz Khanom's house in Shiraz was invaded by Revolutionary Guards with machine guns. When Sarveali answered the door, the guards aimed between his eyebrows.

"Move away, old man. We need to search this spy nest," a bearded guard said and pushed Sarveali from the door. Other guards opened the gate and backed a large military truck into the yard. The guards took gunnysacks from the truck and threw book after book into them, some periodicals yellow with age. As soon as one stripped the bookshelf naked, another broke into the wall behind to search for anything else the family might be hiding. The guard found nothing, and Nima's wailing exacerbated the commotion.

"You criminals! We have done nothing wrong!" the Bibi cried, disappearing into her bedroom. From the window, she watched the guards load the military truck, turning it into a mobile library. All the books from her husband's vast store were removed as evidence of Dr. Darioushi's Western orientation and counterrevolutionary activities.

Sarveali walked into the looted library, which, although his footsteps echoed in the empty room, still seemed sacred. It reminded him of a dear comrade stripped naked, searched, and mutilated. Sarveali had not been able to defend the house and felt disgraced again, as if somehow he was connected to the room's humiliation.

That night, as Bibi Naz Khanom's tears soaked through an entire box of tissues, she told Sarveali that the attackers were after her husband and his allegedly opposition-related documents. "And now that my husband has run away, I must also exile myself across the world to Ecuador, far from my roots. This paper says they've frozen our bank accounts." She looked into Sarveali's eyes with melancholy and despair. Fighting hiccups, Bibi Naz Khanom continued. "I hope they won't harm my father, for that would be the end of the Shirlus, the end of a five-century heritage, and the end of progress in this country, mind you."

Shortly after the conversation, guilty that her husband's political problems would indeed affect Changiz Khan, Bibi Naz Khanom telephoned her father. His house had likewise been ransacked, and the old man said that he was about to lose the little land that remained. Before Bibi Naz Khanom could offer an apology, Changiz Khan cried out to her, "Thanks to you and your *counterrevolutionary* husband, I'm about to lose everything." Listening on an extension, Sarveali heard one of the twins come on the phone. "They tore our naked portrait of Catherine Deneuve into pieces. The death of art is nearing, but at least we've perfected a recipe for homemade raisin brandy."

Chapter 28

Midmorning a few days later, the telephone's screech assaulted Sarveali's eardrums. Hurrying to pick up the receiver, he was sure that the call must herald more bad news. But once the caller began to speak, Sarveali found his intuition incorrect.

He proclaimed, "May God give you 120 years of healthy life, Virasb Khan, what great news!" Holding the receiver to his ear, Sarveali turned to Bibi Naz Khanom and whispered enthusiastically, "Teimour Khan is back!" At the same time, he conjured an image of Teimour Khan arriving in Iran on a white horse with a ruby-encrusted golden saddle to save them all. "God is so kind to his subjects; the other day I was praying for my master's return, and now He's brought him to us."

But as he continued to listen to Virasb on the other end of the line, Sarveali's happiness evaporated. When he heard the words "Imanieh Hospital," it was as if a magician had made the white horse disappear in a cloud of green smoke. He cursed himself, wondering why his hopes and joys always proved so impotent and ephemeral.

"What? My Teimour Khan is ill? Please, don't play a trick like that on an old man like me, especially when it regards the health of your esteemed uncle! Imanieh Hospital?" Sarveali was only fifty-two years old, but he felt like the quintessential geriatric. He called to the Bibi, "Teimour Khan is home, but he's sick and they've taken him to Imanieh Hospital."

"Why did they take him there? That so-called hospital is for peasants and vagabonds! Let me speak." Bibi Naz Khanom took the handset out of Sarveali's hands. "Virasb, Uncle Teimour is in Shiraz?" A small aperture of hope opened for the servant. If Teimour Khan's illness was not too serious, perhaps he would ask for Sarveali to serve him again.

But when he heard Bibi Naz Khanom utter the word "cancer," his knees failed him and he fell to the floor.

"And Niazi turned you away because of my husband's political background? I think I'm going to be sick. Sarveali, here, take the phone." Sarveali dragged himself off the kitchen tiles. Forgetting his own recent encounter with physical suffering, he vowed, *I will be his caretaker until he's ready for the gates of heaven, and if he desires, I'll go with him through the gates of hell.*

Mustering all his strength, he reached for the phone. Virasb continued, "At the moment, my dear sister, we need help from Marx, Engels, Brezhnev, Begin, Henry Kissinger . . . and the corpse of Prime Minister Amir Abbas Hoveyda." Hoveyda was the only name on the list that Sarveali recognized. Until he heard the name of the slain prime minister, he assumed Virasb was listing medications his master would need.

Bibi Naz Khanom called out, "Tell him we're coming immediately!" She ran around the house maniacally, grabbing articles of clothing—first a sweater and then a black scarf. "Sarveali, my uncle is deathly ill and we must go to him, to the Arab ghetto. Can you believe a khan of the Shirlus is hospitalized there? I can't take little Nima with me. Call that old woman . . . the one who used to babysit for the American lady."

Sarveali reacted bitterly himself. "Why is Teimour Khan in such a place? Does he really have cancer? And why did he return without telling us? We could've gone to greet him as in the old days . . . " When Sarveali thought of past welcomes, he remembered his old preceptor, Sheikhak, and the magnificent preparations he had supervised for every homecoming.

Bibi Naz Khanom interrupted him. "Yes, he has cancer, prostate cancer. And worse, France deported him for some reason . . . and don't be so naive, Sarveali, those glorious old days of greeting dignitaries are gone forever."

Sarveali went to get the sitter, thinking all the way, *I wonder how my master looks now. My fair-skinned, honey-eyed master . . . that heavenly smell . . .* He felt a pulse in his genitals, remembering that arousing scent of Creed on Yazgulu. He struggled to regain his focus. *What will I do when I see Teimour Khan again? I'll throw myself at his feet. I'll prove to him that I am his same loyal servant.*

When Sarveali returned with the babysitter, Bibi Naz Khanom wore, for the first time, a long, gray dress and a black head scarf. She said sadly, "I don't know if I can handle this . . . this going back to the Stone Age, wearing a head scarf. The next thing will be a chador again. God, what has our nation done that you must punish it like this?"

She addressed the babysitter. "I suppose the couple you worked for has joined the thousands of Americans fleeing our country, abandoning us, abandoning our king." Sarveali could not help but notice the frustration on the Bibi's face as she blamed her political vicissitudes on America; still, it was unfair to attack the old woman simply because she worked for foreigners.

In the taxi, Sarveali noticed the young driver and his beautiful green eyes looking at the couple through the rearview mirror. He ignored both the driver and his eyes. After all, Teimour Khan, the most handsome of all men, had come back to him. *With Teimour Khan back—even ill—who needed these youths?*

IN THE HOSPITAL ROOM, Bibi Naz Khanom rushed to embrace her uncle. They both began to cry. Sarveali, at the foot of the bed, joined in the room's grief. Teimour Khan, once a pillar of beauty, power, and manhood, had diminished to little more than a skeleton. White as stone, his body made barely a wrinkle under the sheet. As a result of chemotherapy for the cancer, he had lost all his hair, including his eyebrows and lashes. He resembled an eagle plucked for public humiliation.

For a moment, Sarveali could hardly recognize the man lying on the bed before him. But the honey eyes and full, fleshy lips assured Sarveali that the pale ghost was indeed his Teimour Khan Shirlu. Sensing that his master did not wish to be seen by a servant in such a weak and vulnerable state, Sarveali quietly left the room.

Once in the lobby, Sarveali gave way to his mourning at the pitiful sight of his old master. His sobs, like sparrows freed from a cage, resounded off the ceiling. Looking up, he noticed an electric lamp suspended in the center of the ceiling, and, around it, grout discolored from water damage had formed an image in the shape of a raccoon. This vision only escalated Sarveali's hysterical tears. Passersby stared nervously until Sarveali could stand his self-imposed solitude no longer.

He reentered Teimour Khan's room, ready to offer his old master his eternal love and servitude. Their eyes met and as if they had never parted, Teimour Khan called out to him like a muezzin atop a minaret, "Why did you run away like that? Wipe your eyes. How could you flee your ill master in such a cowardly fashion?"

Sarveali was so grateful for the attention that he immediately threw himself at Teimour Khan, kissing his hands and feet, ignoring the khan's gestures of impatience and feverishness. The Bibi paid no attention to Sarveali's gestures of loyalty either, and having taken note of her uncle's misery, began to ask him the whereabouts of her father and brothers.

The patient, who had expended his energy in admonishing the servant, replied slowly. ". . . went to purchase . . . medical supplies . . . This place . . . has nothing . . . more like a . . . self-service cafeteria." He groaned. "One more product . . . of this . . . unholy revolution." He turned to the servant. "Sarveali, I'm so hot. Fan me." Sarveali picked up a magazine and waved it vigorously in front of the exhausted patient's face.

"Why are you back, Uncle?" Bibi Naz Khanom bent over Teimour Khan like a talkative angel, her head scarf grazing his forehead.

More tears trickled down Teimour Khan's pale cheeks as he struggled to answer. ". . . deported me . . . to please . . . the Islamic Republic. And I wanted to be buried in . . .

in . . . Père Lachaise . . . next to Marcel Proust . . . This miserable place . . ." He closed his eyes.

The Bibi regained her equilibrium and took charge. "Sarveali, help me get my uncle up, so you can change these dirty sheets." Delighted, Sarveali rushed to obey. He could not remember the last time he had touched his master. As the two lifted the khan up, Teimour Khan opened his eyes again. ". . . sordid smells. Spots on the sheets like . . . a Miro painting." Sarveali grappled with the sheets as the Bibi held the sick man in her arms. The servant looked at his master and told himself that he had to remove Teimour Khan from this dirty, understaffed hospital to a place where he could care for him forever.

CHANGIZ KHAN, HIS NEW SQUINT-EYED SERVANT, and the twins finally returned, laden with supplies. Each man carried a cardboard box filled with glass bottles. Changiz Khan read the labels out loud: "Sodium Chloride 0.9 percent intravenous solution, 1,000 milliliters, Abbott Laboratories, Abbott Park, Illinois. This could be the last blood-feeding American saline you'll ever receive, my brother. America's withdrawal from Iran will starve us." He barely looked at the pale body now lying on fresh sheets. After he had informed a passing nurse of the medicine, he abruptly announced his departure as if he could not stand even five minutes in his sick brother's company. Bibi Naz Khanom remained to oversee the administration of the medicine.

Outside the hospital room, the men began to speculate. "A conspiracy of Western imperialism forced him out of France," Virasb ventured.

"No, he just lived to the end of his means, spent his very last franc, while I was forced to remain, suffering tragedy after tragedy—land reform, my wife's suicide, seeing my wealth vanish before my eyes. Those khan-hating mullahs—God, I loathe everyone in this country and particularly my brother, who never raised a hand to help me out!" Changiz Khan exclaimed in self-pity. Sarveali felt hot spears puncture his heart. How dare Changiz Khan speak so harshly about his own brother, particularly when he was so ill? He noticed a sardonic smile on the face of the new servant, enraging him further.

"My master, don't you think, sir . . . that perhaps this is not the right time to speak so about Teimour Khan?" This unprecedented remonstrance from a former servant shocked Changiz Khan, and Sarveali recoiled at the tirade he knew would follow.

"Shut up, you addict, wife killer, or I'll strangle you right here!" The twins reached for their father before he could lash out at the servant. "Come, Father, let's go to the car and get some whiskey. Much more pleasant than being in this evil-smelling place." Virasb and his brother pulled Changiz Khan toward the hospital exit.

Sarveali noted the squint-eyed servant, whose frown of disapproval seemed to exaggerate his malformed eyes, and walked back to Teimour Khan's room, lachrymose. He took a seat by the door and watched the patient sleep fitfully as Bibi Naz Khanom stared out the window. He wondered what more bad luck was in store. He had not long to wait. Shortly, the twins returned to say good-bye, already drunk, having left their snoring father in the car.

Bibi Naz Khanom frowned at her brothers and picked up her purse. She spoke quietly to Sarveali, "Would you please stay with my uncle tonight? I need to attend to these merrymakers."

"I will!" Sarveali exclaimed. "I won't leave his side!" The twins and the Bibi left, she struggling to keep them upright,

Lohrasb murmuring, "Yes, let's enjoy the last drop of our Johnnie Walker Red with our sister."

Teimour Khan raised his head from the pillow as they departed. ". . . don't forget . . . a bottle for me . . . the joy . . . of alcohol is universal . . ."

That night, as Teimour Khan restlessly asked for water and tea, Sarveali went over in his mind his confrontation with Changiz Khan. His remark had been intended as a gesture of loyalty to Teimour Khan. Wasn't his old master himself a patriotic soldier now, showing heroic resistance to death? Certainly, facing the end required more strength than Changiz Khan's troubles. Infused with the nectar of euphoria, Sarveali set about cleaning the room, happy that, at least for the night, he did not have to share Teimour Khan with anyone. The well-remembered scent of Creed had been replaced by the clinical smells of alcohol, acetone, and ether, but Sarveali's joy did not notice the difference.

IN THE MORNING, the attending physician added "clinical depression" to the patient's list of ailments after witnessing Teimour Khan weeping uncontrollably and speaking of "the dark abyss that is the well." In his bloodstained uniform, the doctor looked more like a butcher than a clinician. As Teimour Khan's weeping subsided into deep sighs, the physician and Sarveali tried to reposition the patient on the mattress for a more thorough examination. The hospital bed screamed in protest. "Cries from purgatory," Teimour Khan moaned.

Even the doctor seemed alarmed at the khan's ravings. "Look at me . . . as wretched as my country . . . I gladly welcome death." Teimour Khan closed his eyes. Sarveali tried to hold back his tears as he tenderly bathed his master's face.

Later that afternoon, the patient's relatives talked to him about transferring to another facility. The patient did not agree. After trying in vain to verbalize the cause of his dismissal from France, he finally mumbled, "No, no, my dear ones . . . let me die here . . . fate has dictated the end . . ."

"My brother has become a lunatic," Changiz Khan said, as the group gathered once more in the lobby. "And we don't have money to spare anyway. If it weren't for that peasant who returned some of my land, I would be as impecunious as a vagabond."

"Are you referring to the land you immediately sold to buy a new Land Cruiser and a Rolex, and to hire that cross-eyed servant?" Lohrasb asked his father. Changiz Khan sat down heavily on a chair that swayed under his weight. The twins giggled. Sarveali sighed like a mournful wind.

"What if we bring Teimour back to the estate in Kamab?" suggested the practical Bibi. "Sarveali could see to him and perhaps he could use a part of your quarters, Father." She looked imploringly at her pouting father, while Sarveali's heart leapt.

"Yes, let's do that," said Virasb. "We can survey the hypocrisy index of the inhabitants . . ." His brother interrupted him. "Let's load Uncle in the back of the new Land Cruiser, administer him an infusion of whiskey, and be on our merry way."

It was agreed that the next day they would return to Kamab. Sarveali was ecstatic: his faith in both God and Teimour Khan would surely lead to a healing result. *Who needs that butcher in the bloody coat? I can care for my master better than any hospital.* And indeed, that night Teimour Khan slept with a smile on his face. Sarveali convinced himself it was the beginning of a complete recovery.

MIDMORNING THE NEXT DAY, Changiz Khan, Bibi Naz Khanom, and the twins arrived with the butcher-doctor to sign the discharge papers. The physician wrote a few lines on Teimour Khan's chart without looking at him and said, "Mr. Shirlu, I hereby dismiss you from the hospital's custody."

The butcher did not even address my master as His Eminence, Teimour Khan Shirlu, thought Sarveali. But after the doctor left, Teimour Khan seemed stronger. "Now the butcher can return to his slaughterhouse and sacrifice another sheep toward Mecca," followed by, "Take me home, my lovely Bibi Naz and my two crown princes. I believe some whiskey would be soothing for our trip. Let's drink to the last Pahlavi, His Majesty, the fugitive."

The trip home to Kamab went unpredictably well. The last of the contraband whiskey was passed to the patient, who, with Sarveali fussing over him, lay on two mattresses in the back of the Land Cruiser. Changiz Khan drove in silence, while Teimour Khan, with the help of Sarveali, finished the bottle of Johnnie Walker. The twins convinced Sarveali that the whiskey was good for their uncle. "It always dulls pain," they called from the front of the vehicle. Sarveali remembered the *aragh* he had drunk to ward off the pain of having murdered his wife, so he said nothing in protest.

"It's a good antibiotic. It will disinfect my prostate!" Teimour Khan muttered and, rambling on, "In the dark vestibule of purgatory, death is lurking . . ." The twins hooted at their uncle's poetic ditherings. Lohrasb whispered, "Either our uncle is delirious or he's a magnificent plagiarizer!" Changiz Khan drove on silently, as if he regretted his decision to bring his brother home.

When Teimour Khan finally fell asleep, Changiz Khan announced to the company, "We could never live together before. I'm going to regret this." Sarveali paid no attention to Changiz Khan but delighted in each familiar landmark along the way. In less than four hours, they passed the gates of Kamab. Soon the former estate came into view in all its decrepitude, the manor house now enclosed by cement walls two meters tall. The walls seemed to suffocate the building. The Shirlus groaned, but Sarveali gave a sigh of relief. *Coming home is the proper solution for Teimour Khan. Now all will be well.*

Chapter 29

The next months brought Sarveali nothing but happiness. He ministered so carefully to Teimour Khan he felt that had he pursued the profession, he could have become a distinguished nurse. He remembered the dead Bibi and the satisfaction she received from treating the sick of the area.

To Sarveali's relief, shortly after their arrival Changiz Khan and the twins, accompanied by the squint-eyed servant, left for Shiraz to join Bibi Naz Khanom, who disliked living alone while she worked on the official process to emigrate. Sarveali busied himself cooking, cleaning, shaving, and bathing his master, happy to have Teimour Khan to himself. One day, when searching the storeroom—the same room where he had spied on his wife's infidelities through a keyhole—Sarveali made an auspicious discovery: four sealed carboys, two of red wine and two of raisin *aragh*. When he raised the oversize glass bottles wrapped with basketwork and crowned with red sealing wax, he thought only of serving the delights to Teimour Khan.

The first glass of *aragh* so pleased Teimour Khan that he asked Sarveali to dine with him. Even though Sarveali could scarcely eat from nervousness at the great honor of sharing a table with his master, the servant was picking at food that, for the first time in his life, had not been previously rejected by his master. He began to seek out delicacies for the sick man and fed him truffles bought from a local shepherd, which he folded into an omelet. The spoonfuls were followed by sips of the *aragh*, which Teimour Khan called the "Oriental antibiotic." After the truffles, quail eggs, apricot-stuffed partridge, and porridge cooked with eighteen kinds of beans found their way into Sarveali's cooking pot. Slowly the patient's health began to improve. His former ghastly pallor transformed into pink cheeks, and his hair grew back a salt-and-pepper color. Sarveali began to believe that the miracle he had asked for was bringing life back into his master's world.

Some days, Teimour Khan would sit on the front porch and imagine that behind the cement walls the bygone citrus orchard still flourished. "Maybe the French government will come to its senses and unfreeze my funds," he commented to Sarveali. "If they do, I'll buy back all the land behind these walls and bring back the glory of the orchard. And tear down these fucking walls at the same time."

Sarveali could not remember feeling so happy, even in the days when he had smoked opium. Teimour Khan spoke to him kindly, and Sarveali felt that he and his master were two boys left alone to dream out their destinies. When he combed Teimour Khan's hair and saw their smiling faces framed in the old art deco mirror with its beveled edges, he wished that it could transport the two of them back into their youthful selves.

One night, Teimour Khan insisted that Sarveali read him the newspaper. Sarveali thought this was a terrible idea, but he did his best. "Youth . . . arres . . . ted after blo . . . wing old man . . ." Teimour Khan looked at Sarveali with a grim smile. "Concentrate," he commanded. Haltingly, Sarveali read bits and pieces of the article again. "Youth arrested after blowing up old man with a bicycle air pump; elderly man dead of ruptured colon and sepsis . . ." Feeling he was reading much better now, Sarveali gave a surreptitious smile at his master, hoping to amuse him.

But Teimour Khan did not seem amused, just sad. "Like our country. The poor monarch blew modernization and civilization into us, but we couldn't take it. We exploded." Sarveali gave a sigh of relief. Teimour Khan was still responding to the world around him.

On other nights, he did not respond at all. Delirium would strike him as if he were wrestling the diva of death. He would cry out, "They've thrown me into the braziers of hell! I'm burning! Give me the cold water at the bottom of the blackest well . . . Sarveali, remember, 'The truth lies at the bottom of the well.'" Sarveali attempted to soothe his master by bathing him in cool water, at the same time trying to puzzle out the ambiguous message. The next morning, Sarveali took an early-morning walk beyond the wall to the old, straggly eucalyptus tree and the old hydraulic pump, no longer workable, that stood next to an abandoned well. *The truth lies at the bottom of the well. What did my master mean?* When Teimour Khan was better, Sarveali would ask him to explain.

That night, in spite of Sarveali's ministrations, Teimour Khan was burning hot again. Heat seemed to radiate from his face. As a single rivulet of sweat rolled down his forehead and branched out around his nose, he cried out in agony, "Phlebotomize me. Cut my vessels and pull this infernal devil out!" Then, just as suddenly as the fever and delirium came, it vanished and Teimour Khan fell into a heavy sleep. In the morning, he said to Sarveali, "I had a dream last night that Satan cut my blood vessels and placed me in a basin full of brine. I kept screaming for you to throw me into a well of icy water . . ."

THE TWINS OFTEN CAME TO VISIT FROM SHIRAZ, always their irrepressible selves. They brought amusement and comfort to their uncle, so Sarveali overlooked their occasional ridicule of him. He thought of the twins as surrogates, of how Teimour Khan used to be. Often they complained about their father, the arrogant, cross Changiz Khan. Teimour Khan liked these stories best, for he had never lost the rivalry with his brother, even as they had aged.

"He ridicules us constantly," Virasb said. "He always did before, but now it's much worse. We took him to see *Nights of Cabiria,* and he called Giulietta Masina stupid. 'Shoot the bitch,' he kept yelling at Anthony Quinn, until we had to escort him out of the theater. He keeps complaining that poetry without rhyme is like a woman without a bosom, knowing full well how devoted we are to it. We've been after him for months to let us go abroad for our doctorates, but all he says is, 'Do not stir shit! Let it dry and cake!'"

Teimour Khan was sympathetic, but Sarveali was mostly mystified. *What did shit have to do with a doctor?* The khans began to drink from the remaining supply of *aragh,* and soon all of them began to snore peacefully. Sarveali lay awake in the same room, thinking he would never know what his masters knew but that he was completely happy to be ignorant in their presence.

THROUGHOUT 1980, THE ISLAMIC REVOLUTION brought disastrous results, not only for the khans but also for everyone they knew. The clergy continued to rule with an iron hand, in that first year executing several hundred citizens, including friends and relatives of the Shirlus, by firing squad or hanging. Other friends and relatives lost their jobs, homes, and possessions, to be imprisoned or worse. Many fled the land of their ancestors. "Emigration" suddenly became a household word.

One day, Bibi Naz Khanom and Changiz Khan with his squint-eyed servant paid Kamab a visit. The Bibi brought a bottle of Creed cologne as a gift for Teimour Khan. The angelic aroma aroused Sarveali and lifted his spirits, even as it made the room cheerful and bright for a few minutes. Then the Bibi cleared her throat apologetically. "Father is joining Nima and me in our move to Ecuador in three days. We will be meeting my exiled husband at last." Sarveali had no idea where Ecuador was, but he sensed that it was far away and that he would never see his kind mistress or Changiz Khan again. The Bibi continued as if speaking to herself, "It's as if I woke up one day into a world run by the ancient Bedouins." Tears shone in her beautiful dark eyes.

Teimour Khan roused himself. "Don't cry," he said to his Little Princess. "You're going off to help your freedom-fighting husband. It's far better than this 'Mullahstan.'" He rose up weakly in his bed, struggling with his sheets. "And it's far better than a life of ignominy and emasculation."

Sarveali said gently, "If you wish to go to this foreign land, I'll come with you." Teimour Khan fell back onto his pillow. "No, Sarveali, you and I will survive everything here, including this disease." He gave the servant a look that seemed to deny his statement, and Sarveali's old feelings of doom clutched him again.

As the mournful Bibi and the somewhat tipsy Changiz Khan prepared for their departure, Changiz Khan approached Sarveali and said, "You're a fool, but if you've become my brother's professor, who am I to complain? And if you're not too busy reading to him and sharing his idiotic philosophy, write to me sometime, will you? Perhaps you'll become a scribe by the time I get to Ecuador." He handed Sarveali a handful of toumans and a paper giving him a half hectare of the now nonexistent citrus orchard. Sarveali began to weep, which only enraged Changiz Khan, while the twins, seemingly delighted at seeing the last of their father, struggled to open the last carboy for a farewell drink. Despite his tears, Sarveali gently took the bottle from them, saying, "This last must be for my master."

AUTUMN APPROACHED AND TEIMOUR KHAN LIKED to sit on the front porch overlooking the wall and the hot late-summer sky above it. He repeated to Sarveali what he called his "prostate testament." "I want you to make sure that my fucking prostate is donated to the *houris* to play Ping-Pong with." His laughter was rough and slow, like a malfunctioning engine. Sarveali was frightened. Delirium so early in the day was unexpected. On the other hand, he felt like laughing. *Those women couldn't really play Ping-Pong with his master's balls, could they?*

Teimour Khan began to shiver despite the late-summer heat. Sarveali lifted his master from his chair and supported him as they both walked inside the house, the little man having miraculously gained the needed strength.

"I am fatigued by thoughts of winter, but alarmed by this summer heat. When death comes, accompanied by its companion, the inferno, I shall seek the cold of the well." Teimour Khan turned his attention to the salon's ceiling and sighed at the missing pieces of plaster molding, the smoke stains, and the abandoned swallow's nest where the two back walls met the ceiling. "All the flowers from the molding have died and even the swallows have fled."

Hoping to rid Teimour Khan of his gloom and doom, Sarveali fixed a delicious light dinner of *abdoogh*, a chilled soup of fresh mint, raisins, and fragments of bread, all immersed in diluted and iced yogurt, and tried to coax his master to eat. Teimour Khan's mind was elsewhere. He ordered Sarveali to take out a strongbox from beneath the bed. "For you," he said to his servant, "eight 100-touman notes . . . the bottom of the pot . . . the sediment in the wine . . ." He lay back on his pillow and spoke in a whisper. "In the morning . . . don't forget . . . to tie my laces into butterflies."

Sarveali could not eat the soup either. He sat alone in the kitchen, hot tears falling on the uneaten bowl of *abdoogh*, further diluting the mixture. *And to think I believed that coming home would cure him.*

TWO NIGHTS LATER, as Sarveali prepared Teimour Khan for the night, washing him with a mixture of cool water and Creed cologne, he noticed that his master's body was once again bathed in sweat, or "brine," as he had begun to call it. "My immune system is orchestrating its last defense, like our late monarch." As Sarveali watched him anxiously, Teimour Khan said abruptly, "Hold my hand one more time. Don't let me go so easily." Sarveali took the frail hand gently and euphoria flowed through him. *He loves me. He forgives me.* Pulling his cot to the side of his master's bed, Sarveali fell asleep, his hand clasping the sick man's bony one.

He fell into another of his amazing dreams, this one of a white mare similar to the one Yazgulu rode at her wedding. It was pregnant. When it came time for her to deliver with Sarveali serving as de facto doula, the mare raised her right rear hock and, her hoof in midair, strained to produce a foal. Sarveali helped all he could, but no living thing ever emerged.

Sarveali sat up on his cot in fright, his shaking hand no longer clasping Teimour Khan's. The room smelled faintly of Creed cologne and resounded with absolute silence. His master's hand was loosely hanging from the bed; no breath emanated from his body, nor the smallest heaving on the sheets. A sardonic smile had crept over Teimour Khan's face as if protesting his destiny. Sarveali shook his master violently, refusing to believe that death could afflict such a noble person. "Speak to me, my master! Oh, please speak to me. You can't die without me to help you! Why didn't you let me know? I wanted to go with you, to be your servant in heaven or hell!"

Chapter 30

"My patriarch has died! My master is in heaven! Lament, you people, lament!" Sarveali's scream resonated through the empty house. He crawled to a wall, leaned his back against it, pressed his vertebrae against the thick tiles, and buried his head between his raised knees. Unable to produce words or thoughts to describe his feelings, he began to punch himself again and again. He longed for a whip to flagellate himself. Finally he sat without moving for the rest of the day. That evening, he dragged himself to the phone to call the twins, who promised to come with a "dead-washer" the next day.

The *ghassal*, the washer of the dead, and his assistant, a fat young man, arrived the next morning. The twins were nowhere to be found. When the *ghassal* told Sarveali he must start as soon as possible with the enshrouding, praying, and entombment, he cried out, "Bite your tongue!" still denying his master's death.

The *ghassal*, however, immediately went to work. "The soles of his feet should be pointed toward Mecca," he said, gesturing with his right hand. His assistant and Sarveali repositioned Teimour Khan in the proper direction.

"Now raise the head on the pillow to face the holy place."

My master never wished to face those places, Sarveali thought. *But now that he's dead, they're forcing him to.*

"Now you, sir, come help me straighten the limbs of the mort," the *ghassal* commanded. Teimour Khan looked taller than when he was alive. Sarveali remembered the opium den owner telling him about a short addict he had known, whose dead body grew almost a meter after his death.

"Now, prepare to assist us with the washing of your master. Cover his private parts. We will wash him with lotus water perfume, then camphor, and finally pure water. Then I'll perform the anointment process with more fresh-ground camphor. Then we will enshroud him. At that point, we'll perform the prayer for the departed. Then we must transfer the prepared corpse to a coffin and transport it to the cemetery."

An hour later, when the *ghassal* and his assistant were well under way in their preparations, assisted by a dazed and mournful Sarveali, the twins arrived, smelling of whiskey. Trying to maintain some kind of composure, they patted Sarveali on the back in an awkward gesture of sympathy. But, as he had in the Kamab cemetery when he contemplated killing Yazgulu, Sarveali felt like a dried-up lake, drained of tears.

"The last time we had a funeral of a Shirlu Khan, a caravan of five hundred automobiles followed the coffin from Shiraz to Kamab," the *ghassal* said.

"Yes, but those were different times," Lohrasb replied. "We had to pay off a few officials to obtain permission to bury my uncle in Kamab cemetery. They claimed the funeral might cause an agitation. These are indeed bad times."

"Of course, with all these killings, your business must be flourishing," Virasb commented cynically to the dead-washer.

The overweight assistant, silent until now, spoke up enthusiastically. "Well, like the radio said an hour ago, we'll be even busier soon!"

"What did the radio say?" Lohrasb asked.

"Oh, nothing . . . shut up!" the *ghassal* hissed at his apprentice.

But as the small party of three, with no interference from the authorities, prepared to bury Teimour Khan on September 22, 1980, the nation of Iraq was invading the Islamic Republic of Iran. At the Kamab cemetery, a few families had come to visit their dead or listen to funeral orations. One family had turned its visit to the necropolis into a picnic.

"What an obsessive fascination with death and funerals we have. Picnics even in a graveyard!" Virasb commented. But he noticed that the picnickers were listening to a transistor radio. He walked over and interrupted them. "Sir, any news?"

"Yes, we are at war! The bastards, the Arabs . . . I mean, the Iraqis, have invaded us. They're in Khuzestan."

The twins began to discuss the war and what it would mean to them. They seemed to have forgotten about their uncle's burial, but Sarveali could think of nothing but his loss. He remembered, as he waited for the ceremony, how Teimour Khan had once accused him of "killing beauty with a hatchet," but had forgiven him and was holding his hand when he died.

He glanced at the sky. It was suddenly gray, a cluster of clouds covering the earth. *It's as if God is sad at the death of my master,* he thought. *He's sprinkling the world with charcoal.* Lohrasb read a Rumi poem to be inscribed as an epitaph on Teimour Khan's horizontal gravestone:

> *When the rose is gone and the garden folded*
> *Thou wilt hear no more the nightingale's story.*

Quickly the twins set the coffin next to the marble gravestone. "Someone said Khomeini holds a grudge against the American puppet, Saddam Hussein, because he exiled the mullah to Paris. We can hold a grudge against the Iraqis just as well as the old boy." Sarveali began to wail and throw dust on his head and face.

ON THE SEVENTH DAY after their uncle's death, the twins volunteered for the Iranian army.

"Please don't go," Sarveali pleaded. "You are the only two left! You could be killed." The twins laughed at him. "Old man, don't you know that the war could make the most unprecedented film? Imagine the dancing date palm trees, the somber evening breeze, the magnificent carnage! Imagine the millions of red tulips blossoming from our dead!" Sarveali felt the hair on his forearms rise, as the twins used their wild imaginations to tease him in their usual way.

"Imagine helmets holding the brains of those who could have studied astrophysics. Imagine boots on lifeless feet that could have kicked soccer balls . . . I tell you the scene will be magnificent. We must be there to observe and participate . . ." Lohrasb stopped rambling as he observed the terror on the servant's face.

"Besides," Virasb continued realistically, "we cannot allow invaders to ransack our nation, provoked or otherwise.

For now, we have to operate those Chieftain tanks. Otherwise the mullahs, who are used to riding on donkeys, will be helpless in the face of the enemy."

Sarveali was still remembering the twins' words two days later, when he met them at the Kamab barracks where hundreds of young war volunteers and recruits were lined up. He felt the heavy sadness of being the last one left behind. *If only the twins had paid attention to their father, they would not be going to war. Now there will be no more teasing by the crown princes, no more reminders of Teimour Khan.* The twins' faces, with their high foreheads and curled eyelashes, so reminiscent of their uncle as a young man, inspired Sarveali to kiss their hands one last time.

"Be careful," Virasb said. "Don't go back to your prerevolutionary drug habits. You might end up in prison again."

Lohrasb joined in. "He won't. He will stay here to become minister of hygiene!"

And with those words, the twins walked away. Sarveali followed them with his eyes until they disappeared. For the first time since he was six years old, he was alone, without a master, the last sheep in the herd after the shepherd had departed. Hopelessly, he turned back toward the ruined estate. It was only a matter of time before it would be entirely confiscated, now that all the khans had gone. He was alone for the first time in his life, but soon he would have no place to lay his head.

Chapter 31

Two months after the twins departed, with no word from them of any kind, Sarveali was brewing tea on the one remaining burner in the destroyed kitchen. As grateful as he was that the remains of the estate had not been confiscated and he had not been ejected to a hovel in Kamab, the absolute silence of the house without Teimour Khan or the teasing twins was suffocating him. The stillness was like a blanket wrapped so tight around him that it blocked his airways. Even sleeping in his master's Creed-scented bed did not comfort him. Sighing, he left the kitchen for the porch where he and his master had spent so many happy days before his death. He heard a voice say, "Sarveali, have the cook make me some breakfast; then I'll give you the quince seed potion." Sarveali looked all around for the Bibi, then shook his head sadly. *She isn't here; no Shirlu is here, or ever shall be.*

When he had first returned to his lonely home, he sometimes needed to go to Kamab for provisions or just to say hello to other human beings. But everything there reminded him of the old, good days—the school where Teimour Khan had gone, the market square that he, Sheikhak, and Teimour Khan had walked through on the way to school. One day, he met up with a young man spouting rote comments about the old regime.

The young man preached to him. "The glorious Islamic Republic, under the guidance of the Ayatollah Khomeini, has bestowed on us freedom, land, education, distribution of petrol money, the promise of capturing Jerusalem. Down with feudals! Down with the Shirlu khans!" In an agile move that belied his age, Sarveali rose from a sitting position and slapped the young man hard in the face. "Bite your tongue, you insulting dog!"

"I beg for your mercy!" screamed the man. "Are you a khan, I mean, a former one? I apologize. Forgive me! My family is indebted to the Shirlu dynasty!" Sarveali almost laughed in the turncoat's face, because he suddenly remembered the man's father, whose whole family would have starved had he not been given the job of gathering bushes, thorns, and anything combustible to heat the Shirlu estate's bathhouse.

How is it that God has finally brought us peasants back together? Sarveali wondered to himself. The young man fled in embarrassment and Sarveali resolved to visit Kamab as little as possible in the future. It was better to live in the stifling solitude of the destroyed estate.

Now Sarveali found himself walking aimlessly around the barren grounds. He imagined a henna-haired nymphet riding a zebra, as other women with her chanted, "We are playing Ping-Pong with Teimour Khan's prostate." *It must be the extraordinarily hot spring sun,* he thought. *I am old and alone with only my memories, but I wouldn't have lived any other way.*

Such memories sent him to the old storeroom; a few days earlier he had discovered a half bottle of *aragh* buried under an overturned vat. He poured himself a glass. *No ice! Pour it neat,* he remembered Teimour Khan saying. Holding the bottle in one hand and the glass in the other as he wandered and drank, he passed through the cement walls and out to the scrawny eucalyptus tree, whose branches danced to the early spring zephyr. *I should fumigate some of its leaves, so my master can breathe better,* he thought. Next he sat on the abandoned tractor, the same one that had transported him to Yazgulu's murder and then to prison. *It makes a noise like farts when it operates.* He noticed the old hydraulic pump used to draw water from the well next to it to irrigate the old citrus orchard; it was rusting its way into the earth. *If I ladle out some water, will it make refreshing tea for my Bibi?* He staggered over to take a look and fell onto the pistachio-green moss that hugged the contours of the well opening. *I think I'll have another drink,* he thought. But first he removed his sandals and arranged them like buses parallel-parked on the moss's delicate green fur.

He finished his second glass and climbed to his feet. The world turned as black as the mouth of the well; the eucalyptus tree spun like a whirligig. As if the moss beneath him had opened, he found himself falling into a subterranean abyss. He grasped a protruding and sensual adolescent thigh and buttocks, like Teimour Khan's at the height of his beauty and youth. The thigh metamorphosed into a strong, reassuring root of the eucalyptus tree. Two blue eyes and beautiful, henna-colored hair appeared before him, along with a family of bats that exuded an odor like death's halitosis. He heard a series of goatlike screams that he realized were his own. Teimour Khan cried out to him as he fell, "The truth lies at the bottom of the well!"